REA

D0467191

how to
meet
cute
boys

how to meet cute boys

a novel by
Deanna Kizis

illustrations by Ed Brogna

WARNER BOOKS

An AOL Time Warner Company

Copyright © 2003 Deanna Kizis

Song lyrics on page 64 are from Simon & Garfunkel's "Mrs. Robinson" © Charing Cross Music (BMI) 1967.
Song lyrics on pages 91 and 98 are from Duran Duran's "Rio" © 1982 Original Sound Recordings and Tritec Music Ltd. Made by Tritec Music Ltd.
Song lyrics on page 111 are from The Smiths' "There Is a Light That Never Goes Out" © 1986 Sire Records Company.
Song lyrics on page 112 are from The Replacements' "Answering Machine" © 1984 Twin/Tone Records.

Warner Books, Inc., 1271 Avenue of the Americas, New York, NY 10020

Visit our Web site at www.twbookmark.com.

 An AOL Time Warner Company

Printed in the United States of America

First Printing: September 2003

10   9   8   7   6   5   4   3   2   1

Library of Congress Cataloging-in-Publication Data

Kizis, Deanna.
How to meet cute boys / Deanna Kizis.
    p. cm.
ISBN 0-446-53072-7
    1. Young women—Fiction. 2. Women journalists—Fiction. 3. Dating (Social customs)—Fiction. 4. Los Angeles (Calif.)—Fiction. I. Title.
PS3611.I95 H6 2003
813'.6—dc21
                                                    2002192416

Illustrated by: Ed Brogna
Photographs by: Lisa Anne Auerbach
Designed by: Platinum Design, Inc. NYC

For Eve,
who constantly reminds me that
it's good to have friends, even in hell

ACKNOWLEDGMENTS

Thank you to Gregory McKnight, Mike Sheresky, Ian Kleinert, and Jennifer Rudolph Walsh, for agenting it; Karen Kosztolnyik, for editing it; Ed Brogna, for illustrating it; Christian Ablang, Lisa Anne Auerbach, Eve Epstein, Drew Fellman, Elizabeth Flanagan, Harriet Friedman, Gayle Forman, Ali Goldstein, Bernice Hart, Bea Ilumin, Susan Kittenplan, George Kizis, Makenzie Kizis, Jeanne Fay Manfredi, Chris Weitz, Lindsey Wilkes, and all the wonderful women at *Elle* magazine, for supporting it. And a special thanks to all you heartbreakers out there, for inspiring it.

30
DATES FROM HELL

169
THE END?

DOES THIS SHIRT MAKE ME LOOK FAT?
107
TURNING THEM OFF!

how to meet cute boys

PROLOGUE

We've all heard the story of Peter Pan by now. You know, Pan's flying around, doing his thing, when he becomes obsessed with this girl Wendy, and starts showing up at her house at all hours and taking her out on fancy adventures. Until, one day, Wendy wants him to act like a man. She wants him to be *accountable*. So what does Peter Pan do? He flies off with Tinker Bell in tow to continue his life as another immature male and Wendy gets left in the dust. Of course, Pan's story is pretty easy to figure out: Boy meets girl. Girl becomes woman. Woman wants boy to grow up. He can't handle the pressure and bails. The Peter Pan syndrome—that's pretty much every guy I've ever met. But what gets me, what I've been wondering about ever since I first heard this horrifying tale, is this: What was Wendy thinking? Why did she allow herself to be interrupted, distracted, *seduced* by some guy in green tights with a sparkle in his eye? Couldn't she tell that he was just a boy?

CHAPTER

1

"Oh no! You look so much cuter than me."

Kiki had just let herself into my apartment and stormed into my tiny bathroom, where I was putting on my makeup. She scared me half to death, as I was blasting the stereo and didn't hear her knock. *Good thing she hasn't lost her key,* I thought. *Yet.*

"I do not," I said, doing a quick appraisal. Kiki looked like sex on toast, as usual. Her blond hair was down, jeans were snug in all the right places, lips were berry red. Of course, she was wearing another black sweater, which toned her natural vampiness down a bit. (Kiki thinks black sweaters camouflage her boobage.) And, okay, her eyes were *slightly* puffy, but I only noticed that because I already knew what was going on. Overall, I have to say, she looked hot. I looked at myself in the mirror for comparison. Not exactly Kiki, I'm what people call "cute." As in, even if I were wearing nipple clamps, crotchless panties, and holding a whip, they'd say, "That's *so cute!*"

I was going to need more mascara.

"Ben, you *know* you look amazing," Kiki said, watching me apply another coat.

"I really don't."

"Oh my God, fuck you, you do." She spun out of the bathroom and headed toward my bedroom in a huff.

A couple of days before, Kiki had broken up with her boyfriend, Edward. Actually, make that, she broke up with Edward, her rental unit. Renting, as opposed to leasing (or, heaven forbid, actually *owning*), is a common affliction among us over twenty-fives today. You end up dating this guy for months and you're not seeing anybody else, and he's not seeing anybody else (at least, you *think* he's not seeing anybody else), but you don't actually call him your boyfriend because he doesn't actually call you his girlfriend. Then you get in a fight over some dumb thing, like maybe he didn't call all weekend until Sunday, and when you tell him you're upset, he says something like, "Since when is Sunday not the weekend?"

The next thing you know, you're having the I-Think-We-Need-to-Talk Talk (always prefaced with those six crushingly familiar words), and he's broken up with you when you weren't sure you were even going out in the first place. Which is how you end up mourning something you never knew you had, asking yourself questions—*Should I have done this differently? Not said that at all?*—that you didn't even know were serious at the time. The whole thing becomes a downward spiral of regret and second-guessing, something Kiki and I are extremely familiar with. After all, I write the articles about how shitty men can be, she edits the articles about how shitty men can be, *Filly*—the magazine where we both work— publishes the articles about how shitty men can be, and a million-plus women read our articles about how shitty men can be. And yet, we're all still surprised at how shitty men can be. It's a clear-cut case of the blind leading the blind.

Anyway, after six weeks of heavy dating, Kiki's rental unit had initiated The Talk. They'd spent a weekend together doing couple stuff (making seared ahi tuna for dinner, picking out sweaters at Barneys, et cetera). He said things were getting too serious, and she hadn't heard from him since.

I heard the closet door bang open, followed by rummaging. Hangers whisked about; shoes clunked onto the floor. I pictured Kiki standing half naked in front of my full-length mirror, probably trying on one of my tops, possibly with two different shoes crammed onto her size eight feet to see which looked better.

"I look fat," she said over the music.

"Yeah, you're a real cow," I hollered back.

I headed into the kitchen to make her a drink. A *strong* drink. I grabbed the supersized bottle of Absolut Kiki had brought over after I finally broke up with Jack—there was a bit left. (I'd been nursing it alone, I admit it.) I peered into the fridge for a decent mixer, but the only thing I had was diet Coke. But that was okay, I decided, swirling the concoction around in a glass. The vodka would elevate Kiki's mood, the caffeine would keep her awake.

From the bedroom I heard, "I look like a *complete loser!*" A crash of plastic and glass hit the floor, which meant she was into the product samples from publicists that were piled every which way on top of my vanity.

"You're a bombshell, Kiki. Get over it."

"I *loathe* what I'm wearing!"

I entered the bedroom, and she'd exchanged her black sweater for one of my black sweaters. She was stretching it out.

"Well, now you're wearing my clothes, so go easy."

I handed her the drink.

She sighed, "Look at you. I wish I was a brunette."

"Well, brunette *is* the new blond."

"I'm too tall."

"*Short* is the new *statuesque*." I pirouetted around my room, looking for the various things I'd need for the evening and cramming them into my purse.

"Seriously!" she wailed. "You've got that fantastic starving-refugee thing going on—I look like a goddamn giraffe."

Only Kiki could make being five foot eight with 34Ds sound like such a nightmare. She's almost managed to convince me being short isn't all bad—insists everything's more appealing when it's smaller, be it a cell phone, an evening bag, a snack food, or Sarah Jessica Parker.

"Famine is the new fashion!" I declared. "We pronounce it, *fa-meen*."

She still didn't smile. So I said, "Okay, have it your way: You've got *a little bit* of a giraffe thing going on, but you've got bigger tits."

Kiki finally laughed. Downed the drink in a couple of gulps. Chewed an ice cube. Made a face. Her green eyes took on the look of someone determined. Someone who had a job to do, and was going to do it, damn it, even if it was the end of her.

We took her Jetta, because it was parked closer than my Jetta. Before I could sit, I had to clear away a pile of her old bank statements, a ratty brassiere, several diet Coke cans, the calendar section of the *LA Times*, and a half-eaten bag of McDonald's fries, now hard as plastic.

Kiki watched me trying to organize the mess. "Ben, give it a rest wouldja?" she said. "You know you can just throw that stuff in the backseat."

It's the same every time.

IS HE OR ISN'T HE?

BY BENJAMINA FRANKLIN

Ever heard the phrase "They don't buy the cow if they can get the milk for free"? Let's be honest: You give the milk away on a regular basis. But the problem with an enlightened approach to sex is you're probably sleeping with a guy and have no idea if he's your boyfriend. You can't ask. He doesn't say. Here, a Filly quiz to help you find out if you're getting the girlfriend vibe.

1. You're at his house. The phone rings. He:

a. Answers it, explains that he's busy with you right now, then hangs up and says, "Spike and Sofia say hi."

b. Smugly lets it ring. He already signed up for voicemail so you won't overhear messages from other girls.

c. Asks you to get it. He's busy making you a mix tape of your favorite Belle & Sebastian songs.

2. You tell him you suspect one of your "friends" thinks you're a slut. He says:

a. "How could she think you're a slut? We've been together for two whole months."

b. "Why doesn't that smug 'ho just let you date and have fun?"

c. "Now that you mention it, I was wondering why, on our first date, you let me wear your panties as a hat."

3. You're at a party by the pool of your local scenester boutique hotel. When one of his friends approaches he:

a. Doesn't introduce you, mumbling something about how he wants to go check out the modern furniture in the lobby. Alone.

b. Doesn't say much because his friends see you so often they refer to you as "the permanent piece."

c. Makes an introduction and you all make plans to go to punk-rock karaoke next Saturday night.

4. When you tell him you'd like to go for a weekend vacation together, his face most resembles:

a.　　　　**b.**　　　　**c.**

Happy Guy　Non-Committal Guy　Horrified Guy

5. The last time he saw you without makeup on was:

a. Last night. You were only renting movies anyway.

b. When you woke up the morning after your first date. If you'd known you were sleeping over, you would have brought your cosmetics bag.

c. Yeah, *right.*

6. When you go to Blockbuster, you:

a. Get in a flirty, faux argument about which movie to rent.

b. Notice that the new-release section includes the movie you saw with him the last time you two actually left the house for a real date.

c. Proceed directly to the porn.

→ THE FILLY **ANSWER KEY**
In which we refuse to call up so-called experts who write cheesy books for the self-help section but instead just tell you what we think.
Give yourself points as indicated:

1. a=2 b=1 c=3
2. a=3 b=2 c=1
3. a=1 b=3 c=2
4. a=3 b=2 c=1
5. a=3 b=2 c=1
6. a=1 b=3 c=2

6 to 9: He couldn't be your boyfriend less. Your relationship is purely surface, and you're always trying to put your best foot (or, since you're always made up when you two hang out, your best face) forward. The good news: You're in crush mode, the best part of any relationship—you get dressed up, get taken out to dinner, have lots of sex. The bad news: You could be destined to become FWF (friends who fornicate). **Our (Possibly Bad) Advice:** Keep dating. He probably is.

10 to 14: You're in relationship limbo. He'll spend a weekend with you out of town; maybe you've met a sibling or two. But will he become your boyfriend? Or will you run into him at a rock show and find some indie chick sitting on his lap with her tongue in his ear? **Our (Possibly Bad) Advice:** Initiate The Talk. But be aware: If you tell him you want a commitment, he could run screaming out the door, move to Botswana, and you'll never hear from him again.

15 to 18: Congratulations. You have a boyfriend. How do we know? Because it's not so romantic anymore. Sometimes you can't be bothered to put on the good panties before he comes over; he rarely picks up the check. Then again, giving up the trappings of dating is the small price you pay for intimacy. At least, that's what your therapist would say. **Our (Possibly Bad) Advice:** You don't need advice, you're in love. It sucks, right? ℧

Each fall, *Filly*—the fashion magazine of choice for women who prefer sociopathic men and maxed-out credit cards—has a huge bash to celebrate the fashion issue. We hold the event as a thank-you to our advertisers. Of course, thanks to them, nobody actually reads the fashion issue—it's so full of ads you can't find the articles and the magazine weighs about four hundred pounds. The party's usually held in New York. Last year Kiki and I got to fly out there for free, stay at the Mercer, and treat ourselves to expensed dinners at Da Silvano. But this year the party was being held at the Farmer's Daughter Motel on Fairfax. The choice of a campy seventy-five-dollar-a-night dive was meant to be old school, but whatever. At least it was closer to home. *Filly* did this eight-page spread in the issue using Hollywood actresses as models. The actresses were supposed to come to the party, which would then get party pictures in other magazines, which would then make *Filly* even more successful than it already was. Or something.

Outside was a disaster. Photographers were clamoring to get shots of Jennifer Aniston and Kate Hudson. *Entertainment Tonight* was pulling celebrities out of the crowd for the usual "What a great night!" chatting. And then there were all the people who weren't actually invited but were trying to get in anyway. Kiki and I fought our way through the throng, because we certainly didn't want to be confused with what a publicist friend of mine from New York called ham-and-eggers, as in party crashers who wanted more than what they were entitled to (the ham *and* the eggs).

"Name?" asked the bouncer when we got to the front.

"Benjamina Franklin."

As the story goes, my parents came up with it while smoking dope. No wonder they ended up divorced—family life wasn't exactly their thing.

"I don't have time for this," the bouncer said.

"Yeah, but . . . my name *is* Ben Franklin."

He looked at the list, said I wasn't on it, and turned his face away so he could listen to an urgent call coming through his headset. ("We're running out of chicken satay in section three! Again, chicken satay needed in section three!")

I looked at Kiki, flustered.

"Did you tell him who you are?" she asked.

"You're the West Coast editor, you tell him who *you* are."

"Can't." She shook her head from side to side. "Can't take rejection now of any kind."

I tried to get the bouncer's attention by grabbing a complimentary issue of the magazine and waving it in his face. He couldn't have been ignoring me more.

"What do you mean I'm not on it?" I said. "See this?" I opened *Filly* and pointed to my last article, "How to Meet Cute Boys." "I wrote that."

His eyes arrested briefly on the magazine, then moved back into the void over my head. I felt a door-anxiety panic attack coming on. *Am I seriously not going to get into my own party?* I wondered. *Am I a loser? Unsuitable for admittance? Does he* hate *me?* And then, as a kind of coup de grâce, the bouncer said, "If you're not on the list you can't come in," and gently but firmly pushed me aside.

Mother. *Fucker.*

Fortunately, at this moment Hilary Swank arrived wearing a see-through dress and the paparazzi went nuts. ("Didn't she already work that shit at the Oscars?" Kiki muttered in my ear.) Everyone took this opportunity to rush the door, and we were swept up into a wave of unstoppable, fabulously dressed humanity, shoving past the now screaming guards. And just as quickly as we were out . . . we were in.

Kiki and I walked through the courtyard toward the bar, and my eyes turned skyward to hundreds of people making their way up and down the motel's outdoor walkways. It was an "Around the World" party—each room in the motel had a theme. At a glance, I could see a massage parlor, a keg party, and a tiki lounge, all going on at once. I squinted at faces to see if I actually knew anyone, but found myself staring at the same familiar-looking strangers I always see at events like this. We had our well-heeled Westsiders wearing wrap dresses, the hipsters in thrift-shop corduroy, a coterie of agents who'd dashed straight from work and still had on suits and ties. The publicists were in the house, talking on their cell phones and giving dirty looks to everyone who wasn't a potential client, along with *Filly* writers like myself, all of whom were getting bombed. There were the actors, of course, who came hoping to be noticed yet, the minute you noticed them, pretended they didn't want the extra attention. And then there was . . . everybody else. Whoever they were.

I imagine we all had that same desperate look in our eyes. The one that says, *Entertain me. Show me. Seduce me. Shock me. Do something, anything that will make tonight more than just another excuse to leave the house.* But I predicted that everyone, including me, would be let down. There are so many premieres, so many art shows, so many boutique openings, restaurant openings, record-release parties . . . you could go out every night of the week but know deep down inside that you weren't actually *doing* anything. It was depressing when I stopped and thought about it, which I tried not to do. Maybe Jack was right. All these people come to L.A. because they just want to get famous. Or get next to the famous. They want to get on the list. But inside the list there's *another* list, an A-list. And inside the party there's another party, the VIP room. So then people try to get on *that* list, in *that* room. And what they find is the same sorry, bored-out-of-their-minds fuckers as the ones they were so desperate to elevate themselves above in the first place.

And yet. Well, there is that moment. You go to a premiere, you walk down the red carpet, you see all the people standing on the other side of the velvet rope clutching their autograph books, and you think to yourself, *I may be just another hanger-on, a plus-one, a ham-and-egger, but I'm here. And here is always better than there.*

Speaking of which, I spotted Collin, a wannabe celebrity stylist friend who wears a lot of ironic eighties fashions and thinks The Strokes were the Second Coming of Christ.

"Ladies, how's your lifestyle?" he said.

"Excellent," I said.

"Crappy," Kiki said.

"Pretty good party." He nodded, eyes darting this way and that. "Strictly A-list."

(Total bullshit—there were more people at this party than there were on the *Titanic*.)

"Oh fuck," Collin added, "there's Winona Ryder."

Kiki and I didn't look.

"Damn, she's hot," he said. "Damn, damn, damn. Hey—do you think there's a chance?"

"Didn't she date Beck?" I composed my face in a way that would imply that if she weren't into rock stars, she might be interested.

"So," he said. "I met Beck once and he was a really great guy."

"Oh yeah?"

"He was eating with a friend of mine at Ammo. We talked for, like, ten minutes."

Collin always gets annoyed if you question his celebrity bragging rights. It's fun. So I said, "And he was nice, huh?"

"Hey Ben? *Go die.* There are lots of people here I want to meet, and I already know you two, so—later!" Collin dived back into the throng.

Kiki was primed for another drink, so we fought our way to the bar. Souza was sponsoring the party, which meant unfortunately there were only free tequila martinis on hand. Everything else we'd have to pay for, which was out of the question since we hadn't brought any cash. (Nobody in this city ever carries more than just a few singles, which, naturally, are for the valet.)

Kiki and I got two free drinks and she chugged hers while I winced my way through mine. We decided to do a lap. We hit the massage room first, where Kiki got a five-minute neck rub. Opted against the tattoo parlor, which was being patronized by the Gwen Stefani/Orange County/wallet-chain crowd, and headed to the next floor. If there was one good thing to say about the party, it's that there were boys, boys, and more boys. Not that I intended to actually try to talk to any of them. My secret hope was that a cute guy would try to talk to me.

We grabbed another tequila martini from a nearby cocktail waitress and made for the fortune-telling room. I usually avoided fortune-tellers. What if they tell you you're going to die in a terrible boating tragedy or go bankrupt or something? But I was curious to see if she thought I'd ever meet The One. The One I go to places like this looking for. Now, I know that a huge, impersonal party can't really be the right place to find true love. Nevertheless, I keep RSVPing, hoping that, one night, yes, maybe tonight, I'll have RSVP'd my way right into an earth-shattering romance.

I got in line. *Jack would give me so much shit for this,* I thought. He didn't believe in fortune-telling—would have hated this party, too. Of course, he was a financial planner.

As of two months ago, Jack and I were still living together. It was like being married—except not. Because we didn't want to have kids (not yet, anyway), and we still liked to meet friends out at a bar and get bombed now and then. On the other hand, it was generally assumed we'd get married eventually, and the sex had a predictable but comfortable bent. On the surface, everything was great. Jack was making a pretty good living; I'd left the local freebie I was writing for and gotten a new gig as a *Filly* writer. Jack asked me to move in and I did. But every time I wanted to go out with my friends alone, he would make these annoying little remarks. Like, "Have fun hanging out with the other fashionistas, dahling."

"I work at a fashion magazine now, Jack," I'd say. "Besides, it's just a party, like any other party. The only one who takes it seriously is you."

But then I'd always feel bad and invite him to come along. He'd throw it in my face, saying, "No, just *go.* Have a *fabulous* time."

I finally did just go. From his Santa Monica duplex—which I always felt was like living in the land of the multiplying baby strollers anyway—all the way to Silver Lake, which is forty-five minutes and a million light-years away. To Jack, it was the ultimate betrayal. I invited him out to see my new apartment, hoping we could at least be friends, but he refused. When I gave him my address so he could forward my mail, he said, "Oh, aren't you *so cool.*"

The one-bedroom I took was small, but it had hardwood floors and a view of the hills. I tossed the Pottery Barn crap Jack insisted I take half of, bought a couple of Eames chairs from a used-furniture store, and got a nice minimalist vibe going. The neighborhood had coffee shops you could walk to, art galleries, independent bookstores, and quirky bars on practically every corner. There were things to do.

But then, well, sure, a little bit of fear started to creep in. I couldn't figure out what people who weren't in a relationship did with their spare time. Watching television alone was an excruciating experience—I started turning down the sound real low so the neighbors wouldn't hear it and feel sorry for me. It occurred to me that Jack was like this piece of driftwood—a small, resentful piece, fine—but he'd kept me afloat. Without him, I was just bobbing along, getting tossed this way and that, not sinking, but not really swimming, either.

I was almost at the front of the line for the fortune-telling lady. I turned to ask Kiki what she thought about fortune-tellers. Charlatans? Clairvoyant? But she was preoccupied with people-watching—scanning the crowd looking for Edward. Probably terrified that he was there, yet somehow downtrodden by the fact that he didn't seem to be. Kiki caught me staring at her and mouthed the words, *"Kill me now."*

I felt a tap on my shoulder.

"HEY YOU GUYS OH MY GOD IT'S SO GOOD TO SEE YOU WHAT'S UP DO YOU HAVE A LIGHT I CAN'T FIND MY FUCKING LIGHTER THOSE PEARLS ARE GENIUS!" It was Steph, *Filly's* publicist, a stick-thin party thrower/socialite, who, because she spent most of her evenings at events where music was blasting and chitchat was rampant, did her own brand of yell talk and could never focus on one topic. Jack used to call her "Minnie Mouth."

"Hey, Steph. I'm good. Take these matches. Thank you," I said.

"DID YOU GUYS HAVE ANY TROUBLE AT THE DOOR THE LIST IS ALL FUCKED UP CAN YOU BELIEVE HOW MANY CUTE GUYS THERE ARE HERE OH MY GOD I SAW THIS GUY WHO I AM SO IN LOVE WITH HE'S AN ACTOR BUT MY FRIEND SAYS HE'S ALSO A DRUG DEALER AND I CAN'T DECIDE IF THAT'S BAD WHAT DO YOU THINK?"

I let Kiki take this one. "It was hectic, but we got in," she said. "If you really like him then it's probably okay." She shot me a *he's-a-drug-dealer?* look. "But you should probably find out if he's, you know, the right guy for you."

"TOTALLY I SO HEAR YOU WAIT OH MY GOD J'AI IS HERE SHE'S SUCH A FUCKING GENIUS I HAVE TO TALK TO

FILLY TIPS

AVOID SPERMY

How to get the perfect eyebrow in six steps, courtesy of a Beverly Hills star plucker.—*B.F.*

- **1** Determine your face shape. If your mug is a big circle, you want a brow that doesn't go too far across. A small pointy face needs a thin arch. A long, oval face wants wide, thin brows.

- **2** Take a pencil and hold it against your nose, then align it with the inside corner of your eye. Where the pencil hits the brow line is where your eyebrows should start. Now hold it from the end of your nose to the end of your eyelid. This is where your brows should end.

- **3** With a makeup brush, cover the hairs you want to tweeze with concealer.

- **4** If tweezing hurts, numb the area with an ice cube first.

- **5** Tweeze the tiny hairs that grow underneath your arch—they make the area around your eyes look wrinkled. Who needs that?

- **6** Brush the inside hair of your brows upward with a toothbrush, then trim them with scissors to make them even. Otherwise you could get what star pluckers call the dreaded "spermy brow," which is shaped like a, uh, you know. ∪

HER AND SEE IF I CAN GET AN APPOINTMENT MY EYEBROWS ARE A DISASTER BYE-BYE DAHLINGS!"

We watched Steph cut her way expertly down the stairwell and thrust herself in the path of an eyebrow shaper who, thanks to journalists like myself, is now a celebrity complete with first-name-only recognition. Like Madonna.

It was my turn. I walked into the dimly lit motel room, and it took a minute for my eyes to adjust to the candlelight. I made out the fortune-teller waving me toward an empty upholstered chair. I sat at the table, which was covered with glittery scarves, but the presence of two double beds with green and blue comforters and a cheap-looking nightstand sort of detracted from the gypsy ambience. Not to mention that my fortune-teller, who introduced herself as Olivia, looked bored out of her turban. She told me to shuffle the tarot cards; then she laid them out on the table, the bangles on her arms making a fake-gold clinking sound.

"This one," Olivia said, taking a swig of bottled water, "says you are a creative person whose strengths lie in the arts."

Flattering, but not exactly what I had in mind.

"This one says there will be a big change for someone close to you. Maybe family."

Unlikely—my mother dated so often that a new guy could hardly constitute a big change, and Audrey was in a perma relationship with the Commando.

"This one"—she pointed to another—"says you recently had your heart broken, but you're starting to realize that it's all for the best."

No kidding.

"Is there a question you want to ask?" Olivia looked at me and yawned.

Suddenly I realized how pathetic my question really was: Would I ever fall madly in love? Would I ever want to give someone everything I had? Would I ever want to share everything, want him to touch everything, want to tell him everything? They were probably the same questions everyone asked. What the fortune-teller should do was start taking down everybody's phone number and become a matchmaker instead. I shook my head. "No, no questions. Thank you, though."

Olivia was too tired to put up a fight, so she just shrugged, giving me an incriminating, *it's-not-my-fault-you-didn't-come-prepared* look. I felt like I'd wasted her valuable psychic energy, so I put four dollars in the tip jar—my valet money—and met Kiki outside.

"How was it?" she said.

"I'm good at the arts, I've had my heart broken, blah blah blah. Are you going in?"

Kiki peered into the gloom at Olivia lighting a cigarette off a candle and hesitated. "No, forget it. I can't face the future," she said. "Let's go get another drink and obliterate it instead."

With our territory staked out at the bar so we wouldn't have to wait in line for refills, Kiki finally went there. "I'm never going to meet anyone again," she said.

"Of course you are," I said.

"I don't think so. Seriously. I don't even have the energy to try anymore. Edward took the will right out of me."

"Kiki, you can't give up because of Mrs. Doubtfire."

She raised her eyebrows at me, like, *Quoi?*

"He was so hairy he looked like Robin Williams on Rogaine."

"Good one," she said. But it wasn't the direct hit I was hoping for.

"Look, meeting cute boys is easy." I bobbed my head up and down like one of those little nodding dolls. "All you have to do is find someone you might be into, and put yourself in his way. If he's into you, too, you'll strike up a conversation."

"Really." She raised an eyebrow. "Quoting our own articles, are we?"

"A, it was your idea. And, B, you edited it, so supposedly you agreed with it."

"All right, then." She took a look around the courtyard. *"Show me."*

"What, now?"

"Yeah!" She gave me a playful shove toward the masses. "Do it now!"

"You can't be serious."

"Ben, lemme ask you something." Kiki leaned back in her chair and studied me. "Why do you think I keep assigning you those dating stories?"

"I give up. Why?"

"Because if I didn't, *you'd never go out on a date.*"

"Bullshit."

"Bull *true.* You broke up with Jack, but instead of getting busy you just go to parties and watch me and Nina flirt with everyone. So I figured, you're a good reporter, if I give you an assignment, I know you'll do it. And you do. But then you sit at home, right, type type typing away. Never do this; always do that . . ."

I couldn't believe what I was hearing. She was dissing my stuff.

"What?" she said. "I'm not saying I don't love your articles. Look, think of this as fact checking. You claim the techniques in your article work, so show me. Go meet a cute guy."

Okay, so I was just saying that stuff to make her feel better. And I was a little peeved that she'd called me on it but . . . *Well,* I figured, *maybe if I humiliate myself it will cheer her up.* And in terms of my not trying, I don't know. I mean, I've picked up guys post-Jack. Ashton, for one. In a way.

"Ben?" Kiki said. "Are you going?"

"Yes," I snapped. "Jesus, Kiki. You're being really pushy, you know that?"

She just smiled and waved me on.

I didn't seem to have much of a choice, so I insisted we do another lap. I needed time to strategize while I picked out my prey. At first I didn't see anybody. There was this one devastatingly cute boy standing off to the side, over by the motel soda machine. Nothing like Jack. Jack's style was conservative, button-down, premature male pattern baldness. This guy was tall and very thin, pure Hugo Boss. I got a little closer so I could get a better look. His hair was perfectly mussed and just gritty enough to be cool. Kind of a dark blond color. He had huge brown eyes that were wide and looked innocent, but also . . . *self-aware,* if you know what I mean. And maybe just a little aloof. He was like that sexy, self-possessed high school senior you know you're not supposed to be attracted to but you are. And he had full lips that were just . . . Well, I could think of a lot of really dirty things to do with those lips. I mean, those lips could be a novel in and of themselves. He was just standing there, alone, yet perfectly at ease. *How does he do it?* I wondered. He was *beautiful.*

Then I looked at his clothes and was shattered. Navy blue nylon jacket, zipped up all the way, a hint of blindingly white T-shirt underneath. Immaculate khakis, with crease. White Converse AllStars, unscuffed. He could have been a skateboarder/Beastie Boys fan/East Coaster, but I was picking up a very different vibe.

"What about him?" I said to Kiki, with a discreet nod in his direction.

"Gay," she said.

Damn, I was just thinking that.

We did another lap, but it was hopeless. I saw one guy who looked good—hair, with product, vintage-rock T-shirt . . .

"Him?" I said.

Her eyes narrowed. "Not the guy for you."

"Why?"

"He's wearing tapered jeans."

"Right." She was right.

Everyone else was either too buff (I hate buff guys), looked like an actor (never, *ever* date an actor), or had another girl on his arm. The guy with the lips was still in the corner, lighting a cigarette.

"I'm going for the gay guy," I told Kiki.

"Dude! You can't go for a gay guy. That's totally not the point."

But I had a feeling.

I started to sidle. Like I'd said in my article, this *must* look like a chance encounter. I mean, any guy who sees a girl walking purposefully toward him at a party will probably think she's either desperate or a crazy person. When I got in his immediate vicinity, I tried to look lost. Little girl lost, that's what I was going for. I'm no actress, so I probably looked ridiculous. But it worked. He noticed me, started watching me a little. Then, out of the corner of my eye, I saw him scan the crowd. I was surprised, but it looked like he was actually wondering who I was looking for. I took a deep breath and moved in for the kill. I looked in his general direction, let him catch my eye, and said . . .

"I think I lost my friends."

He frowned like he wasn't really sure I was talking to him. Like I was some insane maniac walking around the party looking lost and muttering to myself, which was basically the case. I started to panic. *Abort! Abort!* my brain screamed. *This was a dumb scheme!*

When suddenly I was saved.

"Well," he said, cocking his head to the side and giving me a little smile. "What do your friends look like?"

Now, I could have started lying my ass off, giving fake descriptions and seeing if he offered to help me find them. Or I could have said something vague like, "Oh, I don't know. Maybe they left," and tried to keep the conversation going. *Or* I could have tried the full-on flirt. Very risky.

But then I thought to myself, *You know what? I can* do *this.*

"Actually, they look a lot like you," I said, and grimaced in something I hoped looked like a captivating smile. Now, I know *They look a lot like you* is a total line. But I was improvising. And I could see Kiki just over his shoulder, watching everything, which was putting me off my game.

"Really?" he said. "Then I guess you and I were meant to be friends."

Success! Success! Success!

The conversation grew from there. He said his name was Max. That he owned a T-shirt company, Super Very Good, thus the crispness of the clothes he was wearing, which were from the new line. (He didn't have a close, personal relationship with the ironing board, as Kiki and I had feared.) He said he traveled a lot between L.A., New York, Paris, Hong Kong, and London. He designed the graphics himself. I was impressed, although, you know, I tried not to act like I was. Still, I had to ask him if he knew Radiohead, because they wear Super Very Good clothes. Max shrugged and said, "Oh yeah, we hang out all the time."

"Really?" I said.

"No. Not really. But one time Heather Graham came in to try on samples for a photo shoot and I got to see her breasts."

Okay. I'm what people call proportional when they're trying to think of something nice to say, so this stumped me. But then he leaned forward and whispered in my ear, "They weren't that great."

"Really." I tried to sound all sad for poor bad-breasted Heather Graham. This was *thrilling* information.

"No." He started laughing again. "Not really."

He's gorgeous, I thought. *He's confident. He's making fun of me. I'm in love with him.*

Kiki finally joined us, saying, "Oh, *there* you are! I've been looking for you everywhere!" (Love Kiki.) She did what she could to help me along, laughing at my jokes, acting like we were the most carefree, fun girls in the world even though inside she was aching for that loser Edward. We asked him where he lived. (Silver Lake.) He asked me where I lived. (Silver Lake. Aha!) He asked me what I did. ("I'm a writer. Uh, journalist.") I asked him what he did for fun. ("Nothing. Collect vinyl, I guess.") He asked me what I did for fun. ("Hang out with Kiki.") I asked him why he was at this party. (*"No* idea.") He asked me what I'd written recently and Kiki flipped open an issue of *Filly* and pointed to one of my stories. Unfortunately, it was "How to Meet Cute Boys." (Hate Kiki.)

The article clearly laid out my whole game plan, complete with subject headings in bold, large font—The Lap, The Sidle, The Full-On Flirt, The Pickup. I was busted. But I made a vain attempt at sounding casual. Like I wasn't some hussy who trolled parties and picked up guys for a living. So I said, "Look, I'm not some hussy who trolls parties and picks up guys for a living." I stammered about how, well, Kiki was my editor and she'd assigned it to me so, heh heh, I couldn't really say no and . . .

"Everybody, time to go home! Make your way to the nearest exit! Now, people!"

Of course. This awkward moment had to be when the fire department would arrive to bust up the party. It wasn't an entirely bad thing—for *Filly*, that is. If the fire department's called, the party is over capacity, which means the event is a success. But it was woefully ill timed. A helicopter appeared overhead, shining its spotlight down on people. My new crush and I were suddenly smack in the middle of an Oliver Stone movie, and in the blinding glare I became convinced I had a seriously bad lighting situation going. We stood there, frozen, gawking at one another, while I glanced around looking for a friendly shadow, wondering if my mascara was raccooning around my eyes. Men in uniforms with bullhorns were screaming, "Party's over! Go home!" while hipsters scrambled for their cell phones to call people who were only five feet away so they could plan where they were going next.

I didn't know what to do. According to my own article, I was supposed to close. Get his number. Seal the deal. But it was harder in real life than it was when I was telling other people to do it from the safety of my laptop. "Well, can I . . ." I started to say.

"I'd really like to . . ." he started to say.

"Oh, I interrupted you," I said. "Go ahead."

"No, you go."

"Um. You first."

"Well, you're the one who tried to pull off the I'm-looking-for-my-friends strategy," he said. "Very inventive by the way, so I guess it's my turn."

He leaned toward me, and for a split second I thought he was going to kiss me. The really crazy part is I was going to let him. I raised my chin slightly, my lips quivered forward, and then he said, "Ben, can I have your phone number?"

But I didn't lose my cool.

"Of course!" I said, scrambling in my purse for a pen. I couldn't find one. "Kiki—*do you have a pen?*"

He had one.

"Oh. Thanks." I took it, and I scribbled "Did it work?" with my number on his courtesy copy of the "How to Meet Cute Boys" article. Before we could say anything else, a cop grabbed me by the arm and escorted Kiki and me out the door, past a riot of people fighting for their free Puma gift bags. Steph was standing behind the gift table throwing bags out to the crowd and screaming at the top of her lungs, "IF YOU DON'T FORM A FUCKING LINE YOU DON'T GET A FUCKING GIFT BAG YOU FUCKING CHEAP BASTARDS!"

I kind of wanted a bag, too, but I knew from experience that it would just be filled with a few shampoo samples, a cheesy CD compilation from one of the record companies, and a free Filly T-shirt, so I decided to let it go. I craned my head around to see if I could at least wave good-bye to Max, but he was gone. Not that it mattered. I got what I came for.

"See," I said to Kiki while the cop shoved us out onto the street, where I almost got sideswiped by a departing limousine. I did a little Cabbage Patch victory dance, thumbs up, shoulders swinging back and forth, and yelled, "Meeting cute boys is easy!"

CHAPTER

2

I woke up expecting my haze of happiness to clear like perfume left over from a wish-fulfilling dream. But then I realized, instead of another failed attempt at meeting someone, I actually had something to be excited about. I said his name aloud to my empty bedroom: "Max." It sounded good.

"Max," I sighed to myself as I brushed my teeth. "Max," as I washed my face. "Max Max Max Max Max," as I fought off Freak, who was clawing himself up my pajama leg.

The week I moved in, Freak was conducting World War III in the alley behind my place—trash cans banging, screeching fights, feline yowling that sounded like howler monkeys. A neighbor threatened to call Animal Control, so I tempted the feral beast inside with a plate of chopped-up turkey hot dog. I figured Freak, with his bitten ears, scratchy whiskers, and bowlegged stance, lent a certain flair of authenticity—if you're going to be a single girl living alone in a one-bedroom apartment, you gotta have a cat.

Freak was like every guy I'd ever known. Aggressive when he couldn't get your attention, disdainful if you appeared even the slightest bit needy. *But surely Max will not be this way,* I mused as I went to pet Freak and he slinked off into the living room with his mangled tail in the air. Surely Max would be a non-commitment-phobic male with no skeletons in his proverbial closet, no girlfriend he was cheating on, no past relationship that had scarred him for life.

Max...Max...Max... I sipped my morning diet Coke and spaced out with the Sunday paper spread out on the coffee table in front of me. In my reverie I was off in an imaginary gold Mercedes convertible, cruising the PCH in Malibu wearing oversize sunglasses in a sort of seventies Julie Christie homage. Max was sitting next to me in his zip-up nylon jacket, and I was grinning at something he'd just said. Cut to, me running down a hallway in a T-shirt and his blue boxer shorts, laughing uproariously, with Max chasing me with a bottle of Mrs. Butterworth's syrup because I was being a grump at breakfast. Cut to, me crying. Just breaking down on a rainy street corner in some totally justified paroxysm of pain and frustration and anger with the world, and, for once in my life, the guy I wanted to be with putting his arms around me and saying the perfect thing while he stroked my hair.

Of course, I used to visualize montages like this about Jack, of all people. Before I got too caught up, I decided I needed more information. *It's the age of the Internet,* I thought. *The only responsible thing to do is look up my crush in cyberspace.* So I did a search and found a link to the Super

Very Good Web site, where Max (Max!) hawked his clothing. It was very cool—hyperstylized and heavy on the Japanese pop-culture references. By ten-thirty, I'd ordered two pairs of pajamas that they offered to monogram with my initials, a navy hoodie, five pairs of sweat socks with the Super Very Good logo on them (no idea where I was going to wear them since I hate the gym), a pair of hot pink fishnet stockings (endlessly more practical) and three tiny T-shirts. Then I decided the insanity must stop and logged off.

Oh no, what if Max was trying to call? I checked my voicemail, but no. Well, no, of course not. No self-respecting guy would call the next morning. No self-respecting girl would, either. Not that I had his phone number. All I had was his name, $250 worth of merchandise being FedEx'd my way, and a serious jones. I wondered if that afternoon I should drive around Silver Lake, see if we ran into one another. Maybe, I thought, I'll do some shopping on Vermont, or get coffee on Hillhurst . . . Wait, I was starting to act a little creepy. And while I'm being honest, I thought, it might do me good to ponder another cold, hard truth: I was pretty smooth picking up Max at that party the other night. But I'm woefully unlucky in love.

1. The Actor: Ready for his close-up

5 DATES FROM HELL

Men who are two-timing, cheap, and utterly revolting—what's not to love? A special report from L.A.'s dating battlefield.

BY BENJAMINA FRANKLIN

Here's the deal: Since my boyfriend and I broke up, I can't seem to find a decent guy. Maybe I'm a loser magnet with low standards. Maybe I'm *too* picky. Or maybe it's that I live in Los Angeles, where single women outnumber single guys by 127,000. We at Filly decided to get to the root of the problem. My assignment is to go on five dates with five eligible guys, and strip these men—and myself—bare.

DATE ONE: KENNETH BREEZE, THE ACTOR

How We Meet: I approach Breeze in front of the guacamole dip at a party and tell him to drop the chalupa. He asks me out.
Stats: Was the guy in the AmPm commercial who says, "There better be a jumbo chili dog in it for me!" On a good day looks like Jared Leto.
The Date: Breeze arrives at my house wearing a cream-colored sweater and jeans. I hand him a glass of Merlot, and he insists on taking my new computer for a test drive. But he's a PC person, whereas I'm a Mac person, and this sends Breeze into brand-identity posturing. He peppers me with questions about my G3, and in an attempt to defend my

computer choice, I start gesticulating wildly and, yes, that's when I spill red wine all over his shirt.

Breeze rips off his sweater and starts scrubbing it in the kitchen sink. "How is it?" I ask from the doorway.

"Probably ruined," he says. "And it's Armani."

Ugh.

We go to dinner at Mr. Chow, a trendy Beverly Hills restaurant. Breeze gripes about his latest audition, brags about the directors and casting agents he knows. I start feeling better about myself—he's a consummate

2. The Producer: Likes life in the closet

name-dropper. But when we leave the restaurant, I commit the ultimate dating faux pas: I slip on my heels, butt hitting the ground, feet flying into the air, right in front of the crowd waiting for the valet. Breeze offers me his hand, saying, "Apparently, coordination isn't your strong suit."

Postdate Phone Status: He doesn't call me, I don't call him. I consider this a tie. Even though I spilled, and even though, okay, I fell on my ass, how tacky was it of him to tell me the label on his sweater?

DATE TWO: EVAN KATZ, THE PRODUCER

How We Meet: At a Fourth of July barbecue in Beachwood Canyon. Katz introduces himself, saying he wants to know everything about my life as a journalist for a script he has in development.

Stats: Produces teen comedies for Universal. Has a fondness for wire spectacles. Owns a cat named Robert Evans.

The Date: Katz takes me to a local Italian restaurant, Ca'Brea, where he's on a first-name basis with the hostess. Over pap al pomodoro he tells me about his collection of African art and passion for black-and-white photography. I'm thinking: He's smart, he's got taste, what's the catch?

After dinner, we go to a cocktail party. Katz is a perfect gentleman—even goes to the bar to get me a cocktail napkin when I mistakenly splash scotch on his Prada suit. (I'm a klutz. I get that now.) Everything's going great, until a mutual friend approaches and whispers, "Ooooh, now that you're Evan's beard, you'll get to go to all the great parties!"

Postdate Phone Status: Katz is gay but closeted, so it's a friend thing. Sometimes he brings me to events as his date, while I help him pick out sweaters at International Male.

DATE THREE: ELLIOT EILERMAN, THE MUSICIAN

How We Meet: A setup. I meet a friend for drinks at Snug Harbor in Koreatown, and Eilerman's sitting in my seat.

Stats: Not that I'm mad. Looks a little like Sean Lennon, plays guitar in a rock band that gets some radio play on KROQ. Lame band. Cute guy.

The Date: We hit it off. When he asks if I want to check out his temporary digs in the Oakwoods, a Studio City residential hotel (dubbed "the Cokewoods" by actors who get put up there by Warner Brothers), how could I say no?

3. The Musician: Killing us softly

"HE DOESN'T CALL ME, I DON'T CALL HIM. I CONSIDER THIS A TIE."

After a few hours, he's playing guitar for me and I attempt to do the right thing by asking him what time it is, making excuses about having to work the next day. But Eilerman shakes his head. "I'm not telling you," he says.

"Because? . . ."

"Because if I tell you what time it is, you'll leave."

Five minutes later we're rolling around on his Murphy bed. No, we don't do it; I have a sliver of restraint.

Postdate Phone Status: Did I mention that Eilerman has an ex-girlfriend he's obsessed with? *No?* Well, nobody told me either. Imagine my surprise when he told me he "just got out of a serious relationship."

I did what any self-respecting girl would do: Said I never wanted to see him again, then we went on a few more dates, had sex half a dozen times and, after listening to him rehash their endless arguments ("And I was like, 'What do you mean I never wash the towels? You're the one who decided we should each *do our own chores!'"*), I really *did* never see him again.

DATE FOUR:
ETHAN DAVIES, THE WEB DESIGNER

How We Meet: I'm waiting for my car after dinner at Itacho in Hollywood, and he strikes up a conversation. He mentions that he has a pit bull named Dixon whom he takes hiking every weekend in Runyon Canyon.

Stats: Cute. Brown hair, brown eyes. A little dumber than me. (Question from Ethan: "Like, do you follow the news much?" Answer from Ben: "Well, I *am* a journalist . . ." Response from Ethan: "Oh, yeah. Cool.")

The Date: I meet Davies at the base of the hiking trail. The dog is *amazing.* Doesn't tug at the leash, does fetch. I basically decide that Ethan is a dog-training genius and fantasize about future brunches with him and

4. The Web Designer: Looking for love

Dixon. But then he tells me that his last girlfriend of three months broke up with him after he proposed marriage. He later found out she was seeing another guy the whole time. "Wait," I say, "why were you asking a girl to marry you when you'd only known her for three months?"

"She was from Australia, and she was having a problem with her green card so I thought I'd help her out. Of course, she still owes me about two grand."

Postdate Phone Status: Nonexistent. Davies is one of those rare guys who would do *anything* to be in a relationship, which is why nobody wants to be in a relationship with him.

DATE FIVE: DAVID JETTER, THE SCREENWRITER
How We Meet: We're introduced by the aforementioned Evan Katz, who produced Jetter's first feature, *Geek Out,* which he

5. The Screenwriter: Enormously endowed?

you mind if we split this?" tallies up my portion, but *doesn't* deduct his share of the parking. By the time we get to the candy counter before a movie, and Jetter starts to say, "Do you happen to have a . . ," I just interrupt, "Don't worry, I got it." By the end of the evening, I'm out thirty-two dollars; Jetter's up thirteen.

Postdate Phone Status: Incapable of getting the hint (or picking up the check) Jetter still calls now and then. Whenever he asks if I want to go to a movie/party/dinner I do the math in my head and conclude that it would be cheaper to stay home.

pitched as *"Rushmore* meets *Road Trip."*
Stats: Katz cited Jetter's "enormous endowment" as his main selling point. I accused Katz of sampling the goods, but he claimed to have heard it from an ex-girlfriend.
The Date: Jetter takes me to a Thai restaurant famous for its singing Elvises. It's fun, although Jetter is a strict vegetarian, which means we don't want the same things to eat and this leads to tense ordering negotiations. Even worse, I start to notice a pattern. In the parking lot, the attendant asks for four dollars, and Jetter looks at me and asks if I have singles. "Of course," I say, handing him four ones. When the check comes at dinner, he asks, "Do

Five dates, five chances, five duds. No wonder I'm starting to suspect it might be better to bunker down at home with my cat and the latest episode of *Sex and the City* than to actually venture out into the war zone. Then again, the guy I liked most was a two-timing pig, and the guy I liked least was engagement-ring-toting marriage material, so it's possible that *I'm* the one with the problem. Either way, one thing is certain: These guys could be perfect someones—for someone else. ♡

I decided it was too tragic to sit around fretting over my failed dating life, so I got ready for lunch with the Mother. When I was in high school, we went every weekend. Of course, my baby sister, Audrey, was living at home back then. Now she lived in San Francisco, shacked up (not that Audrey would ever call it shacking up) with her boyfriend.

I threw on jeans, sneakers, and a sweatshirt, and walked a couple of blocks to Eat Well, a diner around the corner. The Mother hated it because they were always blasting punk rock, but I liked the buttermilk biscuits.

I grabbed two menus and took a table near the kitchen just as I saw the Mother striding through the restaurant, mouthing the words, *"No booth?"* She looked fabulous as usual. Even in blue jeans the Mother carried herself like Sharon Stone—*after* the actress married the multimillionaire, gained enough weight to make her look human, and got the chic haircut. I feel like whenever a guy I'm dating meets the Mother there's this tiny *pffft* of disappointment because I didn't inherit her self-possession or perfect bone structure. Audrey looks like her, though.

"Do you see an open booth?" I said as she harrumphed into her seat. "Hello to you, too, by the way."

She smiled. "Be a bitch, why don't you?"

I told her I shared her point of view.

"Sorry," she said. *"Hello."* She spread her napkin on her lap and pretended to study the menu. It was only going to be a couple of minutes until . . .

"So, did you have a date last night?"

There it was.

"No," I said. "You?"

"With Julio."

I had no idea who Julio was, but I let it go. The Mother had no illusions about my lifestyle; I had no illusions about hers. When I was six, the fact that my father had an affair with his racketball instructor helped convince her it was time to get a divorce. So she took her 2.5 children (I always thought of Audrey as being one and a half times the kid that I was), moved us to a condominium in the San Fernando Valley, and took up real estate. As my dad spiraled into a Topanga Canyon, surfing, existential, ride-the-wave-of-life sort of existence, she started an aggressive dating campaign. The guys came and went like clockwork, and Audrey and I were left at home with the asthmatic, diabetic baby-sitter, Ms. Britton-Baff, who never let me watch *Three's Company* because she thought it was too "lustful." I made it my personal mission to torture Britton-Barf, as I called her, by occasionally going into Audrey's room and screaming at the top of my lungs, *"Oh my God! Where are you taking the baby?"* This would send the baby-sitter puffing up the stairs, after which she'd chew me out until she got too winded to go on.

I didn't really blame the Mother, though—she was raised Roman Catholic, got married young, had two kids by twenty-one. Besides, there was an upside: The Mother bought better junk food than all the other moms, taught me how to disco dance in our living room to "MacArthur Park," and when I got suspended for smoking pot in the high school parking lot, yeah, she grounded me. But then, because she knew I'd stolen it from her and didn't want me to tell my dad—who was about to leave on a surfing trip and had a lot of grandiose ideas about how his kids should be parented (even though he was never there to do it himself)—she let me invite friends over for a weekend-long sleepover party.

After we ordered, the Mother sat back and folded her arms across her chest. She studied me closely, like she was sizing me up or something.

"What's up?" I said.

"Not much," she said. "You?"

"Not much."

She hadn't started complaining about my choice of restaurants yet, either.

"Why are you smiling like that?" I asked.

"Am I?"

"You know you are."

"Well, I can't tell you. It's not my place."

I reminded her that she never was one to stick to her "place" so why start now? She looked thoughtful and said, "You know what? You're right. Okay, the big news is . . . Are you ready?"

I rolled my eyes, and before I took my first sip of my coffee, I said, "Born ready."

"Okay, then . . . Your sister is getting married."

I gasped in horror. The coffee was a thousand degrees, too, and I sucked in too much. I could actually feel the roof of my mouth sizzle. "Wait," I said, grabbing an ice cube from my water glass. "*What?* You've got to be joking."

"Not so far."

"My twenty-one-year-old sister."

"The only one you have."

"Is getting married."

"Yes."

"To whom?"

"What do you mean 'to whom'? To Jamie."

"To her commando boyfriend, Jamie."

"Ben, stop it." She slapped her palm flat on the table. "Stop it now."

The Mother may act like a big sister much of the time, but I knew from experience it would be unwise to push her too far. Then I thought, as I often did, *Fuck it.*

I said, "He's a gun-toting Republican from Texas who wants to join the CIA."

"What does this have to do with politics?" she said, waving the thought away. "Your sister is getting married!"

"Have you ever *been* to Texas? They shoot gay people for fun in Texas!"

"Now you're just being ridiculous."

"Besides, you don't believe in marriage."

"How can you say that?" She looked offended. "I've been *married* three times."

"Exactly."

"Please don't ruin this for me." The Mother leaned forward. "I'm thrilled. *Thrilled* that at least I get to see one of my daughters marry the right man."

The jab didn't escape my attention, so I told her for the hundredth time that Jack was hardly the right man. She nodded, like, *If that's what you need to tell yourself...*

"When did this happen?" I asked.

"Yesterday. She was going to call you but, well, you know. Anyway, Jamie proposed to her in the Color Me Mine where they met. He put the engagement ring inside a ceramic mug she was painting. Isn't it just adorable?"

I felt like I was going to throw up.

With that, the Mother kicked off an endless monologue about all the plans she and Audrey were already making for the wedding. I sat there, stunned. *Audrey's too young to get married,* I thought. *Nobody gets married that young anymore.* I didn't want to get married. Why should she want to get married?

But every time the Mother's voice went up at the end of a sentence, I nodded and smiled. I heard, "Something something something bridal shower since you'll be the maid of honor?" Nodded and smiled. "Something something something *very* Martha Stewart?" Nodded and smiled. And *then,* "Something something something who you're going to bring to the wedding?"

Suddenly it occurred to me that I was about to become a cliché thanks to a ring in the bottom of a DIY coffee mug. I was the twenty-seven-year-old sister who would have to bring her best friend to the wedding because I probably wouldn't have a boyfriend to take. Everyone would *tut-tut* over me, convinced that my decision to break up with Jack was a horrendous mistake, and the rumor that I was a lesbian (which I *knew* was being circulated by my Catholic grandmother) would finally gain a toehold. *And yet,* I mused, *Little Miss Perfect promises to spend the rest of her life with a Nazi and she gets a party thrown for her.* This sucked. It *sucked.*

"When is this taking place?" I asked.

"The second weekend in March."

I had six months to get a boyfriend.

"Well . . ." I offered. "I did just meet someone new. I think."

"Someone new. You think. Sounds promising."

The waitress put our food on the table—the Mother's egg white and chicken omelet and my American cheese and bacon scramble. To annoy her, I pointed at her plate and said, "Isn't that like eating the mommy and the baby?"

She ignored me.

My breakfast looked delicious—all hot and gooey and just waiting to be eaten—but I couldn't believe she hadn't asked me *anything* about Max. So I glumly pushed the food around until the Mother finally asked a couple of perfunctory questions.

I gave her all the details anyway. How we met, how he owned his own company, how he hadn't called yet, but how he would call because, you know, the three-day rule, and how he said he wanted to hang out sometime . . .

"Then hang out." She took a bite of toast, like, *That's that.*

I looked at her like, *Is that all you're going to say?*

"What? You know, the first time Jamie saw Audrey, he followed her into that Color Me Mine off the *street?* He asked for her number and called her *that day.* Took her to that cute seafood place on the pier for dinner . . ."

"Yeah, Mom, because *he's a stalker.*"

"And let me guess," she said, taking a sip of her water. "You met this 'Max' person at some party where he was probably cruising around looking to get laid. Honey, when are you going to find someone who can *really* give you what you need?"

I wanted to ask what Max had done to deserve quotation marks around his name, but decided to just give up. The Mother went back to talking nonstop about Audrey's wedding plans. I nodded/smiled until I got a neck cramp, and, finally, lunch with the Mother was over.

Seriously disturbed, I went home and sulked. *Then you should hang out,* I thought. Maybe she doesn't remember what it was like when she was younger, when she probably picked guys because they were into man-perms and liked Pink Floyd. My mom—who used to be cool—was suddenly acting like I should be romancing with gallant frat boys who wore pressed chinos and patronized ceramic chain stores. Yuck.

I stared at the ceiling and blew smoke rings. Maybe this wouldn't be so jarring if she'd been grooming me from day one to hubby hunt. But the first time I told the Mother I was in love—with a boy in a band named Deus ex Machina who wore Dickies and drove a Vespa—she simply said, "Go on the pill, wear a condom anyway, and never confuse sex with love." I entered the sexual arms race armed to the teeth.

As the afternoon wore on, the things she said continued to nag. I put some leftover Chinese food in the microwave and curled up to watch Sunday-night HBO in my pajamas. But after the first few minutes I realized the *Six Feet Under* was a rerun. So I sat there, channel-surfing, eating my food out of the box, and I started to feel more and more pathetic. Like people were walking by my place outside, hearing the TV and thinking, *That poor, poor girl.* I turned the volume down another notch.

Jack was reliable, I thought. *And on a night like tonight he'd have been sitting next to me, which is at least more dignified.* I finished the last of my kung pao chicken and turned off the TV. I figured if Max called that night, at least I could call the weekend a success.

But he didn't.

CHAPTER

3

"Five days," I said, brandishing my drink at Kiki and Nina. I'd been checking my voicemail every day, checking the caller ID, too—not even a hang-up from Max. "Five days is too long." (It came out *daysh*.)

"Maybe he lost your number." Kiki was trying to sound hopeful.

"He didn't loosh my number," I said, with a look like, *Who do you think you're kidding?* "That's like saying, maybe the phone isn't working, when you know, deep down inside, that the phone is *working*."

"Well, maybe the phone *isn't* working."

"The phone company does not rest!" I shook my drink in her face, and it spilled over my knuckles onto the dirty wooden table. *"Boys do not lose numbers of girls they intend to call!"*

"Okay. Okay. Take it easy. It's only been a couple of days since you met the guy," Kiki said, nervously eyeing my fourth scotch like now would be a good time to take it away. *From my cold, dead hand,* I thought.

Besides, that would have been against the whole Shortstop ethos—we were in the kind of dark, dank, smelly Eastside hole where doing your best *Barfly* imitation is strongly encouraged. And I was doing just that. *If I keep going like this,* I mused, *I'm going to end up like Isabella Rossellini in* Blue Velvet, *standing outside naked with my arms stretched out and moaning, "He put his spell into me . . ."*

Just then, the waitress interrupted to tell me I had to take my cigarette outside.

"Even *here?*" I was aghast.

"The city keeps giving us tickets." She shrugged.

But the look on my face chased the waitress away. I continued to puff—calling after her, "This is my last one, I swear"—and sat back, satisfied. Now I could torment my well-meaning friends in peace. "So back to the subject at hand, girls," I said. "*Five* daysh. Days. Not three. Not four." I held my fingers up, and gave them a little countdown. "One. Two. Three. Four. *Five.*"

"It must be really awful for you to wait so long for him to call, particularly when you're feeling fragile about your sister's engagement," Nina said in a compassionate tone.

I turned toward her. "You're right," I said. "It *is* awful. Do you think there's a reason—something about how I look, something that I said— that would make him not want to call me?"

But ever since Nina decided to get her master's in psychology, she answers every question with a question. As in . . .

"Do *you* think there's a reason why he wouldn't want to call you?" she asked, with a concerned look on her face.

"Nina, I don't know if there's a reason why he wouldn't want to call me. That's why I'm asking *you.*"

She ignored this last bit, saying, "It must be terrible to feel like there's something wrong with you."

That would be the "reflective listening" she'd learned last semester.

I looked back at Kiki, exasperated. "A little help?"

"Okay," she said. "Just give me a second to think."

"Take your time." I looked away, worried that someone was listening to our conversation and I'd been discovered for the loser that I was. Just the opposite, though—some sleazy guy at the bar with greasy hair and a motorcycle jacket was giving me the eye. I gave him the finger. He laughed and went back to hitting on the bartender, ogling her bare midriff. Female bartenders in L.A. always show their midriffs so they get bigger tips. It's true. I imagine them at Crunch Fitness, working those abs. They probably make more money than I do.

"All right, I've got it," Kiki said. "Here's the thing: If he's not going to call, then I say fuck him and find somebody else. I mean, maybe he just broke up with somebody. Maybe he's still *seeing* somebody. Maybe he's an asshole." She shook her head. "If any of the above is true, then be *glad* he hasn't called you, okay? It means he's saving you a lot of trouble. So fuck him and find somebody else."

I took a look around the bar. "There's nobody good here."

"Well," said Kiki, "you know, wait a day or two."

"So, what are we doing this weekend?" interrupted Nina, who usually gets bored about halfway through most conversations. (That her lack of empathy may interfere with her career as a psychologist has never occurred to her.) "Maybe we could go do a nice, long day at Malibu, get a tan."

"I can't," I said. "I'm going with Audrey to look at wedding dresses."

"Sunday?"

"I can't. I'm going with Audrey to look at more wedding dresses if she doesn't find one on Saturday." I put my head down next to my drink.

"*Goddamn* her." Kiki banged her hand on the table so hard it hurt my brain. "I'm sorry, but this is the *last thing you need.* Hi? You're twenty-seven. You're single. And your twenty-one-year-old sister, who as we both know looks like a Barbie doll, is getting married before you. It's not okay."

Nina said, "It must feel terrible to have your younger sister get married before you've even found a decent boyfriend."

"Please shut up," I said, only half joking. "I'm *happy* for Audrey."

Nina raised her eyebrows at me. I noticed she'd recently had them tweezed into fine little arches—Drew Barrymore, but full of scorn and surprise.

"You could hurt someone with those things," I said.

I stood, found my balance, and said I had to go to the bathroom. But what I really did was sneak to the pay phone in back to check my voicemail. It was pathetic. But I figured as long as I knew it was pathetic, then it wasn't really pathetic, right? *Right?*

I had . . . Two . . . Messages. The first was sent . . . today . . . at . . . eight . . . twenty-two . . . P.M. . . . Damn, it was from the Mother. "Have you given any thought to what you want to do for the bridal shower? Martha says that starting to plan right away is crucial . . ." I pressed 3 and erased. The second message was sent . . . today . . . at . . . nine . . . forty-seven . . . P.M. "Hey, it's Max."

No way.

"What's up with you? I'm about to head out to some club thing . . .

Hey, Stu? Where's it at?" I heard someone shout back an answer. "It's at Deluxe," Max said.

Where is Deluxe? I thought. *What is Deluxe? Why didn't we go to Deluxe?*

"Okay. Whatever. Want to get dinner or something one night this week? I'll try you from work tomorrow."

"He called?" Kiki asked when I returned to the table with a grin. "See?" she said. "I *knew* he was going to call. I just knew it."

"It must feel good to be validated with a phone call," Nina said with a nod. Then she looked at her watch. "Oh my, it's past eleven." She stood up, and said, "We're going to have to stop."

Like she was my therapist, and our time was up.

ARE YOU, OR ARE YOU NOT, A STALKER?

That is the question.

BY BENJAMINA FRANKLIN

So you think he could be The One, but then the questions start. Why hasn't he called? Maybe you should do a drive-by and see if he's home? Should you call from your cell and ask if he wants to have lunch? If you get the voicemail, should you hang up? Here's the real question you should be asking: Are you a stalker who's bound to drive him away because you can't stop obsessing? Take our quiz!

1. On your monthly phone bill, you pay:

a. $132 for caller ID, voicemail, and long-distance calls to your best friend from high school, who usually wants to discuss why some guy hasn't answered her last Instant Message.

b. $102 for voicemail, charges for the obligatory Sunday-night calls to Mom, and that's about it. You don't chitchat on the phone much because you're way too busy.

c. $167 for voicemail, caller ID (so you know if that hang-up on your voicemail was him), call waiting caller ID (in case that's him on the other line), caller ID block (so he won't know when you call him seven times in a row), and 1-900-2morrow calls, during which you ask a clairvoyant whether or not he'll marry you.

2. When you call your best friend you:

a. Get her voicemail, again. She's sick of listening to you talk about him morning, noon, and night, but this doesn't stop you from leaving a message that says, "Mayday! Mayday! I just drove by his house and there was this strange car in the driveway. Do you think it's another woman?"

b. Ask her how she is, then say you need advice because he hasn't called back in forty-eight hours and you're wondering if you should leave another message with his pot-smoking roommate.

c. Tell her you can't go out on Friday night because you forgot you had plans with the new guy to meet his parents. (Which is weird—it's not like you're his girlfriend or anything.)➔

3. When you throw a party you:

a. Send an e-mail to your friends, plus the guy you're dating, plus a guy who has a crush on you, plus an ex who'll do in a pinch, and prepare yourself to have one hell of a good time.

b. Make up an excuse to have a party in the first place. ("*Of course* I can have a housewarming even though I've been living here for a year.") Casually ask him if he'll come, then call your friends and tell them they have to come because he's coming. Drop $950 on a designer dress from the Colette Web site. Then spend the day of the party desperately trying to whip up spanakopita and lobster spring rolls.

c. Send an Evite to all your friends, including the guy you like, telling them what time and when. Then buy hummus, pita bread, beer, and wine, and make sure you have enough toilet paper in the bathroom.

4. The morning after a first date you're most likely to:

a. Wake him for another quickie, then bid him adieu by saying, "I'll give you a call," even though you secretly suspect you won't bother—he didn't exactly flip your switch.

b. Go to brunch with the girls, where you happily dish on what he was wearing, what he ordered, what he said when he kissed you good night.

c. Skip brunch to stay home by the phone in case he calls, getting so frustrated by 5 P.M. that you call him to say, "So, what? You're never going to call again, *is that it?*"

5. He takes you out to dinner with a group of his friends, and they all start talking about a rock show they're going to that weekend (and you haven't been invited). You:

a. Spend the next day frantically trying to get tickets, and when you do, pretend bumping into him at the show is some kind of crazy coincidence.

b. Don't care. You have a date that night with someone else anyway.

c. Feel hurt but figure it's fair—truth is you sometimes go out with your friends and don't invite him.

→ # THE FILLY **ANSWER KEY**

Give yourself points as indicated:

1. a=2 b=1 c=3
2. a=3 b=2 c=1
3. a=1 b=3 c=2
4. a=1 b=2 c=3
5. a=3 b=1 c=2

12 to 15: You couldn't be a stalker more. You'll do anything—break plans with your best friend, throw a party for no reason—to have access to this guy, and he's probably going to file a restraining order. How about focusing on why you think you need him so desperately? You may realize you don't need guys that much, especially since, if you're always this boy crazy, you probably spend a lot of time alone.

9 to 11: Nobody is normal, but you're in range. Sometimes you get a mad crush that inspires you to buy a dress you can't afford; other times you meet a guy you think could be likable, but eventually decide isn't worth the wear he'll put on the bottoms of your shoes. At least your friends don't think you're psycho—you still have time to listen to their problems—and their assurances that you just haven't met the right guy yet are probably true.

5 to 8: You're so unavailable, every guy you meet probably wants you. But only because they can't have you. You use them for sex, you use them for entertainment, and you use them to make you feel strong. Sound good? Actually, no. Open up a little. You might get hurt, but at least you'll have a shot at being happy. ∪

I called Max back the next day, and he asked if I was free for dinner that night. Now, I should have said I was busy to sound more in-demand, but I couldn't help myself. (Okay, I muttered something about having *had* dinner plans, but said they were canceled. Like he fell for that.) He asked me what I was working on. I didn't feel like I could tell him I was sitting on my couch eating Cheetos, watching *The Princess Bride* on DVD for the umpteenth time, and nursing a killer hangover. So I said I was finishing a story. He said what story, so I lied again and said it was a profile I'd already turned in on an actress who's famous for wearing skimpy bikinis in all her films.

Naturally, he asked me what she was really like. I hate this question. Not because I don't understand why people ask it; I do. But if I really told the world how badly their beloved celebrities behave sometimes, their publicists would never let me interview their clients again. Which would be bad. This particular star was so snooty—acted as though my interviewing her was some sort of assault on her dignity, refusing to tell me why she broke up with her last boyfriend ("I don't talk about my personal life") even though *she* was the one who brought it up . . . I told Kiki I wanted the headline to be "Swimming in the Shallow End." She said no. I guess that's why she's the editor. It's called *diplomacy.*

But you know that sinking feeling when you realize the only voice you've heard for, oh, the last ten or fifteen minutes is your own? I couldn't stop talking. I just went on and on, and on and on, and *on and on,* about this actress. And nobody cares that much, not even me. When I finally came up for air, Max jumped in to say he had to get back to work.

"Oh, right," I said. *"Me, too!"*

As I see it, first dates are extremely important, fashion-wise. One can't try too hard. One mustn't overdress. The idea is to look your best, but the kind of best where it appears that you look that good every day—that you didn't make any special effort. I wanted to wear something intriguing, but not overstated. Sexy, but not skanky. I stood in the doorway of my closet for a full fifteen minutes, wondering, *What is this something?* When I'd spoken to Max, he said we'd "grab something to eat." This meant he wasn't going to make a reservation, and *that* meant I didn't know where we were going. I'd have to wing my outfit.

I put on a dress. Too prissy. I put on a pair of pants with a skimpy top. Too body-conscious. I emptied my closet of everything I owned, tried on every shoe, and *still* couldn't find anything to wear. My clothing crisis was like a tsunami—it swept from my mind any sense of perspective. I actually felt like I was going to cry. Still not sure what to wear, I decided I should at least start on my makeup—I could pick my outfit when I calmed down—but my hands were shaking and I smeared eye shadow all over my face and had to wash it off and redo it. Everything was taking too long—I was supposed to be there in twenty minutes, and I hadn't even dried my hair yet. I didn't think I had enough time to tweeze. I needed King Solomon, reincarnated as a beauty editor, to help me decide which part of my beauty regimen I should skip. *Tweeze or dry?* I wondered. *Tweeze or dry? TWEEZE OR DRY?* I didn't shave my legs but that, at least, was on purpose—I'm a firm believer that if you shaved your legs you jinxed the date. Desperate not to be late, I finally threw my hair in a ponytail and frantically tweezed. I put on an old, standby pair of Levi's that I hoped accentuated the positives and hid the negatives. Next I added a camisole that Kiki once said she thought made my boobs look bigger, and threw on a blazer, a knit scarf, and sneakers. Funky casual—that's what I was hoping for. Too bad I didn't notice until dinner with Max was half over and I made a trip to the ladies room that I was only wearing one earring and my camisole was on inside out.

Anyway. Once I was dressed I made a mad dash for my car. I was going to overlook the fact that Max hadn't offered to pick me up because I was curious to see where he lived. Besides, his place was only a few minutes away.

I wasn't disappointed. It was a large, contemporary house, built in the midfifties, complete with a huge redwood deck, glass all around, and a view of Griffith Park Observatory. *Max may be even more than boyfriend material,* I thought while I parked my car out front. *Max is Move-In-Together material . . .*

He greeted me at the door and gave me a quick tour. The house was filled with a mix of postwar furniture (Saarinen chairs, Nelson lamps) and I-found-this-on-the-street-corner cool. It was perfect. But I didn't say much—I was trying not to talk his ear off after my performance on the phone.

"Okay," Max said, pausing in his bedroom to put his wallet, cigarettes, and keys in his pocket. "I guess we better hit it."

He offered to drive. (Good.) And opened my door for me. (Better.)

In the car, he said we were going for shabu shabu in Little Tokyo, and I nodded like I knew what he was talking about. When we got there, the restaurant looked a little like a diner—white Formica, no-nonsense metal-and-vinyl chairs—except it had gas burners with huge pots on them on each table, in which customers were cooking their own steak and vegetables. Max, who had obviously figured out that I had no idea what was going on, explained how *shabu shabu* means "swish swish" in Japanese and gave me a little tutorial on how to do it, stirring long strips of beef in the boiling water and then dipping them in sauce. I was having a pretty good time. The food was good, even though the hot pot between us made me feel like I was being steam-cleaned. The other problem was suddenly I couldn't think of anything to say. My brain was completely blank—I'd open my mouth and out would come . . . nothing. I pretty much just sat there, smiling at everything he said, boiling my meat, and nodding like the village idiot. It was just that he was so *cute*. He made me feel like a troll. Every time I looked at him, I wanted to die. I really did.

On the drive back to his house, I thought, *You blew it. He didn't even ask if you wanted to go for a drink.* He parked his car outside his house and we both got out. I stood there for a minute, struck dumb, not knowing what to do. But then he said, "Do you want to come in for a minute? I think my roommates are out . . ."

"Really?" I said. (I hoped I didn't sound too eager.)

"Yeah, I got a bottle of wine somewhere."

"I like wine."

"Yeah, well"—he grinned—"most people do."

Inside, Max turned on a couple of lamps. But not, I noticed, all of them. *Maybe dinner didn't go so bad after all,* I thought. *Now if I could just relax.*

"I have Radiohead," he said, shaking a vinyl import and doing a funny little dance.

"Nice dance," I said. "Do it again."

"Noooo way." He put the record on the turntable. "Actually, I'm a really bad dancer."

"You don't say," I teased. I sat on the couch with my feet under me and hoped I looked coquettish.

"Oh, come on now." Max went into the kitchen, and I could hear him rummaging around. He returned with the wine and a corkscrew. "Is there anything you're particularly bad at, besides picking up guys?"

"And look at how bad—I got stuck with you."

"Oh, 'Ha.' " He balanced the bottle on the end of the couch and fiddled with the opener. "No, seriously. What are you bad at?"

I pretended to ponder his question for a moment. A long list popped into my head. Bad at: parking, driving, watching what I eat, quitting smoking, keeping boyfriends, hiding my feelings, spelling, not worrying, not picking at my face, sticking to an exercise regimen, getting up early, driving within the speed limit, thinking before I speak, keeping doctors' appointments, cleaning . . . But I didn't think he was ready for this much sharing. So I said, "I'm sure I'm bad at something, but I don't really know. Bad at thinking up things I'm bad at?"

"Nice try." The cork popped out.

He poured me a glass of wine and sat next to me on the couch. Draped his arm over the backrest, rested his head on his hand. His face was close, but not superclose. I tried not to lose my cool. I had to concentrate.

"Can it be a TK?" I said.

"A what?"

"Oh, right, sorry, a TK. It's a phrase journalists use. When you don't know a fact yet—like, um, 'A Clockwork Orange was released in nineteen-TK'—it means you're going to fill it in later. TK stands for 'to come.' "

"Then why isn't it TC?" He clinked my glass. "Cheers."

"Cheers. Um, I don't know." *I'm so clever,* I thought. *Max forgot his question.* "Like, *lead,* as in the first thing in a story, is spelled l-e-d-e. Head, as in *headline,* is h-e-d."

"Well, I think that's kinda weird, Ben, because, like, in my business, *T-shirt* is spelled T-s-h-i-r-t."

"Omigod, yer *sew* funny."

I wondered if he would ever kiss me.

"What about something about yourself you don't like," he said. "Give me that, and I'll let it go."

"I hate my stomach." I blurted this out before I even had time to think, and I quickly realized this was *not* something I wanted to share this early on.

"Because . . ."

"No. I mean. No. Because. I don't know. It's um . . ."

There was really no way out of it, so I finally just told him the truth. "Because no matter how skinny I get, it's never flat. I know that's scary but it's true. It's a Buddha belly. I hate it."

"Lemme see."

"No way."

"Lemme see."

"No way."

A tickling match ensued. Max tickling me and screaming, "I wanna see your Buddha belly!" Me, laughing hysterically and trying like crazy to fight him off.

Do I really have to tell you how it ends?

"Yeah! Fuck you! How did it end?"

I was curled up on the decrepit old wicker chair that I kept on the patio outside my apartment. There are few times when things have gone so well that I can just savor it and leave Kiki squirming in anticipation. I switched the phone to the other ear.

"Okay, so basically he kept tickling me until I kicked him in the face by mistake and gave him a bloody nose."

"You *didn't*," she said.

"I did. Yeah, I really did."

"You're such a spaz."

"But it was okay. I mean, it wasn't *okay*, but he put some ice on it and was pretty nice about the whole thing. And then, well, I kind of kissed his nose, to make it feel better . . ."

"And then?"

"And then he kind of kissed me to make me feel better . . ."

"And then?"

"And then he kind of asked me if I wanted to spend the night . . ."

"No!"

Yes. Here's what happened: After kissing for a bit, Max popped the question. At first I was taken aback. He was gracious enough to offer me boxers and a T-shirt, and said he didn't care whether or not anything happened. *Yeah, right,* I thought. Of course something would happen. And that would lead to that horrible, too-much-information feeling when you know you've gone too far for a first date. Like this one time—I was with this guy, first-date situation, and we started messing around. Everything was going fine until he leaned over right in the middle of things, grabbed a tube of K-Y out of his nightstand, and squirted a huge glop into my hand. *And it wasn't even a fresh tube.* Icky moments like this, I decided, were *not* going to be a major part of my new single life. But Max laid the best line on me (if, indeed, it was a line) that I'd ever heard. He said, "I just want to spend the night with you, sweet girl."

"Ugh! And you *liked* that?" Kiki howled, making retching noises.

"I know, but picture it. He was being so sincere. He told me he thought I was adorable. He was the *best* kisser I have *ever* kissed . . ."

"Slut!" she yelled.

Oh, hell. What can I say? The next thing I knew I was in his boxers and a Super Very Good T-shirt. He lit candles. We lay on his big bed, with its scratchy comforter. (Why is it that most men have never heard of a thread count?) Shortly after that, the boxers were on the floor. Max kissed my stomach for a full five minutes. I kissed his everything. He was gracious and kind and there was no K-Y in sight. It was bliss.

FILLY TIPS

STEALTH PHONE!

When it comes to guys, good phone techniques can save you from yourself. —*B.F.*

- Never initiate a call. Only call back.

- Never call back right away.

- If you have his cell, work, or home number memorized within the first three months, you're calling too much.

- To avoid seeming overeager during chats, do something else at the same time that requires concentration.

- Banish from your vocabulary the four W's and the H—namely, who, what, where, when, and how. Asking when you'll see him, how you'll get there, what time he'll be home, where he's going, and who he's going with all imply that you give a shit.

- Always end the conversation first.

- But most important, remember, just be yourself! ∪

Max called three days later, thank God. Just as I was starting to completely bug out. And I was particularly proud of the fact that *before* the conversation wound down I called myself from my fax machine, told him I had to take the call, and got off the phone first. *Yes.* I had another date with Max on Saturday night. It was Wednesday. I was sure the wait would kill me.

"Don't you think the sheen on that one is a little *too* white?" I said.

"Ben, she's a bride," the Mother said. "It's supposed to be white."

"Yeah, Mom, I know, but not Colgate commercial white."

Audrey looked uncertain. "I don't know . . ."

"Vhat she vill love ees thees vone vit ze beadwork. Ze beadwork on thees vone es fabulous," interrupted the saleswoman in her impossible, put-on accent. We were in a ritzy bridal shop in Beverly Hills. It was the third store that day and the air-conditioning was broken. Audrey and the saleswoman from hell went back in the dressing room to try on her umpteenth dress and my mother went to investigate more gowns, so I wandered around. The carnation pink and baby blue frescoes on the walls were making me slightly nauseous. A couple of the dresses were okay, though, and I wondered which one I'd wear if it were me. Before I could decide, Audrey emerged in ze beadwork gown and it was hideous.

"Um . . ." she said.

"Well, maybe it's not you," said the Mother.

I said, *"Eet ees a dress zhat could only be vorn by ze bride of Satan."*

Nobody laughed.

Wearing sample shoes that were two sizes too big, Audrey clumped back behind the heavy velvet curtains.

"What's wrong with you?" the Mother hissed, pulling me into a corner.

"What's wrong with *you*?"

"You're not being very supportive."

I decided there was no better time to try the reflective-listening thing that Nina's always using, so I said, "It must be terrible for you to feel like I'm not being supportive."

The Mother pursed her lips. "Should we just take you home?"

I hate it when my mom talks to me like I'm ten. Especially since she didn't talk to me like I was ten when I was actually ten. "No. I want to go look at more dresses. I do. *I do.*"

Surprisingly enough, I was kind of looking forward to the day. I thought it would be really fun and great and girlie. That we'd find the perfect dress for Aud and then go to a restaurant to eat quiche and drink mimosas (what ladies-who-lunch eat and drink, in my mind). But the dresses were awful. The samples were dirty with pen marks and sweat stains from other nervous brides-to-be, and everything seemed designed with the lowest common denominator in mind. Plus, my second date with Max was that night—unlike last time, I wanted to plan my outfit early. (We were going to a rock show, always a fashion challenge.)

Just the same, the Mother was being a little borderline, so in the next store I didn't say a word when Audrey briefly considered a huge, crinoline puffy cream ball thing. It reminded me of when we used to play dress-up. Audrey liked to be one of two things: a fairy princess, or a mommy. I'd tackle my mom's closet and dress up like whatever—the first lady, a corporate attorney, Superwoman. One time I greeted the Mother in her bedroom wearing red heels, pink lipstick, and a negligee I found in her special drawer.

"And what are you supposed to be?" she asked.

"A hooker!" I said. I was six.

The fourth store turned out to be a dud, too. Audrey still had one more appointment, and every time I opened my mouth the Mother looked like she'd just gotten a whiff of the sewer. Fortunately she got paged by a client who wanted her to show him a house in Hancock Park. After bringing us back to the first bridal shop so I could get my car, she said pointedly, "I trust you can take it from here?"

Not a problem.

"Can you believe I'm getting married?" Audrey asked when we were safely inside my car and the Mother was driving in the opposite direction.

I said I guessed I was a little surprised.

"I'm *stressed*," she said. "Mom keeps giving me magazines with little Post-it notes on what she thinks the flowers should look like, what she thinks the cake should look like . . ."

"Well, you're the first daughter getting married. You get to break her in."

I paused to blow my horn at someone who cut me off. "Do you think if I take Kiki to the wedding as my date our relatives will think I'm a lesbian?"

Audrey sidestepped this one.

"Do you think I'm making a mistake?" she said.

"Who am I to say whether or not you're making a mistake?"

"I think you think I'm making a mistake."

"You love Jamie, right?"

"More than anything."

"Then you're not making a mistake."

We drove for a few minutes in silence. Just as I was getting into a song

I recognized they were playing on the radio, Audrey busted out with: "Do you think Jamie is cute?"

"I think Jamie is very cute," I said. "He's got those great eyes. And . . . he's very fit."

"Would you have sex with him?"

"I can't think of a single appropriate way to answer that question."

"I mean, if you didn't know me. If you met him while you were out one night."

"You've had sex with him, right?"

"Of course."

"And you like it, right?"

"Yeah."

"There you go."

"But . . . ahem. To be honest, ahem, he doesn't go . . ." Audrey tucked a stray clump of hair behind her ears.

"Go where?"

"Don't make me say it!" She started pointing toward her seat. "You *know* . . ."

"He doesn't eat you out?"

"Ben-ja-*mi*-na." (This being the response I usually get whenever Audrey and I talk about sex.)

"What? Don't get all shocked. You brought it up."

She cleared her throat again. "Well, I mean, maybe he would. If I asked him. Which I haven't." She inspected a perfectly manicured nail, then folded her hands back in her lap. We were stopped at a traffic light. Her engagement ring from Tiffany's glittered darkly. Her skin and her blue eyes were incredibly clear, I noticed, and her pressed gray pants went perfectly with her lint-free black cardigan. I could try my whole life, but I would never look like Audrey. My life's too messy. She looked young.

"Do you let people . . . do it to you?" she asked.

"Everyone who offers."

"Sha," she snorted. I think it was the first time she smiled that day.

We pulled into the parking lot behind Cupid's Garden. Walking in, Audrey told the ladies-in-waiting that I was the bride-to-be.

"Audrey," I started to say, "what are you—"

But before I had a chance to protest, the saleswoman swished me off to the dressing room, where she whisked my shirt over my head and started measuring away while asking me about my fiancé. So I made it up. He owns his own fashion company, I said. He's a graphic designer, too, I added. He's tall and thin. Has a modern house in the hills. We're going to honeymoon in Africa, I said, and we're going to have two children, Kurt and . . . um . . . Courtney. Isn't that cute? Yes, isn't it?

Audrey started throwing wedding gown after wedding gown through the doorway. I tried on five Vera Wangs before we found The Dress. It was a dramatic, creamy strapless number by Christian Dior with a huger-than-huge skirt featuring enormous pale pink silk cabbage roses tumbling down the back. It was bold. It was dramatic. It was hopelessly romantic. The saleswoman led me out of the dressing room and put me on a little pedestal in front of the mirror. I looked at my reflection and burst into tears. "I love it!" I screamed at my sister, who also started to cry and was clapping her hands with glee. *I absolutely love it!*

The saleswoman handed me a tissue. "Please, hon," she said. "Not on the dress."

Later that night, Max came to pick me up. When I opened the door, he handed me a bouquet of carnations and a bag with SUPER VERY GOOD emblazoned on the side, saying, "This is for you, my dear."

Where does he get these terms? I thought, taking the bag and showing him into the living room. *My dear. Sweet girl. If he calls me baby doll I'm going to dissolve into a puddle of happy mushy femaleness.* I made a crack that nobody gives carnations anymore and Max shrugged. He said, "You can take the boy out of Ohio . . ."

I opened the bag, and in it was a navy blue T-shirt. On it was a big, fat, smiling Chinese Buddha and below him read the words FOR GOOD LUCK, RUB MY BELLY in Asian-style script.

"I *love* it," I said. "But"—I held it up to myself—"what are you getting at?"

Max smiled and gave my stomach a little pat. "For luck. Let's go. We're going to be late."

We were going to Spaceland to see a band I'd never heard of before called The New Year. In the car on the way over, Max explained they were pretty much think-tank-indie-rock types, two of whom used to be in a band called Bedhead, all of whom took their music as seriously as anyone currently studying at Juilliard. Apparently the drummer was a friend who stopped by the warehouse sometimes for free Super Very Good clothes. I was curious, so I asked Max how he got to start his own company anyway. He told me how he'd gone to Rhode Island School of Design, but he wasn't that interested in studying so he left. He'd started the company with twenty thousand dollars, mostly money scraped together from some professional skateboarder friends. I imagined Super Very Good was worth a lot more now. His house, however, was a rental. Max said he didn't feel ready to buy, and he was pouring all his money back into the company. This explained the roommates, Seth and Stuart (Max called them Fred and Barney), whose presence I'd sensed the night I slept over (the pizza boxes and a photo of Britney Spears taped to the refrigerator were dead giveaways), but whom I'd never actually gotten to meet. I was so impressed by Max, by his job, by every blond hair on his head . . .

"Why don't you have a girlfriend?" I asked.

"Oh. God. I haven't had a girlfriend since high school." He laughed. "It's fine. Although, you know, I hate sleeping alone."

I gave him my best sidelong glance. "Don't even try it."

We parked and Max took my hand as we walked to the club. I gave my ID to the bouncer. But then I saw something bizarre—Max's was fake.

Now, I've seen some fake IDs in my life. When I was in college, I put myself through my last year of school by working nights as a bartender. Because I was sick of cleaning up kiddie puke, I used to cut up fake IDs with a pair of scissors I hung on the wall with a big red ribbon. It was one of the only times in my life that I've ever really been in a position of power, and I got a good laugh from the bar backs whenever I did it. But this bouncer, he didn't even notice that Max's "Alaska" driver's license was a laminate, when Alaska doesn't do laminates anymore. I looked at Max like, *What's going on?* His face remained a blank.

At the bar, I ordered the usual scotch and soda. Max got a Sprite.

"So," I said, looking him over. "You an ex-convict or something?"

"What do you mean?" he asked.

"On the lam? On the run? In the witness protection program?"

"No. No. And, no. Why?"

"Well"—I lowered my voice to a whisper—"you have a fake ID."

"So? Until recently, so did you."

He was looking at me like I was being really weird, the straw from his Sprite stuck in his mouth. I was looking at him like he was being really weird, beads of water from my scotch condensing in the palm of my hand. *Why would I have a fake ID for six years?* I wondered, reaching for the napkin. *Why would I have a fake ID when I'm old enough to go to a . . .* And that's when it hit me.

"Max, how old are you?"

"Ben, how old are *you?*"

A beat. I squinted at him and said, "How old do you think I am?"

"Dunno. I never really thought about it. What, are you, like, twenty-three?"

I shook my head. This was bad.

"Okay . . . twenty-two . . . Twenty-one?" He was smiling.

This was not good. This was not good. This was so not good.

I proposed that we both say our ages at the exact same time.

"You're on," he said. He was starting to look a little worried.

"All right. You be the counter."

Max held three fingers up. One went down. Two went down. The third went down and I yelled out, "Twenty-seven!"

Max was silent.

"Twenty-seven!" I yelled again, trying to keep my sense of humor. "Max . . . it's your turn."

He smiled weakly. "Okay," he said. "Don't freak out. It's not a big deal."

"Go on."

"I'm twenty."

It took me a minute to scrape my jaw off the bar.

"You're joking."

"I wouldn't joke about that."

"You're twenty?"

"Yeah."

"Twenty."

"Yeah."

Twenty.

"Um, would you excuse me for a minute?" I didn't know where to go, so I made a dash for the bathroom, knocking over some guy's beer on the way and not even stopping to say sorry. I wanted to splash cold water on my face. Then I got there and realized I was wearing makeup so I couldn't. Instead I snuck a cigarette in the bathroom stall. I wondered if everyone was thinking the same thing I was: *And here's to you, Mrs. Robinson, Jesus loves you more than you will know* . . .

When I got back, Max looked a little green. "I didn't mean to mislead you," he said. "I thought you might be a *little* older than me, because of the writing job and all, but only by a couple of years. You look *young*, B."

I ignored the fact that he'd just shortened my name to one letter, which, I have to say, was pretty endearing.

He asked, "Is it really such a big deal?"

Maybe. Yes. Maybe. It certainly *felt* like a big deal. The first thing I wanted to know was whether or not he'd been lying to me. The company, the house, all of it. But Max's answer made sense. He said he'd started the company his first year in college. He left to run it before the year was out, and that pretty much accounted for what had happened since. He was about to turn twenty-one, he said. In two weeks.

"So I'm a cougar," I moaned, putting my head in my hands.

"A what?"

"An older woman who picks up younger guys."

"They call that a cougar? That's funny."

"It's not."

"Oh, so what, right?" He put his hand over mine. "Look, I'm still the same guy. And, to be honest, I don't really care how old you are. You're too adorable to pass up." I started to melt. He could sense it. "My little cougar," he said, poking my ribs. "Grrrr."

Later, just before Max pulled the boxers off me once again (oh, like you would have gone home), we turned it into a game. I pointed out that when I was having sex for the first time, he was learning how to ride his BMX bike. He remarked that when I was learning how to drive, he had a crush on his baby-sitter, who was my age and was now married with two kids. When I was going to college, he was busy collecting Power Rangers. Max started kissing me. I opened my eyes and was relieved to find that his were shut. This gave me a chance to really inspect his face, or at least the top half of his face. His long eyelashes curled just above his cheek. Up near his ears, tiny hairs glowed, downy. Outside, it started to rain. Big drops that splashed the asphalt like the sky was giving the ground a well-deserved spanking. Through the open window, the world smelled different, like earth and clean leaves. I slid my hands down Max's perfect stomach, washboard without effort, as most twenty-year-old stomachs are, and I could feel him pressing against me just below my navel. It wasn't insistent, but asking permission, so I angled my hips away, saying no. For now.

"Too soon," I whispered.

"Mmmm," Max said, never leaving my mouth. I continued to watch him kiss me, fascinated. I wondered if every guy, while kissing a girl, looked like he could so easily fall in love.

In the morning, however, when I left Max's warm bed, the sunlight an incriminating glare on the freshly washed sidewalk, it didn't seem so easy. *I'm twenty-seven years old,* I thought. *I put on wedding dresses and I cry.* As I unlocked my car door I wondered if, when Max stood on his porch and kissed me good-bye, he could see wrinkles around my eyes. I'd never thought I had wrinkles before, but what if I did? Maybe I didn't look as good as the last girl who'd left his house. She was probably a college senior. Or a waitress from the Back Door Bakery down the street. Pulling onto Silver Lake, I called Kiki from my cell. On the third ring, she answered.

"Kiki?" I said. My voice had a catch.

"Ben? Is everything okay?"

How dismal my situation really was hit me the minute I heard her concern digitally wafting through the air. "When I saw *Star Wars* for the first time, Max . . ." Was I going to cry? "Max . . . was an embryo."

With her shocked silence for company, I started my drive home.

CHAPTER

4

Kiki arrived armed with a fresh pack of cigarettes, a sixer of Amstel, and sunscreen, and arranged the supplies on the decrepit picnic table that sat like an abandoned shipwreck outside my apartment. I checked the SPF number while flicking on my lighter.

"Oh good," I said. "This won't wash off while we do sports."

Kiki smiled. "So how old?" she asked, handing me a beer.

"Twenty years, eleven months, two weeks," I said.

Kiki sat across from me and lit her cigarette with one of those long matches my neighbors used for the barbecue, which I was afraid of since it was gas and I always thought I was going to blow myself up. The crunchy, patchouli-fumigated guy who lived next door grilled veggie burgers on it sometimes, but only when my window was open so my entire apartment ended up smelling like a Phish show on fire. I used it as an ashtray.

"Did you ask your mom if she'll drive you to his b-day party?" she asked.

"He's going home for it."

"So perfect." Kiki stretched out, crossed her long legs at the ankles. "You don't have to stress about getting him a gift that says you're into him but not obsessed, and soon he'll be old enough to go to bars."

"If you're going to be glib, I'm ordering a pizza."

I went upstairs for the phone, brought it back, and dialed the preprogrammed number. I needed a large sausage and mushroom in thirty minutes or less.

"You wanna free salad with it?" the guy said. "Only two dollars more."

"Then it's not exactly free," I said, rolling my eyes at Kiki.

"Huh?"

"Two dollars isn't free."

"Please hold."

I waited an unbelievably long period of time, which allowed me to ponder possible consequences. As in, maybe I should get the salad and skip the pizza since the new guy I was dating was four and probably didn't want to see my fat, tired twenty-seven-year-old flesh . . . He came back.

"So, you want a free salad with that or not?"

"Um, okay, yeah. Make it a salad and a pizza."

I'll just eat the salad, I thought.

"What—you're going to go on a diet now?" Kiki said when I hung up. "Look, everything's going to be fine. No, better than fine. Here's the thing.

So he's a little younger than we thought. That's not so bad. It's *society.*"

"Oh *come on.*" I rolled my head from shoulder to shoulder, trying to get my muscles to relax, and my spine made a loud crack. "You're not seriously going to turn this into a political issue."

"No, listen, if you were a male VP at Sony and he were some hot d-girl nobody would even care. They'd give you a fucking *promotion.* Look, I've always believed that the right guy is just the right guy. Like if he worked at Kinko's, but you liked him, his blue apron wouldn't matter. Or if he didn't make a decent living and lived in a shack, you'd just accept it. Remember, there's *always* something we have to overlook. Back hair, bad parenting, drug problem, weird moles, passive aggression, poor fashion, stamp collection . . . I think you should count your blessings. Max is *cute,* okay? He has a good job. He's got good hair. He might be younger, but what about Susan Sarandon and Goldie Hawn? They go out with younger men and they're *celebrities.* The *fact* remains, Max could be perfect for you. Or not. I don't think age is the issue. Whether or not he's boyfriend material is the issue."

I tried to get Kiki's words to make an imprint on my brain. Then I thought, *When Max is thirty-three, I'll be forty.*

"Have you talked to Good Morning Vietnam?" I asked, opening another beer and hoping a change of subject would do me good.

"Edward? Nooo. But, in a moment of weakness, I called him."

"You didn't."

"Can you believe? Left the most embarrassing message, too—said I had this T-shirt of his and wanted to know if he wanted it back. Total hell."

"*Total* hell. And?"

"He didn't call me back. In fact"—she paused for dramatic effect—"I give up."

"Oh, come on. You don't mean that."

She said she did. No more men, no more dates. I found this hard to believe—Kiki dated more than the Mother, which was saying a lot. She claimed she yearned for solitude.

"Nobody wants solitude," I said.

"I do," she said. "I *fantasize* about it."

"Knowing that if you do it too long you'll miss your peak years and end up childless?"

"Oh, I don't believe that backlash shit." Kiki shook her hand in front of her face. "From now on it's work and home. Then work, then home. I just bought a new DVD player, and I have a gazillion movies on the way from Amazon, so . . . That's it. If I'm meant to meet someone, I will. Frankly, I think the universe will reward me for my restraint."

"You can't act aloof so the universe will get interested," I said. "The universe isn't a guy." I paused. "Now who's going to go out with me and meet cute boys?"

"Nobody." She smiled. "Because you already *have* a cute boy."

After Kiki left, I puttered around, pretending to tidy up. That whole never-leaving-the-house-again thing—she sounded like she could actually be serious. Then again, only a few months ago she'd said she was going to quit her job, become a Buddhist, and renounce material goods in order to achieve a higher level of spiritual awareness. Started showing up at my house with trash bags full of jewelry, black cashmere sweaters, and designer shoes that seemed too dressy for her pilgrimage to nirvana. I stashed it all in the closet and gave it back to Siddhartha when she came to her senses a few weeks later. I've helped Kiki carry her microwave oven to the trash because she was joining the raw-foods movement, and I've helped her go pick out a new microwave when she ate so many carrots the whites of her eyes turned orange. Whenever Kiki gets one of these plans into her head, I play along and hope my best friend isn't about to turn into a raw-foods-eating Buddhist vegetarian social worker.

Anyway. Kiki, somehow, managed to make me feel like everything would be okay. But after she left, a kind of free-floating anxiety took over. I inspected my face in the mirror, and wondered if the sun gave me wrinkles. I lit a cigarette, and started to worry about what it was doing to the elasticity of my skin. I put on a clay masque, hoping to undo some of the damage, and while it dried I thought about those "How Old You *Really* Are" quizzes in *Cosmo*. I pretty much checked off every risk factor in the box and discovered that I was, like, *fifty*. While brushing my teeth, I worried that statistically Max was in a higher-risk group when it came to diseases. We hadn't had sex yet, but we'd done other stuff—how risky was other stuff, exactly? And I wasn't just worried about dying, either. *I made it through my early twenties without getting a single cold sore,* I thought, staring at my reflection in the mirror. *Oh sweet Jesus, what if I get one now?*

I turned in early, and had a crazy dream in which I tried to find Max in a murky swamp. I was holding my breath and diving down into smelly green water. Finally I spotted him. He was drowning. I reached for his hair, pulled him up to the surface. But when I went to kiss him, all I had was his severed head. I woke up, kicking wildly and screaming, "Noooo head! Noooo head!"

★ ★ ★

Ten A.M. Phone ringing. Me sleeping. Phone ringing. Me pulling pillow over head. Phone ringing. Oh, hell.

I picked up the phone. "Who's calling before eleven?"

"Yo! Where were you last night?"

Did I forget to mention Ashton?

"Out."

"Where'd you go to?"

Ashton who ends his sentences in prepositions?

"Uhhh . . ." I pictured the post-Kiki panic attack and leaned over to pick at the middle-of-the-night pedicure I'd given myself after that dream woke me up. I hadn't let it dry all the way though, so I now had a waffle pattern from my sheets on each toe. "Out," I lied. "Rock show."

"Who'd you see?"

"You wouldn't know. There were no synthesizers, oversize cargo pants, or tabs of X. There were actually people there who knew how to play a guitar." I lit a cigarette and rubbed my eyes.

"Gross. So I called you at, like, twelve-thirty, but there was no answer. I called you Saturday night, too."

Okay. So I'm a bad person. All right? A bad, bad person. But Ashton was Kiki's idea. We'd met him at a gallery opening. He asked me if I liked the art; I said no. He asked for my number; I gave it to him. He seemed okay. But once he started leaving messages it didn't feel right. I called Kiki at the office and told her I intended to blow him off.

"No, no, no, no, *no,*" she said. "You're dating now, okay. You gotta give people more of a chance."

"But you were the one who said most guys in L.A. are assholes," I said.

"Which is why you have to make sure you're not tossing out the *one* amazing guy who *isn't* an asshole. Investigate. Let things breathe. Seriously—you shouldn't get rid of any potential partner until after you've had the sex."

So I started dating him, but he was neither amazing nor asshole. The best thing about it was at certain key moments I didn't have to be alone.

I got out of bed and tried to wake myself up.

"Let's go out tonight," Ashton said. *So the question is,* I thought while pulling my bathrobe on over my pajamas, *is it pathetic to go out with another guy because I haven't heard from Max? Or is it pathetic* not *to go out with another guy because I haven't heard from Max?*

"Ben—are you there?"

"I'm here."

I couldn't make up my mind. What if Max called and I had plans? It was hopeless. "Ash," I said, "I'm gonna call you back when I'm not asleep."

"Word."

I fed Freak. Drank my morning diet Coke. Read my e-mails, which were mostly dispatches from the Whip, *Filly's* editor in chief, who thought the tone on my last piece was off. I checked for an e-mail from Max, but there was none. *Oh yeah,* I remembered. He said if we exchanged addresses then we'd just become those people who e-mailed one another all the time and never actually talked. At the time, I thought this was romantic. Now I think I should have pushed. Because you can e-mail casually. But you can never, ever call casually. *They see through you.*

By two, there was still no call. *Maybe I should tell Ashton I'm free . . .* I knew what the Mother would say. ("Just *go*. What are you moping around here for? Get your nose out of that *book*. You're driving your mother crazy.") She'd date through a bad case of polio.

I finally sent Ashton a casual e-mail: "We're on."

I spent the rest of my afternoon wishing I had a real job. I had a celebrity interview to prepare for, but sitting at my computer reading bios on upcomingmovies.com and poking at the keys to write questions more interesting than "What was it really like to work with [insert director name here]?" made me feel like I was wasting my life. I wanted to be *out*. To see the world. I thought about going for coffee, but sitting outside the Coffee Bean & Tea Leaf with all those people circling want ads in *Variety* always makes me depressed. Exercise was out of the question. So I started a load of laundry, which I then forgot about and left in the washer for half the day. (When I finally pulled it out it smelled mildewed and I had to scrounge up quarters so I could wash it all over again.) Then I tried to interest Freak in a toy called the "Cat Dancer" that I'd bought at the grocery store—five bucks for wire with a little piece of cardboard at the end. He just looked at me like, *Why are you jumping around with that wire with a little piece of cardboard at the end?* I started a book about Orson Welles because I want to better myself and not be a total idiot my whole life, but I got bored during Truffaut's foreword and realized I just didn't give a damn. In a last-ditch attempt to jazz up my day I went to Ron Herman, and Allegra, who'd picked out practically every piece of clothing I owned, did her best to make me look cute even though I wasn't really in a shopping mood. She worked on commission, though, so I bought two wool pencil skirts I'd never wear because I didn't actually work in an office, a snazzy-looking top I couldn't afford that was tight and made me feel self-conscious, and—who knows why?—a wristband. When I walked in the front door with the shopping bags, I had my first pang of guilt over the money I'd spent.

Maybe I'll just wear the shirt tonight as a little test run, I thought, pulling the top out and inspecting the tag. *I can probably just tuck this in my bra . . .*

"Heyyy, look at you!" Ashton said when I answered the door. He was admiring my new top.

"Oh." I pulled at it self-consciously, trying to keep my left boob from making an unscheduled appearance. "Thanks."

"The tag's sticking out the side."

He crossed the living room to pet the cat, which I'd told him a million times never to do. Freak happily sunk a claw into his thumb.

"Ow!" Ashton gave me a pathetic, *Mommy-take-care-of-me* look, so I went to the bathroom to get him a Band-Aid. While I was there, I dug through my makeup drawer for a pair of nail scissors so I could remove the offending tag. I realized I was going to have to keep the top at the same moment I decided I hated it.

I bandaged Ash's thumb. He leaned down to inspect my work.

"No kiss to make it feel better?" he said.

"Grow up," I said.

"Never." Ashton smiled. He has perfect teeth.

"So," he said. "I was thinking falafel."

This was something that always bugged me about Ash. He worked at a start-up electronic music label and couldn't really afford to go someplace nice. I got that. But the lack of romance . . . It made it seem like dinner was just a nod to convention before we swapped bodily fluids.

"Don't you think we could go to a real restaurant this time?" I asked.

"What're you *talking* about? Falafel is the *shit*."

"No, it's just shit."

My remark was uncalled for—I was surprised I'd snapped like that—but still. I grabbed my purse and stuffed my keys, lip gloss, and a twenty-dollar bill inside. "I'm sorry," I said. "It's just, why can't we, you know, make a real plan for once. Even if we both paid, we could go somewhere . . ."

Ashton looked genuinely hurt. Even his dark hair, which usually stuck straight up, seemed to wilt. He told me he'd sit in a trash can with me if that was what I wanted to do. It made me feel so guilty I wanted to scream.

This was how I ended up sitting at Falafel King trying to be gung-ho about eating a pita stuffed full of fried balls and dripping with a mayonnaisy sauce. The place only had counter service so I had to keep getting up. I got a napkin, sat down, then realized I didn't have a fork. I got the fork, sat down, and discovered I'd finished most of my diet Coke. I got the diet Coke, sat down, and found that my napkin had fallen on the floor. Adding to the up-down-up-down ambience was a nearby trash can piled high with the remnants of other people's dinners. The garbage smelled exactly like what I was eating. And it didn't escape my attention that I'd been worried that Max was too young for me, while here was Ashton, who was my age, yet he still preferred restaurants that served on paper plates.

Oblivious, Ashton launched into a story about some party he'd gone to with his friend Dezi, a DJ at a club on Sunset. I didn't like Dezi because he never remembered me and he called everyone "bro."

I pretended to listen. The last time I'd seen Ashton, I'd been talkative and flirty and had some pink in my cheeks. Sure, it was just the promise of no-strings-attached sex that put it there, but it was *there.* Now all I could think about was Max. I was worried that by now he'd decided I was too old for him, and he'd never call me again. *Maybe I need true love,* I thought. *And all the excitement, insecurity, and self-loathing that only true love can bring.*

Ashton said, "Do you have any friends you can set Dezi up with?"

"What?" I was back on planet earth.

"Dezi."

"No! I mean, I don't think so."

We ended up back at my place on the couch, where I pretended to enjoy another one of Ashton's Crazy-Night-Out-with-Dezi stories. When it was over, he slid his hand up my thigh. I shifted away.

"I think I have a headache," I said. I couldn't believe that lame excuse had left my mouth.

"Take some Tylenol." He was now kissing my neck.

"I'm too tired to get up."

"I'll get it for you." His hand was back on my leg.

"You know what"—I pushed his hand away with a little more force than I meant to—"I want to just go to bed. Alone."

I could see confusion in his eyes, and, maybe, some slight hurt somewhere deep down. *He knows I'm cheating on him,* I thought, which made no sense, since we weren't going out. But I also felt like I was cheating on Max, which also made no sense, because I didn't even know if I was ever going to see him again. "Look, I'm sorry," I said. "I just feel off today. Okay?"

"No, I understand."

Ashton got up and smoothed down his pants. I looked away—his erection was incriminating. "You go snuggle up in bed, get some sleep, and I'll talk to you soon." He gave me a kiss on the cheek and rumpled my hair. Then he let himself out.

The second I heard his steps going down the stairs I ran to my answering machine. *I've acted in good faith,* I thought. *Surely there will be a call from Max on my voicemail, rewarding me for being such a loyal future girlfriend.* But there was no message.

I took off my new shirt, the shirt I despised, and wondered if there was any way to reattach the tag. Well, of course not. I wondered if there was any way to reattach Ashton to my lips, because if I felt lonely before, now I'd fallen into the pit of despair. *Maybe I can call Ash on his cell and say I've taken an Advil and feel much better,* I thought. *Or maybe I can tell him the truth and he'll come over to console me.*

Maybe not.

"What am I doing?" I asked Freak. Who opened his eyes drowsily from on top of the television, where he sleeps because it's always warm. He mewed softly, and fell back into his own dreams.

"Um. What was it like to work with Wes Anderson?"

I was sitting on the stone-walled patio at Orso, a power-lunch location for agents from the William Morris Agency and execs from New Line, trying to conduct a captivating interview of Chandra McInerney, star of

Waiting for Godard and *Minimall*. My tape recorder was whirring on the table between us, my notepad was in my hand, but I was failing miserably. It had been almost a week since the night Max and I had found out our mutual ages and I still hadn't heard from him. I was distracted to the breaking point. Meanwhile, Chandra McInerney was hardly the kind of person you'd want to look vulnerable in front of. She had a multimovie deal at Miramax, designed a clothing line on the side called Gummy, and graduated from Brown. She talked like Missy Elliott even though she was a freckled blonde with stick-thin arms, a ski-slope nose, and a girlish gap between her two front teeth that sent male film reviewers into paroxysms of ecstasy. I'd see her at parties now and then—usually surrounded by a crowd so hip they looked like they were cast at a model call—and it seemed like she'd be popular and stylish even if she weren't famous. Of course, in L.A. it's considered very uncool to slobber over celebrities. When you see them all the time—at the supermarket, hiking in Runyon Canyon, shopping on Sunset Plaza—you cultivate this idea that, deep inside, they're just like the rest of us. But then you get near someone like Chandra and realize they're not like us at all. I was completely terrified of her.

Chandra ignored my question. She looked me up and down and said, "Girl, do you know your hands are shaking?"

"They are?"

"You need protein, muthafucka." She snapped her fingers and a waiter, who'd been ignoring my repeated requests for a glass of water, miraculously appeared. Figuring protein couldn't hurt, I took Chandra's advice and ordered the chicken. She asked for a salad and a bottle of mineral water.

"Two glasses?" the waiter said pointedly. I realized he hadn't brought me any water because I didn't ask for the bottled kind. I nodded meekly.

"You could be coming down with something." Chandra narrowed her eyes at me. "Why don't I just give you the quotes, mkay?"

I was so flattered by her attention, I threw journalistic integrity out the window and actually heard myself saying, "Okay."

"Okay. Here's the thing, G. I want to keep doin' small movies, because that's the only way to stay on top," she said. "Like viral marketing. I'm a *virus*. I have to spread slow. Don't want to blow up too fast. If I do, the public will reject me the same way they rejected P. Diddy, mkay?" She paused for the waiter, who was back with her salad in record time, and continued. "On my love life? *Fuck* my love life. My last boyfriend was off the hook—he was an alcoholic and a fuckin' slob. Homeboy was good in bed, knowwhatImsayin? But I practically checked myself into a fuckin' *hospital* when I found out he was fucking my best friend." She paused, stabbed at her salad, took a bite, and continued. "On my lawsuits: Yeah, I sue. *So sue me.* You fuck with me? I got an entire *law firm* at my disposal, so fuck *you.*" Paused, stabbed, chewed. "On my fashion line: I don't talk about that. That has nothing to do with star-power crap and everything to do with keeping it real, mkay?" She sat back. "That enough for five hundred words?"

"Um, yeah. That should actually do it." I looked at my notes. "And Wes Anderson?"

"He's a fuckin' genius, what do you think? Girl, you're turning green." Chandra rummaged in her purse, pulled out an industrial-size bottle of stinking yellow vitamins, and thrust the tablets toward me. "Take these," she said, lighting a cigarette and inhaling deeply. "They're organic."

But before I had a chance to swallow the pills or take a bite of my chicken, which had just arrived, she was standing up. "Franklin, yo girl's got ADD, knowwhatImsayin? We out."

Chandra was already saying good-bye to a group of execs two tables over when I realized *We out* translated to "Interview over." I paid the check (seventy-five dollars for a lunch I didn't get to eat) and followed her outside, half convinced I wouldn't even get to say good-bye. But Chandra was waving at me to get in her customized Range Rover. I slid into the passenger seat, and she said, "Pay the man will you? I'm outta cash."

Movie stars never carry any money.

I handed the valet a five, and Chandra peeled out and headed up Beverly. In between rolling calls on her cell she told a story about the time she thought she had a life-threatening disease. My ears perked up, because the Whip is always telling us that readers love anecdotes about celebrity illness. But it turned out it was just an ulcer. A very *serious* ulcer, Chandra emphasized, that, she said, "coulda fuckin' fucked up my whole digestive system."

"You have health problems?" I asked.

"Girl," she said. "You have no idea."

I didn't know we were going to Yellow until she pulled into a spot outside.

When Chandra walked through the door of the boutique, everyone stopped for a barely perceptible moment to look. Then they made an obvious attempt not to notice her. Chandra, in turn, arranged her face into an expression of tolerant oblivion. It was like watching two different species interact on *Animal Planet.* Chandra introduced me to the store's owner, as her "favorite new fuckin' person in the whole world," and I was thrilled.

While ladies-in-waiting picked out different clothes for Chandra to try, she pulled me into the dressing room so we could talk. I couldn't believe I was standing there looking at Chandra McInerney in her Cosabella underwear! I remembered how Max had said he got a glimpse of Heather Graham's breasts that time, and I couldn't wait to tell him about my new best friend. That is, if I ever got the chance.

Chandra tried on various outfits, and I made a conscious effort to maintain eye contact, so it wouldn't seem like her being almost naked was making me uncomfortable. On the blurry sidelines of my vision, I could see she was as skinny as a model—collarbone jutting out, ribs countable—but she was even shorter than me, like she shrank. Most actresses are shrunken—the mummies you see at the natural history museum. Sometimes they eat so little their heads look too big for their bodies (something that gives Kiki the heebie-jeebies), their forearms get hairy from all the extra testosterone in their system, and their teeth get soft. But clothes look *so good* on them. While she changed, Chandra crowed to the owner about some "fuckin' hot" clothing designer they both knew. I wanted to find a way into the conversation, but before I could, she said, "Girl, I gotta split, but you can get a ride back with one of the girls here, mkay? I have a meeting at the Peacock."

She meant NBC.

With a superfast wave of her arms that made her look like someone out of *The Matrix,* Chandra was dressed and storming toward the exit before I'd even picked up my purse. Halfway out the door, she shouted back, "Peace, dawg."

I was assured that one of the buyer's assistants would drive me back to the restaurant so I could get my car. The girl in question didn't even try to get a conversation going, obviously thinking I was just some groupie. I guess she didn't see when Chandra programmed my number into her cell.

I was transcribing the tape from my Chandra interview when the phone rang.

"Hello?" I said.

A voice said, "Hey, wanna go see Jon Brion on Friday?"

"Who is this?"

I knew who it was. But I was being passive aggressive because there really isn't anything else to be after a week's gone by and you haven't heard from the guy you'd spend every minute of every day with if it were up to you.

"It's Max."

"Oh. Hey." I said it like I'd been doing so much more than calling Kiki up every morning, noon, and night and saying things like, "Just in case you were wondering, day five, hour one hundred and twenty. No call." (She'd say, "Repeat this to yourself five times: 'I am an attractive woman who's friends with celebrities and has much better things to do,' and call me later.")

"Hey," he said.

"Hey," I said, just to be disagreeable.

He said, "Hey."

The pause started to stretch itself out. Then it made itself comfortable and took a seat. *Then* it started browsing through a magazine. I waited for him to fill the silence with an apology for not calling, or, perhaps, the requisite excuse about being really busy. But Max said nothing. For a moment I thought I could hear him typing something in the background. *Is this guy actually dicking around with his computer while he's on the phone with me?* I thought, suddenly so irritated I wanted to chuck the phone at the wall. But then a little voice in my head whispered, *Don't blow this. You're not prepared to blow this.*

"You know how I feel about Jon Brion . . ." I began, trying to shift my tone.

"Oh . . ." The typing sounds stopped. "You like him?"

"Well, *yeah.* How he plays piano? And the guitar? And the drums? All at once? His version of '99 Luftballons'? So good?" *(Why? Am I talking? Like this?)*

We arranged the particulars. What time he was getting out of work, what time I should get to his house. I tried to think of something charming to chat about and . . .

"Listen, I gotta try to get out of here," Max interrupted, just as I was beginning what I thought was an impressive riff about why Brion's lo-fi rock is really the most po-mo thing an artist can do.

"Oh! Me, too! Busy, busy!" *Painful.*

The first thing Max said when he opened the door was, "I don't think that jacket will look good on you, man. It came out really huge and only fits big dudes."

"Wha—?" I started to say. Max held up his index finger. Oh. He was on the phone. He waved me into the house and continued his conversation.

"Yeah? You gonna check that party out? Nah. Think I'm gonna go to this show . . ."

Max ignored me while I wandered around his bedroom, looking for someplace to sit where I'd seem like I belonged. The bed, which I noticed he made perfectly—no creases in his duvet, thank you very much—seemed too flirtatious, so I perched myself on the stool next to the drum set in the corner. I ran my finger over a cymbal, checking for dust. Nope. He practiced.

"Yeah?" Max said. "Well that makes sense because she's, like, a complete nut job. She used to go out with that guy who works in reception, Eddie. Ummm-hmmmm. Ummmm-hmmmm."

I watched him pace around the room. He checked his pockets for his cigarettes, found them on top of his dresser, got his lighter from the bedside table, lit the cigarette, all with the phone tucked in the nook between his shoulder and his ear. His hair was mussed, like he just woke up. His clothes were all Super Very Good. They hung on him like he was a hanger. I kept expecting him to end the conversation, to tell his friend I was there. But he kept introducing one new topic after another. I had received no kiss.

"Hey, whatever happened with those vinyls you were ordering for me?" he said. "No that's cool. Thanks man. Not too much. Work's been killing me. Well, it doesn't matter if I run the company. Heh, heh. Seriously. Hey, guess who I ran into the other day?" He was now flipping through his records, maybe looking for something to put on the turntable. Yes, that's what it was. He put on a record. Badly Drawn Boy. Good choice. But he had to be kidding. Whenever I tried to talk to Max on the phone, he acted like he hated it, like he had a million other things he needed to do. Now he was just chatting away.

"She's good."

I perked up.

"My mother loves you. You know it. Heh, heh . . ."

IS IT A LOVE CONNECTION?

A budding romance can be bliss, or it can make you want to sharpen your nails into fine points and claw out your own eyes. Here, plot the course of your new romance.—B.F.

start here

THE PARTY: He makes eyes, you exude pheromones. He asks for your number...

IF IT WAS THE WEEKEND...

IF IT WAS A SCHOOL NIGHT

You go home alone & he calls! Make small talk that drips with sexual innuendo until he asks you out.

You drink too many Jack & Cokes and go home with him that same night.

THE HOOK UP! How much happens here depends upon how shameless you are.

IT'S A LOVE CONNECTION! Give mom the good news: You actually have a boyfriend! (Until you break up, that is. When this happens, proceed to START.)

"I'M NOT READY FOR A SERIOUS RELATIONSHIP."

OR

Time to initiate "The Talk," in which he tells you whether or not he wants a commitment.

False alarm.

Finally, I heard signs of the end of the conversation: "Okay. Well then, I'll catch you Thursday. Right, at Fred Sixty-Two. Good French toast. Cool."

He hung up, and I looked at him like, *Are you aware that I've been sitting here for four thousand years?*

He said, "Don't you look pretty."

I couldn't help but smile.

Later that night, I was back in Max's arms. The show was amazing—turned out he knew the singer so we got to go backstage. And then, after we got back to Max's house, and after I put on his boxers (again), and after he took them off (again), I said yes.

I just couldn't wait anymore. And I was fairly certain the timing was right. We'd had a lovely evening—no awkward pauses, no weird jokes about the other night. And being with him felt so *good.* He was tender, but not in a cheesy way. And passionate, but not in a forced way. When he held me, I felt like I could stay there forever. Like I could lie there, starve to death, have the ravens come and pick my bones clean, and I'd be completely fine with it.

After, Max said, "So I was thinking, B." His breath near my ear gave me the shivers.

"Hit me." I tried to nuzzle even closer.

"I was *think*ing . . ."

I held my breath. *He's going to tell me it's all going to be okay,* I thought. *That he's not freaked out by the age difference.* Max rubbed his hand up and down my arm, fingers trailing . . .

"You were thinking," I said.

"Yeah, I was thinking that maybe since that party on Friday won't really get going till eleven we should stop in Koreatown and play some video games."

"What?"

"It's on the way." He paused and craned his neck to look at me. "You don't like video games?"

I've owned every home system known to humanity, from Atari to Sega to PlayStation 2. But this was supposed to be the moment when he told me how things were going to be. When our relationship would come into focus. When I'd get some sense of what I could expect. *Maybe I should just bring it up myself?* I thought. *Point out that, since he was just inside me, maybe this isn't the best time to talk about the arcade?* But then, *Don't blow this. You're not prepared to blow this.*

I smiled into the dark.

"I'll tell you what, Max," I said. "I particularly love House of the Dead, not to mention Time Crisis Two, but I'm also fond of the old school. I can Tron, I can Mario. And if you really want to see something, then get me to an air hockey table."

"Then I'll tell *you* what, B." Max sat up and reached over me for a glass of water. The little hairs on his chest tickled my arm. "I've got five dollars that says I could kick your ass in air hockey."

I scoffed. "You may as well give it to me now."

"And why is that?"

"I was the air hockey interstate trimural champion for fifteen years in a row."

"Pac Ten, huh?" he said, and he laughed.

For some reason, I wanted to hear him sleep. I lay perfectly still and waited for his breathing to get slow, low, and deep, and when it did, it made me happy to the point of giddiness. Something about how he seemed so relaxed. So mine. So right there. *There's so much there, there,* I thought. And this made sense to me. It really did.

CHAPTER

5

I love Duran Duran. They're so eighties and weird and if Max knew I'd die. But I couldn't help driving in my car, thinking about Max, and blasting that song "Save a Prayer" over and over. I mentioned this to Kiki, and she said, "Some people call it a one-night stand, but we can call it paradise."

Once I'd resigned myself to how old he was—make that, how old he *wasn't*—I consoled myself with the fact that at least I had all the hand in the relationship. I'd tell the Story of Max in the coming years, and it would be like he was my last hurrah. I'd talk about how I was getting up there and guys my age and up were starting to get paunches and taking "recreational" Viagra. Or, even worse, they'd go buy a BMW, get a hip haircut, and start going obsessively to the gym. Kiki once dated a twenty-nine-year-old television executive who would only eat boiled chicken for breakfast (with a well-packed bowl of marijuana on the side) because he was on the high-protein diet. And what, this was acceptable just because he was so rich he kept his chicken and his chronic stashed in his stainless-steel Sub-Zero fridge? So Max was going to be my nonchicken guy. My fabulous young boyfriend who could have sex for hours and who wouldn't get fat. There were other forecasted benefits as well . . .

"He's younger than you, so naturally, he'll worship you," Kiki said over beers at The Shortstop, sneaking a cigarette and trying to keep the smoke away from Nina, who'd quit and was being very holier-than-thou about it.

Nina waved her hands around her face like she was warding off a mosquito, and added, "Yet he's socially potty trained, owns his own business, and should know a thing or two about how to act at parties."

"I'm all for it," chimed in Collin, looking over his shoulder at a girl in a sailor-striped top and mandarin jacket. "Is she famous?"

Me, Kiki, Nina: *"No."*

"Yet," Kiki added, turning back around, "because of his youth, he can't *really* be as experienced as you . . ."

"But that's positive," interrupted Nina, "in that the women he's *dated* couldn't have been as smart as you or as successful as you, either. Or as good in bed."

"He'll be amazed by your fabulous connections and all the parties that you're on the list for," Collin volunteered. "Speaking of which, I was wondering if you could get me into that Playboy Mansion party next week."

"She can't take *you*," Kiki said. "She has to take Max. He'll die when she says hello to Hef, shows him around the Grotto . . . It's a real opportunity."

Max's age had been making me feel insecure, but while listening to my friends plotting away, I was suddenly swimming in vast seas of self-confidence. *Yes, yes!* I thought. I could bring Max to the Playboy Mansion *and* introduce him to Hef because Steph was his event planner—he'd be *so* impressed. And when Kiki rightly pointed out that when I met The One I'd have to break things off, I realized that the best thing was nobody would really blame me. I'd magnanimously explain to Max that even though I adored him, I was older, and therefore had more pressing biological-clock concerns that simply couldn't be ignored. He would pine for a while. Okay, maybe a whole year. But then he'd realize my leaving him was the natural order of things. Years would pass, and one day Max and I would have lunch and he'd almost tell me that he was still in love with me but I wouldn't let him. I'd change the subject gracefully to my husband's new film, or how my toddler was faring at Les Enfants, and frankly, he'd love me for that, too, because I would be teaching him how to have dignity. And I would have dignity.

This would be my future—provided I didn't take my romance with Max too seriously, of course. Kiki insisted it was simple strategy. Keeping my feelings in check, she said, would help me not get hurt by a younger man who couldn't be trusted with my heart. But being self-possessed would *also* be intriguing to Max, making him more and more likely to come through in the end. I couldn't lose. Even Chandra, who'd called the next morning and given me precisely three minutes of her time—until she had to go scream at her assistant for giving her "the wrong pen"—was on board. "Hit that shit, Franklin," she said, after I'd told her I'd entered into a tryst with someone who could only just legally drink. "Hit. That. Shit."

Max and I settled into a wonderful routine. We had plans to have plans two nights a week. On the weeknight we went to whatever big party was happening, or Max took me to a rock show. He always knew the best bands to see, and we usually got backstage passes because Max seemed to be friends with an awful lot of musicians. On the weekends Max and I avoided the crowds, who would take over all our favorite spots, and ordered in. Usually Thai food. We'd rent a movie that we'd never watch because we always ended up having sex halfway through, and since his roommates were always out at bars looking for girls, we had the house to ourselves, which meant we could make as much noise as we wanted. It was perfect.

Except. The other night, we were supposed to have dinner with a few of my fancier friends, one of whom promised to procure "the New Coppola" (yet another relative of Francis Ford who had been recently unleashed on society). But since the New Coppola flaked—something about jetting off on the family Gulfstream IV to Paris, you know how it is—Max and I ended up at yet another list party. This one was promoting a new kind of cell phone from Motorola. But anyway. It was being sponsored by Tanqueray, and Max seemed to be having a good time. I caught him staring at me while I sipped my gin daiquiri, and he said, "You know what I like about you, B?"

I pretended to think. "My allergies?" I said.

"Those keep me awake at night."

"The pimple in the middle of my forehead?"

"Your third eye? Hardly noticed it."

"The fact that I purposely put my faults on full display in hopes that you'll find them charming instead of revolting?"

"I was thinking about something else."

"I give up."

"I like that I never worry about you." He shrugged.

"You never worry about? . . ."

"I worried that night that your cat got sick and you had to take him to the vet. I was worried that mean little thing was going to die and you'd be inconsolable. But other than that, I mean, I don't worry about *you*. I can just do this . . ." He shrugged again and smiled. "I dunno, B. I just don't worry about you."

I grinned and patted his arm. But inside, I repeated his words to myself. *I don't worry about you.* I thought, *Don't worry about what about me? Don't worry how about me? Should Max worry about me?* I looked at him. He was sipping his Sprite—he loathed alcohol, which I personally found achingly cute—and smoking his four thousandth cigarette. He looked so harmless. Vulnerable. Sweet, even. *No, it's good,* I thought. *It's good that I don't cause Max any stress. That he's so comfortable being with me.* I decided I would be the one Max didn't worry about. I would make Max happy.

My wildest dreams were confirmed when I took Max to that party at the Playboy Mansion a week later. We were checking out the Grotto, an underground labyrinth of faux lava hot pools where bunnies supposedly cavort naked, and Max was disheartened—we'd only seen one transsexual with his top off. So I sent him off in search of silicone while I caught up with Steph, who launched into a monologue that ran along the lines of: "NO WAY CUTE GUY IS HE YOUR BOYFRIEND I AM SO SERIOUSLY BUGGING RIGHT NOW BECAUSE THE PARKING SITUATION IS FROM FUCKING HELL WHAT ARE THOSE CHAMPAGNE

GLASSES DOING IN THE GROTTO SOMEONE COULD GET HURT WAIT THERE'S MILLA JOVOVICH MILLA! MILLA! . . ." Just then Max reappeared, thrilled because he'd found triplets in G-strings, and put his arms around me. "You're the coolest, B," he whispered in my ear. "Now that I've seen naked girls at the Playboy Mansion—and I still get to go home with you—I can die a happy man."

I just smiled, thinking, *This whole younger-guy thing is really going to work out!*

The next day I figured it was finally safe to ditch Ashton. It didn't take any histrionics. I simply told him during dinner at another lunch-to-late-night restaurant that we were becoming too dependent on one another for people who obviously didn't want to be in something serious. That the best thing, really, would be for us to focus on our friendship. We parted on good terms, both of us assuring the other we'd "get together soon" even though we both knew that wasn't true. It occurred to me that Ashton was probably seeing someone on the side—he gave up rather quickly. But what the hell. I was too happy to care. I thought, *I genuinely hope he's happy with whoever she is.*

I was awakened by a leaf blower wailing away somewhere down the street, a long *waaaaaaaaaa* that both got on my nerves and made me nostalgic for the childhood I'd spent stranded in the suburbs. I opened my eyes and could tell immediately that Max's house was empty—the air was completely undisturbed by any other living thing. I rubbed my head, which was still cloudy, and sat up. The night before Max had taken me to see Ryan Adams, and the band was so wasted they played the longest set I'd ever heard. Then we had to say hello to the lead singer, whom Max knew. Made me wonder. Since when did *Max* know all the cool people? As if reading my mind, he explained that Super Very Good was popular with the musician crowd. Anyhow, Adams chatted us up for a full hour, telling funny stories about growing up in the South and his father's taxidermy hobby—stuffed raccoons hanging over his bed and terrifying the shit out of him when he was a kid. We didn't get home until after three.

Still trying to wake up, my eyes focused on the clock—11:30 A.M., shit. But next to it I saw a tall glass of apple juice and one perfect chocolate-covered cherry, both left there by Max, just for me.

I thought, *I think I'm in love with him.*

Then, *I hope he doesn't find out.*

I squashed both thoughts like a bug.

Max's alarm had gone off at seven-fifteen as usual—he always got up earlier than I did because he had a real job. I vaguely remembered opening my eyes and seeing him sitting on the stool in front of his drums, smoking a cigarette without any clothes on. (Unlike me, he never seemed embarrassed about being naked.) Later, I think after his shower, he kissed me on the cheek and I could smell the cigarettes and toothpaste on his breath. Max smoked two packs a day. I'd never seen anyone smoke so much. When I asked him if he ever thought about quitting, he laughed and said, "Yeah right—I'd need, like, a nicotine *shirt.*"

I liked the weekdays, when I could wake up in his house alone. I showered in Max's shower. Soaped myself with Max's soap. I made his bed. Perfect—no wrinkles, just like he did it. I walked around and looked at his things. Not snooping, because to snoop you have to open drawers and read journals, stuff like that. His records and CDs, hundreds of them, were neatly catalogued in multiple bookcases against one wall and alphabetized. I checked to see how many of them I also owned, but his collection was so extensive I realized he had everything I'd ever heard of, plus at least five hundred more. I stared at the posters on his bedroom walls. The inevitable Andre the Giant print made me smile. His collection of Japanese manga figurines—sexy little girls wearing mini skirts with big cartoon eyes frozen in that perfect moment of tension between childhood and maturity—gave me pause. On a bookshelf there was a watch collection—a whole shoe box full of, from what I could tell, faces dating back to sometime in the fifties. I didn't know Max collected watches. Finally I left a mix tape I made for him as a surprise on his pillow. I found a Post-it on his desk, drew a big smiley face on it, and stuck it on. Max was always getting me little things. Satisfied, I drank my juice and put the chocolate in my purse. (I wanted to save it.) Then I called Kiki and talked her into leaving the office to meet me at Madame Matisse for lunch.

I sang the whole way over. *"Some people call it a one night stand but we can call it paradiiise!"*

Kiki was waiting outside. She took one look at me and summed up how I felt. "You're peaking," she said.

"I am?"

"Totally peaking." She nodded. "Look at you. You look great, although personally I think you're too skinny."

"You're high on crack. Have you *seen* my stomach?"

"Oh my God you're the craziest person in the world. Your stomach is practically *concave*."

While we waited for an outdoor table to open up, we continued our ritual—the one where we extolled one another's virtues as a way of keeping at bay paralyzing self-esteem panic attacks while bolstering overall self-confidence.

"You're the one who's about five hundred feet tall," I said. "*With,* may I add, a body I would kill kittens for."

"Oh please." Kiki cupped her boobs. "Look at these—they're *disgusting.* And anyway, the only one who thinks you don't have a good figure is you. Plus, your hair looks great. You have no zits. *And* you have a new boyfriend who's obsessed with your very existence. You're totally peaking. You're fully realized. Fully *actualized.*"

A couple of Emo-core kids wearing regimentals cleared out of the smoking section. When the table was ready, Kiki waited for me to choose which seat I wanted. She always gives me the best seat. I don't know why—pure generosity, I suppose. That and the fact that she knows I'm fussy about where I sit. I can't stand to have my back to the door, and I hate facing mirrors because then I can't stop looking at myself and thinking negative thoughts. "Thanks, honey," I said, taking the chair with the best view of the hills. As I sat down, it occurred to me that the only time I didn't take the best seat was when I was with Max.

"He's not my boyfriend," I said, opening a menu.

"He's *so* your boyfriend." Kiki rolled her eyes.

The waiter came to take our order, and Kiki convinced herself—against my advice—that all she'd need to get through the day was a paltry, no-frills green salad. I asked for eggs, bacon, potatoes, and fruit, knowing that she'd eat much of my breakfast.

"He just hasn't told you he's your boyfriend yet," Kiki said. "You got bacon, right?"

"Yeah."

"You know I can't resist bacon."

"Well, it's the other white meat."

"Exactly. Look, very soon Max will introduce you to somebody as his girlfriend, but"—she got serious and started pointing at me—"don't try to bring that about, do you hear? Ben, *keep your cool.* Wait it out. Remember, guys only want to do something when they think it's *their* idea. Let him start to wonder if you're seeing anybody else. I promise, it will drive him crazy and eventually he'll want to lock you down. It's always the way."

I thought about back when I first started dating Jack. Yeah—I got a little gaga. Not scary gaga, but let's just say that it's a good thing caller ID and *69 were invented, because they stopped me from indulging in the call-to-see-if-he's-there/hang-up/call-again/hang-up routine. This time, Kiki was right. Max would have to try to win my affections. It made sense, because I was fully realized as a complete and totally effective person.

That night I was going to an engagement party for my sister and her fiancé and I felt great. I was not depressed, morose, or brooding. It was kind of refreshing.

Those in the pop-culture realm who've decided irony is dead have never met Audrey, because for her it's an entirely new concept. Her engagement party was being held at a cheesy roller-skating rink in Glendale that hadn't been redecorated since 1980. It had worn carpet-covered benches, metal lockers, and neon signs on the walls that said things like SKATE FEVER and ROLL WITH IT! To get into the groove I wore a denim mini skirt and a vintage Joan Jett concert tee. I was feeling no pain—Kiki and I stashed a flask of Beam in a locker as a kind of high school homage.

I did miss Max, though. He had to work, poor guy. I could just picture him, slaving away in his . . . Wait. I had never seen his office. Did he have a cubicle? A door that shut? Oh well. It wasn't our night, and we hadn't broken the two-evening-in-a-row barrier yet, which was completely fine with me. Besides, I figured it was too soon to introduce him to the Mother—that would seem too couple-y. I told Kiki, and she was very proud.

"Hi!" Audrey, beaming. She was wearing denim jeans with the cuffs turned up and a little cardigan sweater. Her outfit made me feel like I was dressed up for Halloween. She looked at my mini skirt and said, "Are you going to be able to skate in that?" I wasn't falling for it.

"Actually," I said, "I intend to skate *backward* in it."

Audrey shrugged and pulled me over to meet the bridesmaids. I couldn't keep the four of them straight—Anna, Diana, Traccy, and Casey. All from her sorority. All blond. All with overenthusiastic expressions that made them look like they were in a continual state of surprise.

"We've got spar-kel-ics!" Diana—or was it Anna?—said, smearing glitter gel on my arms. She handed me a paint-penned shirt that read ALWAYS A BRIDESMAID . . . JAMIE & AUDREY ARE ENGAGED! surrounded by little Bedazzled hearts. I noticed that of Anna, Diana, Tracey, and Casey, three of them were wearing engagement rings and one of them had a wedding band. But I reminded myself I was determined to be the comfortable older sister with the new almost-boyfriend, who was thrilled beyond belief at her younger sister's upcoming nuptials.

"These are genius," I lied, pulling the shirt on over mine.

So I was going around the rink, shaking my thang to Hall & Oates's "Whoa, Here She Comes." Every now and then, I'd wave to Kiki, who refused to skate, claiming she was over the height requirement. It was all going fine until Anna, Diana, Tracey, and Casey skated by in a daisy chain and one of them grabbed my wrist, screaming, "The bridesmaids who skate together stay together!" Next thing I knew, I was being pulled along at ridiculous speed. Faces at the side of the rink were whizzing by and suddenly I thought I saw . . . Oh no. No no *no*. I saw David Factor, a guy who'd completely blown me off right before I met Jack, standing in front of the lockers talking to Jamie. I'd totally forgotten about him.

Basically, I'm not in the business of screwing around with my sister's significant other's friends. But a couple of New Year's ago I'd visited Audrey and Jamie in San Francisco. They threw a huge party, and in walked David Factor, wearing a white button-down, probably with a Dave Matthews CD somewhere in his car, carrying an unfortunate J. Crew barn jacket. There was once a time—high school through early twenties—when I wouldn't have looked twice at a guy like this. I'd have inspected his cultural references, promptly deemed him an asshole, and moved on. That year, I was trying to be less judgmental. And I can honestly say—post-David-Factor, post-Jack—that you try to become a good person and all the world does is shit on you.

Anyway, David Factor and I ended up in Jamie's rec room, making out on the Ping-Pong table. (My sister gave me a somewhat judgmental look before going to bed, but I was tipsy enough not to care.) I was wearing a tiny cocktail dress that I hoped made me look like Heidi Klum (it didn't), and San Francisco in January is freezing. So I asked David if I could borrow his barn jacket. He gave it up gladly. We made out until the wee hours. When I finally walked him to the door, he said he'd call to see what we were going to do for the rest of my weekend in the city.

I passed out in the jacket.

I told my sister and Jamie about our hook-up the next morning, and eventually they seemed genuinely happy for me. But the thing was, David never did call. I was mortified. Audrey was mortified by association.

Now here was David Factor, who should have been in San Francisco where I left him, and since I'd decided not to bring Max I'd have to face him without a date. Suddenly my mini skirt, which kept riding up to panty-revealing length while I skated, seemed like a really bad idea. I tried to extricate myself from Anna, Diana, Tracey, and Casey so I could compose myself before David saw me.

"Let go of my hand!" I yelled over the music.

They didn't hear me.

"LET GO OF MY HAND!"

Still nothing.

So I twisted my wrist quickly just before we hit a turn and broke free. I went careening toward the carpet, which, when the wheels hit it, stopped me cold and I tripped and crashed face-first into the Space Invaders video game.

"Fuuuuck!" I crumpled to the ground, clutching my knee. David and Jamie saw the whole thing.

"Ben, God, are you okay?" Jamie rushed over with this annoying grin on his face. "Lemme help . . ."

"I'm fine! Thank you! Just . . ."

"No, come on. You just fell. It's no big—"

"Go *away* please." I gave him the hand. As in, *Talk to the hand.* Where I picked up this ridiculous gesture, and why it appeared now, I had no idea. Jamie gave me a look that said *What's up your ass?* and skated off. Great.

I limped over to an empty bench and sat down, trying not to cry.

"Ben? Is that you?" David Factor, standing right in front of me.

"Oh *HI!*" I said, like this was the best ever. "I wasn't expecting to see you here." (Sounded like a lie, even though it was true.)

"I moved back after graduation." *(Math in head: That would be last June. It's October. He's owed me a call for almost two years.)* "I was thinking about moving to New York, actually, but"—he gave me this phony, self-deprecating smile—"I'm starring in a play now with Tim Robbins's theater company, so . . ."

"Oh yeah?" I thought, *If I could take his skates, tie them together, and push him down a flight of stairs right now, I'd do it.*

"Yeah, and Spielberg came to one of my shows and word on the street is he wants to discuss some projects he has."

Word on the street.

"Oh. So I . . ." I racked my brain for what to say next. It came: *Say it was great seeing you, say it was great seeing you, say it was great seeing you and walk—no, skate—away.* Except I said, "You never called me." *Shit.*

"Well, I . . ." His eyes were darting here and there, looking for an escape. And I got this impulse. *Fuck this guy,* I thought. *I'm fully realized, and I have a new cute almost-boyfriend—he's not here, but still. Why not take control of this situation and laugh in David's face?*

"Why didn't you call?" I asked, raising an eyebrow.

"You don't want to hear that."

"I do."

"Trust me, you don't."

"You're an actor. *Act* like an adult." I smiled like, I imagined, a cat with a squirming mouse in its teeth.

David was holding his breath. He let it out in this big *huuhhhh* sound and smiled. "You know what? You're right. Okay . . . Well, I was going to call you, but then . . . Something kind of creeped me out."

Maybe I didn't want to hear this.

"The jacket." He let the words hang between us, waiting for me to grasp the thread.

"The jacket I borrowed?"

"Yeah. We were having a good time. But then you *had* to 'borrow' my jacket"—he made a *quote, unquote* gesture here—"like you were cold so I would *have* to leave it there, and then I'd *have* to see you again to get it back. If we're being honest, then, it turned me off."

I explained about the tiny cocktail dress and San Francisco's winter weather patterns.

"Oh *come on!*" he said. "Are you telling me that you didn't have *anything* like a jacket or a sweater that you could have run up the little stairs and put on?"

Little stairs? This guy was condescending to me and I was starting to suspect he was some kind of crazy misogynist. I was suddenly painfully aware that I was wearing a shirt emblazoned ALWAYS A BRIDESMAID . . . I looked for Kiki, who would have easily cut this guy to pieces, but I couldn't see her. So I said, "I. Was. Cold. Okay? That's all. I was just a little cold."

"If you say so." David Factor laid a hand on my shoulder and the touch burned. Then he said, "It was great seeing you." And he skated away.

I tried to fake it for another half an hour, with a cherry Icee my mom brought over to put on my now very swollen knee. ("What's bothering you now?" she said, handing it to me. I ignored the question and gave her a big, fake smile. She looked scared and left.) But eventually I got so cold, thanks to the mini skirt and the Icee and my self-immolation, I made excuses and went home. I obviously wasn't going to borrow one of Jamie's friends' jackets. *Whatever happened to chivalry?* I wondered, limping around my kitchen, making myself a frozen pizza, and trying not to hit my knee. *And how perilous is dating anyway? How can anyone possibly negotiate so many land mines without making a mistake?* If I'd blown it with David Factor so innocently, how could I not be blowing it with Max the same way? I'd mistakenly left a tube of lip gloss on Max's nightstand the last time I slept over. Was he sitting at home looking at it and thinking about what a loser I was? Did I call Max too frequently? Hold his hand too often in public? Stand too close to him when we were picking out videos at Blockbuster? I thought, *Do I seem, just because of the way I am, desperate?* Was I desperate?

Then it hit me.

Oh God. Oh God. Oh *no*.

The mix tape.

FOR FUN, FREEDOM, AND IN THE NAME OF RESEARCH, TURN THEM OFF!

BENJAMINA FRANKLIN goes into the field to see if she can get guys to hate her.

Why do some men run hot, then suddenly turn cold? Not long ago a seemingly interested party asked for my number but never called. This got me thinking—what turns guys off the most? My mission is to find out. I will not rest until every man I meet finds me incredibly unattractive, just so you can read, learn, and do the opposite.

CHANNELING GLENN CLOSE

After a canvassing of my male friends, I found they pretty much all think women are too needy. But surely there are guys who would do anything for a damsel in distress . . .

Setting: As Needy Girl, I take myself for drinks poolside at Hollywood's Mondrian Hotel.

Cute Boy #1: [A blond, with a good body but disappointing sunburns, approaches.] Need a light?

Me: Thanks. [I try to look sexy in Marlene Dietrich fashion.] Wanna sit?

CB 1: Sure! So . . . what do you do?

Me: [Looking stricken.] Actually, I was an assistant, but my boss fired me because I said I wouldn't get him lattes on my way to work.

CB 1: That's bullshit! Jesus, what are you going to do now?

Me: I don't know . . . [Choking back a sob.] Oh, God, you don't know anybody who needs an assistant, do you?

CB 1: Not really. [Looking a little uncomfortable, but still game.] So, are you here with anyone?

Me: I'm not here with a guy, if that's what you're asking. I haven't had a date in . . . oh . . .

[Reaching into purse for a Kleenex, blowing nose.] You like me, don't you?

CB 1: You seem nice enough.

Me: Are you single? Can I stay over?

CB 1: Um, actually . . . [Cute boy is weighing his options; should he persevere, or am I a psycho?] You know what? I think my friends are leaving.

Me: Can I come?

CB 1: We're just going home. [He gets up to leave. I grab his arm.]

Me: Don't go! Please! Can you give me a ride home?

CB 1: I'm seeing somebody, okay? *[I hold on like my life depends on it.]* Let go of my arm. Seriously. *[Starting to freak out as I sob onto his wrist, finally wrenching his arm free.]* Okay then, 'bye. Take care of yourself . . .

He starts to back away slowly, as if from a wild animal. Walks to his friend and I overhear him say, "Dude, that chick's, like, a total bunny boiler."

HIS EYES SAID NO BUT HIS BODY SAID... MAYBE

"I think some girls come on too strong," says my friend Dan Shapiro, a writer for *Details,* over lunch one day. "Sometimes I feel like they just want to use me for my schvantz."

I laugh so hard that the pizza I'm eating comes out my nose and tell him most guys would kill for guilt-free sex. He disagrees. We put a ten-spot on it.

Setting: In the role of Total 'Ho, I cruise the sandwich counter at Wild Oats, a chic health food market, during lunch hour.

Cute Boy #2: *[Wearing a suit with tie undone, talking to the guy behind the counter.]* I'll take a tuna sandwich. What kind of bread do you have? *[Rye, sourdough, or wheat.]* Sourdough. Can you toast that? *[They can.]* Cool.

Me: I just love a hot tuna sandwich, don't you?

CB 2: Excuse me?

Me: I said, I just love a hot tuna sandwich, don't you?

CB 2: Um, yeah. Do you come here often? *[Suddenly aware this sounds like a cheesy pickup line . . .]* I mean, do you work nearby?

Me: I live nearby—just around the corner.

CB 2: *[Looking confused.]* You work at home?

Me: Where you going to eat that sandwich?

CB 2: At my desk. I'm a lawyer, actually, and I have a pretty heavy caseload . . .

Me: Maybe I could help you release some of the tension. *[I reach up to massage his shoulders.]*

CB 2: Wait a sec . . . *[Shifts away so I'll stop touching him.]* Are you making fun of me?

Me: *[Looking longingly into his eyes.]* Let's go have hot, meaningless sex.

CB 2: Wow. Uh, maybe some other time. I'm really flattered, though. *[Taking his sandwich.]* I have to go back to work now. But . . . can I get your number? *[I scribble it down on a napkin under the words "Anastasia. Anytime. Anywhere" and he puts it in his pocket.]* Okay, well, nice meeting you, Anıka.

He calls "Anika" the next day, leaving directions to the Beauty Bar, where he'll be at 12:30 A.M. on Saturday night, in case she wants to meet for a drink. Dan owes me ten bucks.

"AFTER A CANVASSING OF MY MALE FRIENDS, I FOUND THEY PRETTY MUCH ALL THINK WOMEN ARE TOO NEEDY."

I WANT MONEY THAT'S WHAT I WANT

In L.A. you see a gazillion girls at trendy clubs talking to wealthy-looking guys who buy them free drinks and appear to dig their crass attitude. Meanwhile, when I go out on a date I'm usually worried if he pays too often he'll think I'm only after his dough. What gives? Does being a money-grubbing bi-atch turn them away, or turn them on?

Setting: Les Deux Cafes, where I act like a Money-Grubbing Bi-atch on a date with the guy I'm actually seeing. Because I want him to keep dating me, we'll ID him as Cute Boy #3.

Cute Boy #3: *[Upon reading the menu, which prices salads at $14; the chicken, the cheapest dish, is over $30.]* This is a nice restaurant.

Me: Isn't it? I was thinking that we should go to nice dinners more often.

CB 3: Yeah, if it's a special occasion . . . Is this a special occasion?

Me: Just another night out.

He asks me if I want to split a salad, I tell him I'm getting the foie gras, then the steak.

Me: So, I was thinking. You should take me to Hawaii. There's a hotel I want to

check out that's supposed to be fabulous. *[I smile fetchingly.]*

CB 3: *[Laughing.]* What do you mean "take you"?

Me: You don't want to take me on vacation? *[I do my best imitation of a pout.]*

CB 3: You don't want to take *me* on vacation?

Me: You're the guy. I would think that you would want to pay. You're buying me dinner, right?

CB 3: Didn't you say you wanted to take *me* to dinner? *[Lighting a cigarette, looking disturbed.]*

Me: *[Smiling sweetly and shrugging the way I suspect money-grubbing girls do.]* I forgot my wallet.

CB 3: Are you mad at me or something?

Terrified that if I go one step farther he'll never talk to me again, I apologize profusely, telling CB 3 I'm doing research for an article and can expense the check. I ask him if my money-grubbing made him feel like more of a man. He assures me it didn't. I then ask if he would continue to date me if I always acted like this, and he says, "I adore you, B, but I don't think I could afford it."

DO I LOOK FAT? NO, SERIOUSLY, DO I LOOK LIKE A COW?

"I hate how gorgeous girls are always asking me how they look," confides Art Ablang, a marketing exec for a shoe company. "They complain about their appearance but really they're fishing for compliments." This is a tough one—what girl doesn't worry that her ass looks too big in her new pants? And self-deprecation *can* be charming . . .

The Setting: As Self-Conscious Suzie, I stroll Melrose Boulevard on a Saturday afternoon wearing a T-shirt that reads DOES THIS SHIRT MAKE ME LOOK FAT?

Me: *[Approaching Cute Boy #4, who's window-shopping and looks like Johnny Depp.]* Does this shirt make me look fat?

Cute Boy #4: *[Giving an accusatory stare.]* Why?

Me: I'm just wondering if you like it.

CB 4: *[Extremely hostile.]* Go away! I don't want to have this conversation!

Humiliated, I proceed to the nearby Starbucks and Cute Boy #5, who's drinking an iced coffee and reading the paper.

Me: Does this shirt make me look fat?
Cute Boy #5: Oh. I don't think so.
Me: Do you like it?
CB 5: It's kind of ironic. I think it's funny.
Me: Does my ass look fat in these pants?
CB 5: Not really. *[Laughing.]* You sound like my ex-girlfriend.
Me: Did she annoy you?
CB 5: Well, we broke up. *[Goes back to reading paper.]*

Now I'm walking down the street, and I come across Cute Boy #6, who has a crew cut and is walking in the opposite direction. He reads my shirt from a distance, staring as I get closer. Before I can say anything, he points at my chest and says: "Yes."

It seems one guy's nightmare is another's potential scam. When I was Needy Girl, Cute Boy #1 didn't give up until I started to act like the psycho from hell, and Cute Boy #2 *did* call Total 'Ho and ask her out for a drink. Then again, the guy I'm currently dating would probably have stopped returning my calls if I didn't have a really good explanation for why I was being a Money-Grubbing Bi-atch. And as for all the guys who saw my FAT T-shirt, I think we can safely say asking them how I looked antagonized them beyond all reason. Just the same, I spend so much time trying to hide all the annoying and embarrassing things about myself, it was liberating to let my inner craziness out. So why not put all your faults front and center and stick like Krazy Glue to the one guy who can still stand you? Because honestly, we all have a *little* bit of Needy Girl, Total 'Ho, Money-Grubbing Bi-atch, and Self-Conscious Suzie in each and every one of us. I say, ladies, *let your inner bitches and 'hos roar.* U

6

When I woke up I was still obsessing about the tape. I stood in my dining room and stared with deep resentment at the CDs I'd recorded, still coverless and stacked (probably getting scratched) on my dining room table. There were five serious trouble spots:

1. "Venus as a Boy," Bjork. Mellifluous, romantic meditation on how the guy she's in love with is so beautiful he could be compared to da Vinci's *Venus de Milo.* Shit.

2. "Gigantic," The Pixies. Some say it was Kim Deal rhapsodizing about the size of her boyfriend's penis; others claim she was singing about her immense feelings for him. Big problem either way . . .

3. "There Is a Light That Never Goes Out," The Smiths. Sample lyric: "To die by your side, is such a heavenly way to die." A particularly bad choice.

4. "God Only Knows," The Beach Boys. Maybe I'd squeak by on this one since I'd spied a Brian Wilson autobiography on his nightstand the last time I'd slept over.

5. Last, but certainly not least, "Answering Machine," The Replacements. Sample lyric: "How do you say I love you to an answering machine?" Better question: What was I, fucking nuts?

I may as well have stood up on his Eames coffee table, bared my chest, beat it like a mad gorilla, and screamed "I LOVE YOU, MAX!" five times. I may as well have hired a plane to fly over his house to sky-write it at five thousand feet. I may as well have gotten Casey Kasem himself to show up at Max's damn office to do an in-person "I love you" dedication. Unwittingly, I broke my own rule. *My own damn rule.* Never say I love you! Never!

Next possible steps . . . I could casually ask Max how he liked the mix tape and gauge his reaction. I could be counterintuitive and start using the L-word in Max's presence constantly (I *love* this song on the radio, I *love* pizza, I *love* Q-tips) so as to demystify and disempower it. Or I could pretend the mix tape didn't exist.

I called Kiki at the office but she was MIA. Where could she be? In a panic, I called Nina on her cell. She said she had just enough time between classes for coffee, so I met her on the patio outside Starbucks near UCLA. Surrounded by students with interesting facial hair who were somberly poking at their laptop computers, Nina listened as I ranted.

"The Pixies song is going to just *fuck me*," I said, head in hand. "It *fucks me*."

"I don't know that group," Nina said, taking a sip of iced chai. "But I think you're dodging the main issue here."

"What main issue?"

"The fact that you've made a declaration of love and now you are uncertain of how it will be received." She removed her straw and absently chewed the end. She was still not smoking, which made me murderous.

"So what do I do?"

"I would advise you to address this problem head-on. Tell Max that while you do have feelings for him, you hope that he doesn't read more into the tape than what was intended, as you were thinking about it and realized that he might."

"But, if I do that, then isn't it like I'm saying, *Oh, in case you're wondering whether or not I'm in love with you I'm really not,* in which case I'm going to sound like I really am?"

"I'm not following you, Ben." Nina leaned in. Her voice took on a soothing cadence that grated on my nerves. "Talk about how this conversation is making you feel."

I took a deep breath. "What about my idea that I should pretend the mix tape doesn't exist? What's wrong with that?"

"I think you're going to find it difficult, because it's not what your psyche wants." She sat back.

"What does my psyche want?"

"What do *you* think your psyche wants?"

"Please don't start that. You know I hate that."

"Listen, Ben, you're being very defensive, and I have a class starting in a few minutes so we're going to have to wrap this up. All I'm saying is that, on some level, *you* wanted to confront the issue. *You* created this situation, intentionally, even if it was unconsciously."

For some reason, this made me angry. So I said, "Nina, are you going to be experimenting with people soon, or are you going to stick with rats? Because, at this point, I think rats are the safer option."

"Are you being passive aggressive because you're angry with me, or because you're angry with yourself?" She leaned forward again. "Or perhaps your sister?"

"What are you *on?*"

She ticked the reasons off for me. "She's getting married. You're not. You're angry with her on a macro level because she makes you feel inadequate. Which makes me think you may be turning your relationship with Max into a kind of competition. Or you may be trying to get him to compensate for your own feelings of inferiority. And when I tell you this, you take your anger out on me. It's called transference, Ben, and I think it's very interesting."

"I'm not *transferring* shit!"

Nina raised her eyebrows and sat back with her arms folded across her chest. I decided if she told me I was having a breakthrough I was going to scream. Then I realized I had hurt Nina's feelings.

"Okay, okay," I said. "I'll be a willing patient, a good patient, and I'm asking you, please . . . Why would I have intentionally created this situation I'm in with Max?"

She didn't answer.

"Earth to Nina?"

She looked over my shoulder at the street.

"Oh, so you can be passive aggressive but I can't be a transferer, or whatever you call it?" That did it.

"All I'm saying is *you wouldn't have created a whole ninety-minute tape full of fucking love songs unless you wanted him to know that you love him so you could find out if he loves you back!* Jesus fucking Christ!"

A table full of Delta Gammas in monogrammed sweatshirts turned and stared. Nina rubbed her temples, trying to get back into her professional place. She took a deep breath, smoothed her brown hair into its low ponytail. "Look, this is the entrée you needed to open up a discussion that may give you the results you want," she said once she regained her composure. "Or not. But if you talk to him about it at least you will know where you stand. Which was probably your goal in the first place."

"I don't know . . ."

"I know this isn't what you want to hear, Ben, but a cigar is never just a cigar." Nina got up, removed the cigarette from my lips, and put it out in the ashtray, saying, "You should really get a prescription for Zyban. An additional benefit is it might help with some of the free-floating anxiety."

"I'm sorry, Nina," I said.

She smiled. "I forgive you." She checked the time. "Oh fuck. I'm late."

With that, she packed up her battered copy of Freud's *Civilization and Its Discontents,* her chai, her cell phone, and she left. I watched her head toward campus. It was funny—as Nina strode down the sidewalk, all the other passersby quickly stepped out of her way.

Can't you see that I love you!

THE *OTHER* FOUR-LETTER WORD

A Three-Part Lesson in Love

BY BENJAMINA FRANKLIN

You can't say I love you first to a guy. Every girl knows this.

How do we know?

Experience.

When I was fourteen, my first boyfriend was a theater geek. I adored him. He was the Sebastian cellophane to my bilevel hair cut. (It was the eighties, therefore *my hair* was the eighties.) We met at theater camp, and for three whole weeks, we spent every afternoon together. But then fall came, and Tina Totino, aka "The Rack"—who had matured at an incredible rate—reappeared at school like the Angel of Death with the most enormous tits I've ever seen. My theater-geek boyfriend informed me he wanted to take Totino to the homecoming dance. He said he "had to play the field while he still could." (This being the melodramatic, self-important verbiage used by a fourteen-year-old boy experiencing the bracing, but nonetheless exciting, *thrill* of breaking his first heart.) And I, in a moment of desperation and naïveté, screamed, "How could you do this? *Can't you see that I love you?*"

LESSON #1: Screaming *Can't you see that I love you?* makes men feel like they're trapped. Being held against their will. Emotionally blackmailed into staying in a relationship. So they take The Rack to the dance.

When I was twenty, I met the snowboarder/punker/computer-programming major who would do the most romantic of things, like show up outside my dorm in a limousine, while dressed in a tuxedo, and take me to McDonald's for a Happy Meal. The sex was fantastic—he was *this* big. And he could play Nirvana songs on his guitar. I waited for six months for him to tell me he loved me. But after *six months* of exclusive dating (!) I could wait no longer. I took the initiative and said, "I love you." And I waited for him to respond in kind.

LESSON #2: I'm still waiting.

When I was twenty-five, I met the man I thought I was going to marry. I was wrong. Even though he had a stable job, was an excellent cook, and had a really nice condo, it got to the point where we just couldn't stand one another. And yes, one huge wrinkle right in the middle of our

I POPPED THE QUESTION: "DO YOU LOVE ME?"

perfect-on-paper relationship was that I turned to him one day, after *a year of living together,* and brought up That Which Must Not Be Said Aloud. This time, I slyly avoided making a blanket declarative statement, and instead I popped the question: "Do you love me?"

LESSON #3: *No, no, no, no, NO!* You cannot think that asking, "Do you love me?" is *any different* from saying you love them. Because why would you ask someone if they love you if you, yourself, do not love them? Well, you wouldn't. Nobody would. Not only that, guys don't say, "I *do* love you!" in response. They say, "Why do you ask?"

Wait months. Wait years. *Wait forever.* He'll never, ever, *ever* say "I love you" with any frequency or conviction unless he thinks it's his own discovery, his own declaration, hell, his own *concept.* Erase the word *love* from your vocabulary the same way you would erase hideously dirty slang before you go to Sunday brunch with your Irish Catholic grandmother. Remember: Love, when it comes to romance, is the foulest of four-letter words. **U**

After coffee with Nina, I walked back to my car, grabbed the latest parking ticket off the window and shoved it in the glove compartment with the rest, and headed toward Beverly Hills where I was meeting the Mother and Audrey for yet another fitting. Instead of turning on NPR like usual, I left the radio off and pondered Nina's advice. It seemed a little hard-core. I mean, she always acts like you should confront everything head-on, but she never seems to actually do this. Oh, sure, Nina confronts her friends. She confronts her superiors even. But when it comes to guys, she's all armor. *Every time* I see Nina she's dating someone new. A student from her Psychobiology of Emotion and Stress class. A professor she thought was "brilliant." The guy from behind the wheat grass juice counter at the Erewhon health food store. The WB Network television producer she met at the . . . actually, I don't remember where she met the TV producer. Oh, right. Hatha yoga class. She sleeps with them all right away, it lasts a week, *maybe* two, and probably just about the time the guy is starting to think that he needs to find a way out, she completely loses interest.

The student she was dating brought her a carrot juice to class one morning. The professor gave her an A minus on a paper she was fairly certain only deserved a B plus. The guy behind the counter of the health food store just *seemed* too excited to see her when she dashed in to purchase frozen Boca burgers, and the TV producer invited her to the Emmys. Based on these transgressions, Nina decided each of them seemed just a little bit north of needy. And she hates needy. Makes you wonder how she can stand to be friends with me, frankly. But anyway, she becomes unavailable in every way, and then the guys become incredibly interested. They call and e-mail and show up at her house in the middle of the night declaring their love and asking, *why, why* won't she just give them a chance? This confirms the suspected neediness, and Nina always feels relieved that she caught it when she did. I may rush toward intimacy. But Nina runs from it like a vegan from a barbecue.

I parked my car at a meter spot and freaked when I discovered twenty-five cents bought only seven minutes in Beverly Hills. I had enough for half an hour. I put the new parking ticket on my windshield just in case and walked inside, where the Mother informed me exactly how late I was while I sat there watching Audrey getting pinned. I wasn't really sure what the point of my presence was—what, really, is one's function while someone is getting a dress altered? I tried to be enthusiastic while we discussed how the fabric on Audrey's gown was draping. But my mix-tape hell—and the fact that I was still playing the songs endlessly in my head—made trying to concentrate on Audrey like trying to watch television with the radio on. Twenty minutes passed and I started to worry that I was probably about to get yet another ticket. "Do you have any change?" I asked the seamstress. She shook her head briskly, and continued to pin and tuck, pin and tuck.

The Mother, at least, was making up for me. As she circled Audrey, who was actually standing on a pedestal, she gushed over the hideous sateen, dye-to-match pumps on her feet. I found it hard to believe that they didn't realize these were the exact same hideous, sateen, dye-to-match pumps teenage girls buy for high school prom. And when the Mother thought nobody was looking, I spied her inspecting a pearl-encrusted veil and trying it on her head. This from the woman who swore the next time she got married (which really could be any day now) she'd do it at city hall exactly like she did the last three times.

★ ★ ★

Next we went to lunch (I did get another ticket, by the way), and Audrey brought along a file—an actual *file*—filled with wedding ideas from *Martha Stewart*. Pertinent articles were mounted on pieces of pastel construction paper, and they were color-coded. Green for "Floral Ideas," pink for "Bride To-Do," blue for "Groom To-Do," et cetera. I leafed through them, reading the notes carefully written in the margins in Audrey's curlicue script. For "unexpected fragrance and texture," she could stick fresh herbs like rosemary, thyme, or sage into her bouquet. Instead of a greeting line, which could seem too formal, Aud was thinking about writing individual "thank-you scrolls" that yours truly could hand out during the reception. There was even a page on tiny "throwing hearts" that Aud wanted to order, which, the clip read, have a dash of romantic appeal *and*, unlike rice, have the added benefit of not making birds' stomachs explode.

"Martha, Martha, Martha," I said, crossing my eyes.

"Oh come on, you know you love it," Audrey said.

"She doesn't love it," the Mother said, "because she's a bi-atch!"

"Did you just say 'bi-atch'?" I asked.

"I heard it on the radio!" She and Audrey dissolved into giggles. I was lunching with the Gilmore Girls.

"So," Audrey said, spooning chilled asparagus soup away from herself—Audrey being the only person I know who actually eats chilled soup—"are you bringing this Max guy to the wedding?"

"I guess so."

"But you haven't asked him."

"No."

"You *should*. I'm dying to meet him." Pause. "I hear he's younger?"

I shot my mother a look. "A little."

"That's okay."

I told her I was glad she'd found a way around it.

"So? . . ." Audrey was looking at me expectantly.

"So? . . ."

"Mom tells me you've been all abuzz with bridal shower plans. I'm *dying* to know what they are."

"Oh . . ."

The Mother was wearing a cruel little smile.

I hadn't done a thing. Well, that wasn't completely accurate. At home, on my desk, was a notebook I'd bought at an art supply store that I planned to fill with lists of all the things I'd need to do for the wedding. I'd mulled over which book to purchase for forty-five minutes. Would it be most useful if it fit in my purse, or if it was oversize and then had more space for me to write? Would the pad be best with perforated paper, so notes could be neatly ripped out? Or would that make me lose important information? Finally I chose a lavender, linen-covered notebook that neither fit in my purse nor was oversize, because I liked the color and the way the expensive, coddled-cream paper felt when I ran my finger over it. I brought the book home, and wrote "Audrey's Wedding List" on the first page in the special black pen I bought to go along with it. I felt excited and mature.

I hadn't picked it up since.

Audrey was still staring at me. I got a brief respite when the waiter brought her chopped salad, my gourmet cheeseburger (that's Muenster instead of American cheese, to you), and the Mother's grilled tenderloin. I realized everything Audrey ordered for lunch was cold and green.

"Okay," she said. "I'm ready."

"I'm thinking . . . *tasteful!*" I waved my hands in front of my face like a magician saying *Abracadabra!* Audrey's eyes lit up. Encouraged, I continued.

"Classic! Refined! Polished! Not . . . *genteel* . . . No. Not . . . *prim.* Certainly not. But . . . elegant. *Elegance is everything!*" I startled an old lady sitting catty-corner to us, who was dining with a friend, whispering back and forth over the last twenty minutes about God knows what.

"That sounds wonderful!" Audrey said, like she was surprised. "Mom, doesn't that sound wonderful?"

"*Won*derful." The Mother sliced into a piece of steak.

"Audrey," I interrupted myself, "why are you doing that?" She was carefully picking up garbanzo beans with her fork and knife and placing them in a neat row at the edge of her plate.

She leaned over conspiratorially and said, "Carbs."

"Right."

"So?" she said. *"What else?"*

"I'm thinking . . . Cream. And . . . *Lavender.*"

"Oooh, I *love* lavender. I briefly considered it as one of my wedding colors, but then I decided maybe it was *too* girlie."

"Well, for a wedding lavender is completely inappropriate." I was starting to enjoy myself. "I mean, you have to consider whether or not the color will date, and lavender is kind of an inaccessible shade, really, when you think about it, once you involve the groom. Doesn't have that masculine practicality . . . But for the bridal shower, lavender is *perfect.* It's feminine and it adds a certain brightness to the occasion."

"I totally agree," she said. "Will the invitations be lavender as well?"

"Invitations?" I took a sip of my soda to buy myself some time. "Yes, those will be in your shower color scheme. As a way of . . . *introducing it.*"

"You don't want to shock people," the Mother offered. She was being sarcastic, but I rolled with it.

"Exactly. Now"—I laid my hand over Audrey's, like I was about to tell her the most fabulous secret—"I don't want to go into the actual invitation design because that's a surprise. But . . . What time will it be? 'What time?' you may be asking yourself . . . And ask you should, because"—the Mother looked extremely amused—"it will be a brunch. Yes! A ladies-who-lunch brunch! At Mom's house! And there will be quiche! Individual quiches for everybody! And mimosas! Right? *Mother?*"

"Oh," she said. "Of *course.* And tell Audrey who will be making all that quiche."

Nice try, Mom. I smiled and said, "I will."

They said it together: "*You* will."

"Relax. I got a recipe—off MarthaStewart.com?"

I guessed right because Audrey didn't correct me.

"I totally know what I'm doing. Remember, the theme of your bridal shower will be"—I waved my hands around again—*"elegance is everything."*

She looked happy enough to burp babies.

I thought, *I'm a genius!*

That night was movie night. Max and I were lying on his bed, and he was engrossed in *Shakespeare in Love.* Gwyneth Paltrow's body looked bigger than it probably does in real life since he'd gone to Circuit City the previous Sunday and bought the largest flat-screen television they had. It was so large Max had to completely remodel his bedroom—everything was somewhere else. He'd also bought a new comforter because I'd happened to mention last weekend that I thought his room got a little chilly at night.

"I don't want you to ever be cold, B," he said, patting the spot on the bed next to him and putting his arm around me.

So Gwyneth was having a bad hair day, prancing around saying "Anon this" and "Anon that." Meanwhile that actor—the one with the dark hair—was putting lots of emotion into his eyes while he watched her trounce around on stage. Oh, it was all very romantic. On the television. But in Max's room, not so much. You know that black-hole-of-deadly-silence thing guys do sometimes? The one where you keep looking at him, wanting him to say something, but he keeps staring straight ahead at the TV? And you know that he knows that you're looking at him, but to ask him why he's being so quiet would make you sound like a fifties housewife so you don't? It was *that* black hole of deadly silence. Before we'd started the film, I'd tried to get him to talk. Told him an edited version of my sister's engagement party—all while trying to gauge whether he was wondering why I hadn't invited him—but he didn't take the bait. Just said, "Sounds like it was a fun time." (Insert black hole of deadly silence here.)

"Max?" I propped myself up on one elbow. "Is there something wrong?" (Code for, "Did that mix tape freak you out?")

He pulled his eyes away from the TV. "I'm watching the movie," he said. (Translation: "I don't want to talk about it.")

He settled back and gently pulled me back down onto the bed with him. He didn't, however, try to put his arm around me again.

I just noticed it. That's all I'm saying.

I sat back up.

"It just seems like something might be wrong . . ." I took the remote from his nightstand to pause the film, but it had a million buttons since he now had his TV, VCR, DVD, and stereo all working off one superremote. I pressed a button and the movie turned off, the cable turned on, and Howard Stern appeared, interviewing some porn star who was perched on a stool, topless.

"Oh, leave it, this is Butt Billionaire!" Max said, craning his neck around me and staring at the almost-naked girl. "If the guy gets all the questions right, he gets to go into a room alone with her and do her up the . . ."

At this moment a guy in a T-shirt that said CHUCK THE LOSER—GET WITH THE BRUISER! failed to answer the question, "Name the president who was impeached for Watergate?"

"This is disgusting," I said. "That guy's so stupid he could never get laid in real life so he has to go on this show."

"That's the whole point." Max was cracking up. He yelled at the TV, "Nixon, you moron!"

"Max, I want to talk to you . . ."

I looked at the remote and at least the power button, which was red, was obvious, so I turned off the television.

Something flashed behind his eyes. Annoyance?

He said, "We have to *talk?*"

"I don't want to *talk* talk," I said. "I just want to know what's going on."

"We're having a perfectly nice evening, watching the movie."

"But we never actually watch the movie . . ."

He ignored this.

I tried switching tacks. "Don't you want me to take my clothes off and dance around naked or something?" I said.

"Yes."

So he got the joke. But he wasn't smiling.

"Well, tell me what's up. Then I'll start dancing. What are you thinking?"

"I'm thinking . . ." He paused, then muttered under his voice, "That things were going so well." And he lay back on the bed.

I assured him that things were going well. I just . . .

"You just what?" He stared at the ceiling. He wasn't even looking at me.

"I just want to talk to you about . . ." Suddenly I wasn't sure what I really wanted to talk to him about.

He was looking back at me now. And his face resembled the face of a patient person, a real honest to God decent human being. But his eyes— the eyes that usually had smiles in them—they seemed closed off. Guarded. His mouth was set in a purposely expressionless way. His expression was impossible to read.

"Look, if you don't want to talk . . ."

"What, exactly, are we talking about?"

Now he seemed *really* pissed. Which somehow seemed a little unfair.

"Maybe I should just go," I said.

Flustered, I got up and started looking for my shoes. *I don't have to take this,* I told myself. *I can walk out the door right now and we'll see how he feels then.*

"You're going," Max said.

It wasn't a question. It was a statement.

"Looks that way." I tried to match his measured tone, but my words had a slap to them. I put on one shoe, then the other. Out of the corner of my eye, I could see he was staring at the ceiling again. I started looking for my keys, and for a moment I panicked because I couldn't find them. The whole fucking room had been rearranged, which meant I hadn't put them on the dresser like usual. He said nothing, and ignored the comedy as I tripped over the end of the rug and banged my elbow—loudly—on one of the cymbals on his drum set. Finally I found my keys on his desk, which used to be by the window, but was now by the door, where the dresser used to be. For some unknown reason, I was compelled to voice this out loud.

"The *dresser* is no longer in the same place," I said.

No reply.

"Just in case you were wondering," I said.

Now I was ready to leave. I was standing in the middle of the room rubbing my elbow and I felt like an idiot. Max didn't even sit up.

"Ben," he said to the ceiling, "if you walk out that door, I am not going to follow."

I didn't know what that meant. That following me was beneath him? Or maybe that I was acting like such a maniac there was no point, because who wants to go out into the night chasing some crazy woman, running down the street elbows akimbo and babbling about the placement of furniture?

I said, "So you want me to stay?"

"I never told you to *leave.*" He rubbed his eyes. "Look. I'm tired. I've had a long day. I want to watch the movie. With you. And then I want to go to sleep." He finally added, "With you. But if you walk out that door, I. Am. Not. Going. To. Follow."

And that's when it occurred to me that this statement was essentially a dare. A game of chicken. Not a particularly nice thing for Max to do. But I have a personal philosophy: Never play a game of chicken unless you know you're going to win. This wasn't going the way I wanted tonight to go at all. I remembered what Nina said—that I wanted to know if Max loved me. I looked at the stereo, but the cassette holder was empty. I thought, *He probably hasn't even listened to it.*

I sat back down on the bed. The room was silent. His roommates, Fred and Barney, were out at some party as usual. Thank God, since I would have been mortified if they heard us fighting. Not that I'd ever actually met them. Finally, Max said, "Should we watch the rest?"

I said okay.

He turned the TV back on, and I lay down and adjusted my pillow so I wouldn't be in his way. I looked at him. "Sorry," I said. "I don't know. I guess I'm just a little stressed today maybe?"

"It's all right," he said. "Just watch."

He was asleep before they even got to the part where the guy finds out that Gwyneth Paltrow's a she. I watched the rest by myself even though I'd already seen it, then tossed and turned all night. Max slept with his back turned to me, which he never does. By the time I woke up, he'd already left for work. The first thing I did when I opened my eyes was look next to the alarm clock to see if Max had left me anything. But there was no candy. And no juice.

CHAPTER
7

I didn't think it was possible to actually die of embarrassment. But there I lay, reading the proof pages for *Filly*'s next issue and wondering if a girl could actually choke to death on her own tongue. *And if I don't choke to death on my own tongue,* I thought, *then I'll kill Kiki with a sharp screwdriver.* Or maybe I'd do us both in with a blowtorch—then the Mother, *Filly*'s new advice columnist, could write all about it in the next issue. *A certain someone she knows,* my ass. That the Mother should start writing a column for the magazine was all Kiki's idea. And I think if I hadn't been so drunk when she thought it up at the bridal shower—and so generally distressed about Max's and my first fight—I would have put a stop to it right away. But now, with the first "Ask Ben's Mom" column already written, it was probably too late.

ASK BEN'S MOM

After listening to the endless tribulations of my daughter (not to mention those of her friends), I can't help but wish my eldest, Benjamina Franklin, would listen to me. Nobody knows better than a mom how to deal with romance, sex, finances . . . Of course, many gals (like a certain someone I know) are too stubborn to ask their own mothers what to do. Starting now, you can ask me.

Dear Ben's Mom,
What's wrong with women today? I'm so *sick* of reading in magazines about men, men, *men*. I can't watch another episode of *Sex and the City* because all they care about is men, men, men. And I may never go out to dinner with my friends again because all they talk about is friggin' men, men, *MEN*! Did women's lib just *not happen*?
From,
Seriously Fed Up
P.S. I've read your daughter's articles in *Filly*. Do you blame yourself?

Dear Fed Up,
I understand your frustration. A certain someone I know cares more about the boy in her life (and I do mean boy) than she does about eating right, about furthering her career—he even comes before doing the laundry! Set a new example. Make clean underwear *your* priority. Exact revenge on the men who treat you badly, reward the ones who treat you well. Set your sights on career and self. Beat up muggers. You could start your own women's movement.
Love,
Mom
P.S. No, she's accountable for her own actions, however deranged they may be.

HE DOESN'T KNOW MY G-SPOT FROM MY ELBOW...

Dear Ben's Mom,
How do I get a red wine stain out of my favorite white shirt?
Thanks,
Total Klutz

Dear Klutz,
1. If the stain is fresh, cover the area with baking soda or salt. Brush it off. 2. Blot with mineral water. 3. Rinse the spot with rubbing alcohol. If the stain is as old as I am, just do steps 2 and 3.
Love,
Mom

Dear Ben's Mom,
How do I tell the guy I'm with he doesn't know my G-spot from my elbow?
XO,
Itching for Action

Dear Action,
It's time you learned an important trick that I've employed with my last two husbands: Don't tell him, *show* him. Literally. He'll enjoy a peek between the sheets, and you can do something you're good at.
Love,
Mom ♡

Let's go back to a little over a week ago. In the days following Max's and my argument, I wasn't feeling particularly good about myself (no surprise there), and he wasn't much help. It was your basic relationship purgatory. We weren't talking about what had happened—Max seemed like he wanted the discomfort we suddenly felt with one another to just blow over. I guess I figured things would go back to normal. But they didn't.

Oh, he called. And I returned those calls. We'd chat for a while and I'd wait for Max to ask me out. He wouldn't. Finally, sick of waiting, I asked him if we were on for our usual Saturday night. (I cringed when I heard the word *usual* come out of my mouth.) He said he had to go to Las Vegas on Friday for some streetwear convention, he'd be gone for a week, and he didn't have a second before then. Those were the words he used: "Sorry, sweetie, but I don't have a *second.*" This was the first I'd heard of his trip. *Why didn't he tell me sooner?* I wondered. I told myself Max was probably just stressed and that's why he hadn't mentioned it before, but anxiety seized my heart like ice. Had I blown it the last time I saw him by acting so needy? If so, couldn't he give me a get-out-of-jail-free card just this once? I couldn't ask. As anyone who's ever dated a guy will tell you, the definition of *insanity* is trying to talk to a boy about the same thing twice and expecting a different result.

So I obsessed. Would Max and I work out? Was it over? I had to live with the circling doubts—once he went away I had no way to tell if things were about to get better, or worse. I figured I should at least try to distract myself, so I left messages for pretty much everyone I knew, hoping a social life would emerge. Surprisingly enough, it did. Chandra called, asking if I'd be "down with" lounging by her pool the next day. I practically did verbal back flips I was so eager to accept. ("I would *LOVE* to! Thank you *SO* much! It will be *SO* fun!")

The following morning I set off to find Chandra's Mediterranean manse high in the hills of Laurel Canyon. I knocked on the door, and Krantz, a man of indeterminable sexual orientation with a hairless, gym-toned chest and wearing a Burberry plaid swimsuit, answered.

"Oh," he said, blocking entry. "Are you the assistant from Team Todd?"

"No," I said. "I'm a friend of Chandra's."

As though I hadn't spoken, he said, "You're delivering a script?"

"*No.* I'm a friend? Of Chandra's?"

"*Who* are you?"

This continued until a person named Kate with a perfect body and a belly chain appeared. "Fuck, Krantz, leave her alone," she said. "Chandra told me she invited some writer girl."

Krantz looked me up and down. "So you're a *journalist,*" he spat. "I handle all of Ms. McInerney's publicity"—he stepped aside—"so *behave.*"

I followed Kate into the backyard, trying to figure out who was who. Kate turned out to be Chandra's Kato—a noncelebrity who lives rent-free in the house of a famous person, does odd jobs, acts as a confidante but isn't exactly a friend. Chandra, apparently, was finishing up a consultation with her guru and would be out shortly, so Kate-o played hostess, introducing Laura, a redhead wearing shorts that revealed the practically albino skin on her legs, who volunteered that she was "VP of development at the studio" and sat in the shade all day while applying sunscreen.

Once Chandra was "centered," she joined us by the black-bottomed pool. Her posse clearly wanted her attention, and didn't enjoy new competition.

"*Love* this fucking pita bread," Laura said from her corner, dipping it in the mushy eggplant caviar Kate was passing around. "And, Chandra, your stomach looks so fabulous I'm . . . speechless."

"Artuuuurrrrro," Chandra purred, patting her abs.

"Who's Arturo?" I asked. I was paddling about on a raft and being generally ignored.

"Private trainer," Laura said. "Forget it—you'll never get an appointment."

I started to say I didn't want an appointment, and wondered if now would be a good time to ask Chandra for some Max advice, but Krantz interrupted.

"So, spill," he said to Chandra. "What's the latest?"

"I've been. *So stressed,*" she said. "Like, everyone keeps doggin' me about this new movie and I told James, like, I'm going to pull a fuckin' Ed Norton on him, commandeer that editing room and fix the fuckin' thing myself, knowwhatImsayin?"

"So the film isn't working," Krantz said.

"What do you mean?" Chandra lowered her sunglasses to give him the evil eye. Marooned on my raft, I thought, *This could get interesting.* "Bitch, what are you saying, that I think I'm not good in my own muthafuckin' movie?" she said. "That's cool, dawg." Chandra got up and stormed into the house, returning with a bottle of mineral water, but she kept yelling at Krantz the way there and back. "You're sitting there?" she hollered, her voice echoing off the red Spanish tiles. "Saying this movie will *harm my career?* And you're my fuckin' *publicist.* What *THE FUCK?*" She twisted the cap off the bottle like she was breaking a chicken neck.

"That's not *remotely* what I meant, McC," Krantz wheezed. "The movie is amazing—you're in it, I mean, *hello!*"

"Don't be fronting, Krantz," said Chandra, arranging herself back on her lounge.

"Seriously, you owe it to Chandra, as her publicist, *as her friend,* to tell her the truth," said Kate-o.

Laura jumped in, saying, "Krantz, you are so fucking fired!"

It was like watching a group of sharks start feeding on one another.

"I am telling the truth." Krantz was starting to sweat.

"Awright, chill. I'm letting it go." Chandra reached for a bottle of suntan oil. "But Krantz, you gotta learn how to represent, knowwhat-Imsayin?" She stabbed her oily finger in the air. "You gotta think about my interests every time you *open your big fucking fat fag mouth.*"

I couldn't believe she'd said that. But everyone else looked away like they hadn't heard.

Then, "What do *you* think, Franklin?"

Here was my chance to get beaten to a pulp. "Well, film is art, right?" I said. "Art is subjective . . ."

Laura snorted.

Kate said, "Art? She attached herself because the studio offered her eight mil!"

"Yo, and 'cause I got da biz on with my costar," Chandra said, adding, "Onscreen of course."

"Yeah, journalist present," Laura snickered.

"I'm *not* here to—" I started to say.

"Everything that is said today is *off the record,*" Krantz interrupted, spraying flecks of eggplant caviar in my direction. He turned to Chandra, nodding. "Now she won't be able to print anything even if she wants to."

This shut me up for the afternoon. I realized I'd never get a chance to talk to Chandra about my Max dilemma, but figured it was safer to be ignored anyway. The oddest thing, though, was when I left. Chandra acted like it was the main event. "Thank you *so much* for coming," she said, walking me to the door. "I *need* my friends around me right now, Franklin. You *know* how hard this is for me."

"How hard what is?" I said.

"Oh, everything." She waved her hands around the beautifully appointed room, like, *See how much I have; see how difficult it can be.* "Look at this." She held up her arm and scratched at it. "I think I'm breaking out in a *rash.*"

I told her I didn't see anything.

"You don't see anything *yet,*" she said, and closed the door. As I was walking to my car, I could hear her yelling, "*Kate!* Page Dr. John!"

I got home, checked my voicemail for a call from Max (no), then checked my e-mail for a message from practically anyone. There was an invitation to a porn site called "Young and Tight." (Fucking Collin. Lately he'd been forwarding me porno links, which he thinks is the height of comedy.) Also a quick note from my dad with a digital picture of him and his surfboard standing on some Costa Rican beach. (It was signed, "Love, The Big Kahuna.") And finally a passive aggressive jab from the Mother regarding the bridal shower—she was "just checking" to see if I needed any help since I was "getting such a late start."

I'd procrastinated enough to antagonize her, so I spent the evening trying to find a Martha recipe for quiche lorraine. (There was one, naturally.) Then I made a shopping list for the shower in my beautiful notebook. I placed an order for flowers from the chichi-est but most cost-effective florist I could find. (The arrangements would be cream and lavender, *of course*.) The shower was practically taking care of itself, so I decided I'd earned an evening off. I ordered in a sausage, pepperoni, and mushroom pizza and a six-pack of diet Coke, and consumed both while watching *The Goodbye Girl* on AMC and marveling at how hot Richard Dreyfuss was in that movie, even though he's so short.

It wasn't until I was waiting in line to buy groceries from the gourmet market the following day that I realized I'd made a terrible mistake. The shopping was taking longer than I thought it would, Bristol Farms was incredibly crowded, and I still had the flowers to pick up and all the cooking to do. My cell phone rang, and I literally spazzed out trying to get to it in case it was Max. With the contents of my purse dumping out on the floor, I looked at the caller ID, but it was just the Mother. She had the phone instincts of a sadist.

As I turned the ringer off, I noticed a woman in line in front of me staring my way with a bemused look on her face. Curious, I inspected her purchases while I unloaded my cart onto the conveyor belt. I spied a tray of gourmet cookies, a packet of turkey hot dogs, four Wolfgang Puck frozen pizzas, and a six-pack of diet Coke. *Finally!* I thought. *A sympathetic ear.*

"It wasn't him," I said, holding up the cell phone with an *aw-shucks-you-caught-me* smile.

"Excuse me?" she said.

"You know how it is. He calls, he doesn't call. You think he wants a commitment, he starts acting like he doesn't. Sometimes I think men won't be happy until we're all acting like maniacs, strapped to the walls of some mental institution with paper slippers on, know what I mean?"

The woman picked her purse up out of her cart and clutched it to her chest. "Actually, I don't," she sniffed. "I married my first beau. And it's lasted fifteen years."

She turned to face the front of the store, and I had to stand behind her in line for the next ten minutes while trying to pretend we'd never spoken.

It took three trips from my car up the stairs to my apartment to get everything inside. In between trips, I checked but no message from Max. I'd thought leaving the house would change my phone karma. Like how when you're in a restaurant, starving, and waiting for the food to come— if you go to the bathroom, your meal will usually be sitting there waiting for you when you get back. But this technique doesn't really work with phones.

"I don't see why I can't get the out-of-town hi. *At least,*" I said to the Mother, shifting the phone to the other shoulder so I could sift flour for my light-as-air quiche crust.

"The *what?*"

We'd been talking less than two minutes and she was already annoyed.

"It's, like, the *holy grail* of phone calls. He's in Vegas, this totally new environment, but even with all the extra stimuli he calls just to say hello. The OTH—it was the only thing keeping me going."

"Ben." She sighed. "Your lips are moving, but you're not really saying anything."

"I am *too* saying something. I'm saying my relationship isn't going well, *Mother.*"

"*Then why don't you end it, Daughter?*"

I told her that wasn't a very helpful suggestion since I had no intention of breaking up with Max, not that we were going out. Plus, I added, this wasn't a very sympathetic thing to say.

"Well *I don't know what else to suggest,*" she huffed. "What did you expect? This kind of behavior is simply what happens when you date a guy half your age."

"He's not half my age," I argued. "He's half your age."

"He's still too young for a serious relationship."

I took a deep breath, counted to five, and started cracking eggs into a mixing bowl. "I don't think his age has anything to do with it, if you really want to know."

"Fine."

"You know, maybe you should just tell me everything's going to be okay," I said, furiously beating the eggs. "That's really all I want to hear."

"Well, *of course* everything is going to be okay," she said. "Your life will end just because this relationship might not work out? Please." I heard the knock on the door. "Just a minute!" she called out. "Ben, I have to go."

"Where are you going?"

"My date's here."

"You have a date?"

"With my Pilates instructor."

"You take Pilates?"

"I'll see you tomorrow."

I was obviously hatched out of some kind of pod. There's simply no way that woman ever gave birth.

FILLY FEED ✿

cut around dotted line

SO YOUR LIFE'S NO ROSE GARDEN. THAT DOESN'T MEAN YOU CAN'T EAT ONE. BENJAMINA FRANKLIN GIVES US THE DIRT ON HER BEST DESSERT.

1 pint vanilla ice cream
3 cups caramel sauce
1 bag Oreo cookies
6 Styrofoam cups
6 mini terra-cotta pots (avail. at any nursery)
3 plastic straws (cut in half)

Rinse clay pots, dry overnight. Cut Styrofoam cups so they will fit inside each (so ice cream doesn't melt out the bottom). Fill each pot with one layer caramel sauce, ice cream, then caramel sauce on top. Take Oreos and crush until they resemble soil; spoon on top of caramel. Put a straw in each, place a rosebud inside, and serve. Serves 6.

The day of the shower was a nightmare. It took four trips back *down* to my car to load everything up. In between each trip I checked my voicemail for the OTH. No such luck. Meanwhile, I devised this inspired dessert idea that involved miniature terra-cotta pots I bought at the nursery. I envisioned a tiny, edible rose garden, and I figured this extra touch would *really* make Audrey crap her pants. But I forgot to rinse out the pots, which were clay and should have dried overnight, so I had to pray no one would notice there was real dirt along with fake dirt in their ice cream. Then I ran to the grocery store to buy the fresh roses, but they only had the expensive cabbage kind, which wasn't what I had in mind. I bought them anyway (sixty bucks for twenty-four, and I only needed sixteen). And *then* I hauled it all over to my mom's condo in Calabasas, which is only, like, four thousand miles away. The Mother, true to form, opened the door looking gorgeous. Navy blue suit, pretty camisole peeking out at the nape. Her pristine condo—white fluffy carpet, beige slipcovered furniture, rattan accent pieces—smelled fresh and clean.

"You're wearing *sweatpants?*" she said, standing in the doorway, looking me up and down.

"Hi, fuck off, wanna grab a bag or something?"

"That's a nice way to talk to your mother." She took some bags out of my hands and fixed me with a smile. "Fuck you, too, darling."

I explained that I'd be changing my clothing after I warmed the quiches in the oven, tossed the wild greens salad in the homemade Dijon vinaigrette, arranged the fruit salad on platters, assembled the flower pot desserts, uncorked the champagne, mixed the mimosas, and made the coffee—all in the next forty minutes. The Mother, with a bemused look, said she would make the coffee, drinks, and salad dressing, and plucked the recipe from my hand. Then she shoved me toward the bathroom and encouraged me to groom. I'd just managed to shower and towel my hair dry when guests started to arrive.

"Oooooh!" Audrey said, inspecting the spread as I laid it out on the buffet. "The quiche looks fabulous. I *love* the flowers . . . What are those flower pots for?"

I hugged her, suddenly overcome with happiness and my first two glasses of champagne. (The Mother mixes a mean mimosa.) Grandma arrived, choosing a seat in the corner where she told anyone who would listen about her mole biopsy and gave me queer looks. The bridesmaids, whom I secretly dubbed the "So Sisters," gushed over all the girlish touches. ("Oh my God those quiches are *so* cute!" "Oh my God this salad is *so* yummy!" "Oh my God those flowers are *so* gorgeous!") Even Jamie's mom came. A grand woman whose name I can never remember. She picked at the nubs on her St. John suit and looked severely disturbed when I gave Aud the requisite vibrator with a note that guaranteed her a lifetime supply of D batteries.

All day I fussed over Audrey like a perfect maid of honor, getting a mimosa for her, and one for me. And one for her, and one for me. Aud opened a huge present that contained a KitchenAid ultra power mixer— the Rolls-Royce of bridal shower gifts—and she squealed with delight, so I squealed with her. "Rock on!" I yelled, jumping up and down while punching my fist in the air. "You got it!"

Between gifts and dessert, I found myself in the kitchen, watching the Mother make coffee. I was so grateful (I was so wasted), I started rhapsodizing to Kiki about how much I loved the woman who gave me life.

"She gives the *best* advice!" I said. "The fucking *best!* Right, Mom?"

"I'm glad you're starting to realize that," she said.

"You know what Mother always says? Move *on*. Move on! No out-of-town hi? Who needs it?" I snapped my fingers in the air: *"Move 'em on out!"*

"I love it!" Kiki said, clapping (she'd been matching me, as I matched Audrey, drink for drink). *"Genius."* She turned to the Mother. "You are a total genius."

"Now if only you girls would *take my advice*." The Mother rapped her knuckles on the Formica counter with each word for emphasis.

"Mmmm . . ." Kiki said. "But I mean, my mom gives me advice and I don't listen. I just don't. Dunno why." She shook her head and scratched at the quiche she had somehow gotten stuck on the knee of her Prada pants.

"Well. I'm not actually your mother, so you just might listen to me," the Mother said. "Ben's mentioned your little problem with that producer fellow, and *you* need to move on. Have a one-night stand. Or find a husband like Audrey did. Men are *everywhere.* All you have to do is leave the house. Take a walk, and you'll find one."

"You really think so?" Kiki said. And then . . . if only I could turn back time, as Cher would say . . . she said, "You should write a column for *Filly*! An advice column! Instead of asking their own mothers, who our readers won't listen to anyway, they could ask *you.* Ben, wouldn't that be great?"

"A-*ma*-zing." I sighed, gleefully sticking rosebuds into the fake Oreo dirt. "*Bril*liant. I *looove* it."

So that's how it happened. And even though I was supremely annoyed, I didn't have the heart to tell the Mother I didn't want her to write the column after all. I could have told Kiki, but I doubted she could do much about it; apparently the Whip thought the Mother was Candace Bushnell meets Ann Landers. *It's my job,* I reminded myself, pushing the proofs aside and laying back down in bed, *to immolate myself for the entertainment of others.*

Then there was the question of my actually "moving on," that brilliant idea of the Mother-turned-dangerously-empowered-advice-columnist. (She'd already sent me an e-mail asking if I knew any good lit agents.) It wasn't working. I spent the morning wondering if Max, who was surely back from Vegas, got a lap dance while he was away, and how long he'd wait to call me. The phone rang and I leapt for it. Just Nina, calling to tell me about some guy she'd picked up at a Jungian seminar last night. After discussing his finer points, along with possible weak spots (she thought it was suspect that he asked for both her cell and regular phone numbers, as opposed to just one or the other), we returned to my topic of choice.

"I have a question," I said. "Do you think Max got a lap dance when he was in Las Vegas?"

"I don't see why he wouldn't," Nina said. I could hear her grinding coffee in the background. "I'm sure Max, like every other man, enjoys the fantasy that strippers provide."

"What's that?"

"The idea that a beautiful, naked woman exists just to satisfy his most secret desires and that she secretly prefers him to every other man in the club."

"You mean, men don't just desire the woman, but they believe she wants them, in particular?"

"Precisely."

Somehow this was more disturbing than the scenario I'd come up with on my own.

"But why would he want to be desired by someone he pays," I said, "when I desire him for free?"

"Because. With a professional he can have a pair of enormous fake tits in his face without commitment or obligation, which he can't have with you. Most guys find a stripper the perfect antidote to an actual girlfriend."

It was getting worse.

"Nina?"

"Yes?"

"Do you think breast size is important?"

"Do *you* think breast size is important?"

I was way too hungover for this. So I said, "Do *you* think that *I* think that *you* think breast size is important?"

"I don't know, Ben," she said. "Do *you?*"

I hung up on her.

The phone rang again and I answered right away. "I know, I'm sorry," I rushed in, before Nina could bite my head off. "I'm having a shit day, my mom gets more action than I do, *and* she's getting more assignments."

"Have I been gone that long?"

"Max?" I said.

"Hey."

"I thought you were Nina."

"What's this about your mother?"

"Don't go there. So . . . how are you?"

"Good," he said. "How are you?"

"I don't know. Wait, did you get a lap dance?"

"What?"

"In Vegas. Lap dance. Did you get one?"

"Damn, B." He laughed. "Cut to the chase why don't you."

"Seriously, did you?"

"I don't like lap dances."

"Come on."

"No, really. Those girls wear too much makeup, their hair gets in your mouth. Your friends watch you get a hard-on, which is just plain weird. I'm way too much of a control freak for that sort of thing. You?"

"Did I get one or do I give them?"

"Do you *give* them."

"I should think so." This was a happy turn of events. "Definitely."

He laughed. A deep, rich, filthy chuckle. *He still likes me! He still likes me!* I grabbed a pillow and held it tight. Max proceeded to tell me about his trip, how much money he'd lost at craps, and about how his friends dragged him to the Olympic Garden strip club, which he insisted was lap-dance-free. I chose to believe him (at least he had the decency to lie convincingly about it) and filled him in on the near disaster but ultimate success of the bridal shower. I left out the horror of the magazine column, though. Didn't want to give Max a heads-up that my mom was advising me to dump him. And then, miracle of miracles, he said, "So I have an idea."

"Does it involve a G-string?"

"Depends on what you want to pack."

Did he just say "pack"?

There's only one thing better than the out-of-town hi (besides an invitation to move in together). The weekend away.

CHAPTER

8

Palm Springs was Max's idea. Not because Palm Springs is that great, but more because in L.A. we don't have the equivalent of a Martha's Vineyard. All we have are acres of empty desert filled with serial killers. A place once called home by Charles Manson and the Dinah Shore golf tournament, featuring a town overrun with spring-break-esque partyers who come to cruise up and down five sweltering blocks of cheesy gift shops while wearing HARD ROCK CAFÉ T-shirts. Put it this way, the OD scene in *Less Than Zero* wasn't set in Palm Springs for nothing.

Nevertheless, I left home with visions of Bob Hope's tan, martinis, and Neutra houses dancing in my head. Max was going to lavish me with attention for *two whole days in a row.* Unprecedented.

He was being very cute. Arrived at my house to pick me up holding a bottle of sunscreen tied with a bow, and he brought a stack of CDs he thought I would like to listen to on the drive. Even the traffic on the 10 and the guy in the Nissan next to us who picked his nose for two solid miles didn't get me down. Nor did those creepy steel windmill things that you have to pass on the way. The tall stalks, with their two knifelike propellers, generate electricity. But to me they look like the dangerous vestiges of some otherworld civilization that the government is trying to keep hush-hush.

We finally arrived at the hotel—a midcentury marvel with a turquoise pool, an Eames marshmallow chair roasting in the sun, and tasteful cacti planted around like impassive aliens. At the check-in desk, my heart leapt when the extremely tan concierge said, "Suite Two-Oh-Four, Max and Ben."

"Yay!" I said.

"Did you just say, 'Yay'?" Max asked.

I shrugged, but inside I let out an orgasmic *Yay! Yay! Yay!*

The concierge let us into our room and Max immediately stretched out on the king-size bed and started looking for the remote. I carried my suitcase toward the closet and, after unpacking the four skirts, three sundresses, two pairs of jeans, and four pairs of shoes I packed so I'd be ready for anything, went to inspect the bathroom situation. I was hoping there'd be a noisy fan or a radio inside that would camouflage any nongirlie activities. No such luck.

"Do you see the remote in there?" Max yelled.

"In the bathtub?" I yelled back.

"Well, it's not out here."

I came out and looked around. "Wait," I said. "Do you see a TV? Hold on, here's a note."

I picked up the printed card that lay on top of the dresser, where a TV *should* have been, and read aloud, "Dear Guest. Welcome to the Resort at the Desert. We want you to enjoy everything our soothing environment has to offer, so all rooms are without television sets. Also, please be PC and do not smoke in your room. A $200 fine will be charged for smoking."

Max looked pale. "Be PC?" he asked. "So the fact that I smoke makes me, like, as bad as a homophobic racist?"

"Smoke on the patio, evil one, and enjoy the soothing environment."

"Hm."

With that, Max went outside with a plastic cup filled with water to use as an ashtray. He didn't look happy. I wasn't so psyched, either—I'd picked the hotel because *Filly* once did a photo shoot here and everyone said it was fabulous, which meant if anything went wrong it would be my fault.

After washing my face and carefully reapplying my lip gloss, I went outside and found Max smoking glumly in 110-degree heat.

"Look at this, B," he said, holding up the cup of water. It was almost empty.

"Did you spill?"

"Hunh-unh." He shook his head and exhaled. "It's *evaporating*."

Max lay down to take a nap while I read the information booklet and discovered the hotel didn't have room service, either. I resolved to keep this little factoid to myself for as long as possible. When Max finally woke up, we drove into town and had dinner at a gourmet Mexican restaurant the concierge recommended. The place was very popular, and self-consciously trendy. There were muted taupe linens and hand-ground blue corn tamales; they had a gas fireplace that was on, along with the air-conditioning. The menu boasted one hundred different exotic drinks. Max seemed tired, so I tried to engage him by babbling about the ridiculous thing I'd done while he was taking a nap earlier.

"So I go outside?" I said, pausing to take a sip of my persimmon margarita. "And the hotel has this, like, welcome-to-the-desert whatever cocktail thing by the pool where you schmooze with the owners?"

"Uh-huh." He was pushing his tamale around on his plate with a morose look on his face.

"And so the guy who was at the front desk, who it turns out runs the joint, was there with his wife. And she looked a lot like that socialite Jocelyne Wildenstein from New York?"

"Who?"

"The one who had so much plastic surgery she looks like a cat?"

"Right."

"So I was standing out there and I noticed that the other couples looked like they were at least fifteen years older than we are. Oh, I mean, than I am. Twenty-two years older than you."

Max didn't laugh. I persevered.

"You know, the kinds of people who wear gold jewelry with their bathing suits? And they were getting *bombed* on the complimentary cocktails while lounging around in the sun. So the owner guy, who introduced himself as 'Stephen, with a *ph,*' asked me where you were. And I said, 'Oh, he's in the room crashed out like a vampire who will die if exposed to daylight.' "

"That's funny."

"Thanks. So Stephen proceeded to tell this story about some woman who checked in last summer wearing dark sunglasses and all-black, and stayed in her room for two weeks with the heat on."

"That's crazy."

"Exactly. And when her DO NOT DISTURB sign had been on the door for days and nobody had seen her, they finally opened her room and found that she'd overdosed on heroin. Total bummer, right?"

"Gross."

"I know. But here's the thing, so Stephen with a *ph* is telling this story, and I'm starting to feel a little light-headed from the martini I'm drinking, which, mixed with the heat, has become a toxic substance and is congealing my brain." I laughed. "So I say, 'Oh, well, don't worry about me and Max. We don't do smack. We just smoke the chronic.' "

"That's not funny."

"I *know*. What was I thinking, right? Wait, it gets worse. So Stephen looks at me and goes, 'Are you aware that the gentleman sitting next to you'—he motions to my left at this sunburned/mustached/mirrored Aviator sunglasses guy—'is on the vice squad in downtown Los Angeles?' "

I rolled my eyes at Max. "I was so embarrassed. And nobody laughed. I think that cop guy is going to stake us out."

"That's great, B," Max said.

"Wait, are you mad?"

"No."

"You usually think it's funny when I make an ass of myself."

"I'm just a little out of it."

After dinner, at least, Max rose to the occasion. We got back to the room and he dug around in his backpack and pulled out a Ziploc baggie filled with tea lights. He scattered them around the room, looking a little sheepish.

"Too corny?" he said, lighting them with his Zippo.

"I like corny." I stretched out on the bed and watched the flames make jumpy patterns on the ceiling.

"Well, since there's no TV . . ." he said.

"And no smoking . . ." I said.

"Ben, what are we going to do?"

We found activities that I deemed most suitable. And Max finally seemed to relax. After, I was snuggled up in his arms, and he said, "So I told my friends at work about our trip, and how we're going to get massages and marinate in the Jacuzzi and all that. And the girls were all, 'Oh, I wish *I* were your girlfriend.' "

I tried not to cry out. Out of nowhere, he'd said the G-word. Exactly the way Kiki had predicted. But even though my heart was doing cartwheels of ecstasy, I kept my cool. I said, "I guess they're going to have to get in line."

There was this long pause. Then Max said, "I guess."

Suddenly he didn't seem so relaxed.

"Well, I'm . . ." I was about to say, *I'm your girlfriend.* But maybe I wasn't out of the woods quite yet. So instead I said, "Maybe *I* want to be your girlfriend, too."

"Oh B." He pulled me closer, gave me a little hug. "That's a really big topic."

"I know," I said. Except I didn't know. So I said, "Wait . . . I'm sorry, what was the point of your story?"

"The point?" He pulled back and looked at me. "Look, B, I'm not seeing anybody else if that's what you're asking."

"I'm not asking. I just—I guess I'm asking if we're on the same page."

"I think we both know where this is going."

He said it so confidently I shut up for a second. I didn't want to push. *He's not seeing anyone else,* I thought. *That's good.* But for some reason I couldn't let it go. I wanted to hear the word *girlfriend.* I *had* to.

"What if I saw somebody else?" I said. "What would you do?"

"I would assume that you didn't want to be with me. I would be upset, but the truth is that you can't make anyone do what they don't want to do."

"That's it?"

"What would you want me to do? I'm not going to challenge some guy to a duel." He laughed softly and poked me in the shoulder. "En garde."

"But would you be miserable? Would you want to die?"

"I don't know about *die.* Look," he said, fiddling with the ends of my hair, "if you want to be with someone, you make the time. But if you want to see other people, I think you should, right?"

Now I was confused. I wanted to be his girlfriend. Instead I was getting his permission to date someone else. I pulled my head away and looked at him.

"But I don't want to see anybody else," I said.

"Then we're on the same page." Max gave me a kiss on my forehead. And promptly fell asleep.

After staring at the clock for an hour, I was about to drift off when . . .

"I don't think I feel well."

It was Max's voice coming through the pitch black.

"Do you want me to get you some water?" I propped myself up on an elbow and reached for his shoulder.

"No." It was muffled.

"Advil? Do you have a headache?"

"Hunh-unh."

"Stomachache?"

"No."

"What then?"

"I think I may be coming down with something."

Selfishly, I couldn't help but think, *On our weekend?*

Then he said, "I need some juice."

I had to break it to him about the room service. And no, there was no minibar, either. But even though I was finally exhausted, I offered to drive Max to a liquor store. We got up and dressed, and proceeded on this morbid little pilgrimage around downtown Palm Springs, past the spring-break-esque partyers, past the drunken disco dads and their trophy wives, until we found a gas station with a soda machine on the outskirts of town. Max got a Sprite, and he drank it in silence while we headed back to the hotel.

"Are you sure you're okay?" I said.

He said, "Let's not make a big thing out of it."

It was the boyfriend/girlfriend talk. Had to be. *Good God,* I thought, looking out the window at the Joshua trees sliding silently by, *why did I initiate The Talk?*

★ ★ ★

"This isn't cream, Ben."

It was the following morning, and I was browsing through the free Palm Springs magazine, chock-full of ads for various golf courses so minty green they looked like they were spray-painted. Max was staring into a creamer with the look of a man who had just been horribly betrayed. He said, "This is nonfat milk."

Although the hotel didn't feel the need to provide a single convenience, their semisincere yet somehow passive aggressive attempt to make it up to us was to place a tray of hard fat-free bran muffins and lukewarm coffee outside our room in the morning. I don't really like bran muffins, but I was trying to be a trouper so I took a couple of bites. Not too many though, since Max has never seen me in a bikini before and I didn't want to look bloated.

"That sucks," I said.

"I can't not have my coffee," he said, with complete earnestness.

"Well, but you *have* coffee."

"With nonfat milk. In my world, that's not coffee."

"Okay, let me call," I said brightly, dialing the front desk. Stephen with a *ph* answered, probably wondering if we needed a new bong, crack pipe, syringe . . .

"Hi, this is Room Two-Oh-Four," I said. "Do you by any chance have real cream for the coffee? Really? *No* cream?" I looked at Max and he was making this circular motion with his hand. "What about whole milk. Do you have that?"

Max shook his head.

"Oh, okay, never mind, we need actual cream."

Stephen said there was a grocery store about five miles away. "Where is that?" I scrambled for a pen. "Make a right. Yeah. Two lights. Left. Ummm-hmmm. Right. Right. Left. Wait, how far away is this? Uh-huh. Right. Next light. Okay, thanks."

I hung up. Max looked like he'd just swallowed the whole world's worth of misery.

"I'll get it," I said.

"No, I'll get it," he moaned, lying back down on the bed. I took this to mean he still wasn't feeling well.

"Come on, it's fine. I'll just go get it. It's only, like, five minutes away."

I got dressed and grabbed the keys to the car. Outside, it seemed even hotter than it had the day before, and the steering wheel burned the palms of my hands while I drove. I passed a bank that had one of those giant thermometer things outside and the red line was spiked on 114 degrees. Squinting at the street signs, I realized I couldn't have been more lost. It was crazy, because all of Palm Springs is basically this grid, but all the streets are named things like Rio Noches and Rio Dios and the Spanish-style buildings all look exactly the same. Finally I found the store just as the sweat was starting to streak down the front of the sexy little summer dress I'd bought special at Fred Segal. Inside, I realized I'd never bought cream for coffee in my life since I drank it black. *Is half-and-half cream?* I wondered. *Or is that like half cream and half something else that in Max's world won't really be cream?* I didn't see anything with just CREAM on it, and I started to panic. His whole day and my entire life's happiness depended on buying the right thing. So I bought half-and-half, whipping cream, and actual whipped cream in hopes that one of them would be okay.

I got back, palms burned and pits sweaty, and laid the purchases before Max, explaining that I wasn't sure which one he would want.

"That's so cute," he said.

Then he held up the half-and-half and poured an inch in his coffee. I was relieved to see that he looked half happy.

I was starting to suspect that a weekend away was meant for people who were much more comfortable with one another than Max and me. Things just seemed *off.* I felt silly brushing my teeth next to him, putting on makeup in front of him, trying to decide what to wear while he was in the room. After the cream debacle, Max again wasn't feeling well, so he decided to take another nap. I said I'd be relaxing by the pool when he was ready to face the world. The temperature was just this side of hell but I was happy enough standing in the water and browsing through the stack of magazines I propped on the adobe tiles at the side. *Max will come out soon,* I told myself, browsing through *Elle.* Then I flipped through *InStyle.* Then *Vogue, Glamour, Cosmo, Allure,* and *Filly,* which I think is important to read since they pay my rent. By then I could feel a sunburn spreading over my shoulders and the back of my neck. I didn't want to end up looking like Mr. Vice Squad detective, who came out of his room to glare at me with his beet red stomach hanging over his Speedo, so I headed in to see how Max was doing.

He was out cold. I checked his forehead, but it felt cool. I hovered, trying not to wake him, but I was unsure what to do with myself. I'd done the swimming, I'd done the magazines. It was too warm to try the sauna. I could have called Kiki, but that seemed like too much of a defeat. So I wandered around the room, tidying things up even though I'd already put all my stuff neatly away. I was getting more and more desperate for Max to wake up. Restless, I went for a walk around the hotel, peeking into the gift shop where they sold sea-foam green robes monogrammed with the hotel initials. Stephen, who worked the cash register—in addition to being the front-desk guy and the bartender and the towel boy—eyed me suspiciously. "Haven't seen the young man all day," he said.

"He's not feeling well."

Stephen was making me nervous—the guy was everywhere and I was afraid he'd summon the cop to check my body cavities for stolen towels—so I went back to the room. I tried making innocent little noises to rouse Max, casually knocking over the ice bucket, which made a much bigger racket than I thought it would. But it didn't work.

"I knocked over the ice bucket," I said. He didn't move.

"The cop is here and he intends to strip-search me with a flashlight so he can peer into all my body cavities."

Still nothing.

"Then he's going to do you."

Max stayed asleep.

"I think I'm in love with you," I said, thinking this certainly would startle him into consciousness.

It didn't.

Of course, that was a stupid thing to do considering the circumstances. "Just kidding," I added. I huffed down into a chair, and cracked the Philip Roth book I'd bought in another misguided attempt to become a member of the intelligentsia. The book was painstakingly slow. It was four o'clock.

I tried to wake Max at seven. He muttered, "Five more minutes."

I tried again at seven-thirty, and he said, "I think I need another half an hour."

At eight-thirty I was starving, so I said, in what I hoped was a bemused tone, "Hey, Max. I'm dying of hunger over here."

He roused himself, and in a kind of sleepwalk that reminded me of the zombies in the Michael Jackson "Thriller" video, he dressed himself in the same T-shirt and jeans he'd worn for the trip yesterday. Obviously it wasn't going to be a nice dinner. We drove around looking for someplace where they'd have chicken soup (as if anyone serves chicken soup in Palm Springs). I finally convinced him to stop at a pizza place.

Max obviously wasn't in the mood to talk. So while I ate my slice, I pretended to stare at the television they had blaring in the corner. "Look!" I said to Max. "TV!" He didn't laugh. When we got back to the room, Max said, "Sorry, I'm just really under the weather, B. I feel terrible." And he crawled back into bed.

Terrible about ruining our trip? I wondered. *Terrible as in, sick? Terrible because he doesn't want me to be his girlfriend?*

We left first thing in the morning, driving by all the enticing outlet stores that lined the freeway. The same stores we'd both said we were dying to go to on the way down here. That was less than forty-eight hours ago. When I was happy.

HORRORSCOPE

He's so cute, isn't he? His eyes, his hair, his shitty personality. Yeah, you heard me right. Most things end, and it's better to know how in advance. Here, love warnings from the stars.

BY BENJAMINA FRANKLIN

	THE GOOD	THE BAD	THE END
ARIES	He's a chauvinist, which turns you on because until recently you were dating a guy who drank flavored coffee.	Wait until he starts asking where his dinner is.	Babe, you're the best, but he's got room for a lot more notches on his belt.
TAURUS	He's smart, shy, a secret pervert.	He'll make you miserable if your relationship doesn't go the way he wants.	Mixed signals—he'll leave you, come back, leave, come back. When you've finally had enough, expect to do all the dirty work.
GEMINI	He likes to chew the rag even more than your best friend.	All this talk never goes anywhere.	He's such a flake, he'll probably forget to deliver an "it's over" speech.
CANCER	Sensitive, sex-obsessed, the perfect scam.	He's completely anal and ridiculously insecure.	If you dump him, he'll obsess about you forever. If you don't, expect to be smothered to death.
LEO	He acts like he's already famous.	He treats you like just another fan.	Imagine trying to get your way with Madonna—a consummate Leo—but add a penis to the mix.
VIRGO	He's preppy, self-deprecating, and practical.	Therapy five times a week would only scratch the surface.	He's defensive, so he goes on the offensive. Be prepared for a tongue lashing (and no, not the good kind).

→

	THE GOOD	THE BAD	THE END
LIBRA	Isn't he adorable? Thoughtful, kind, soft-spoken . . .	. . . which is only a ruse to hide how insanely judgmental he is.	A dissertation on exactly what you've done wrong, what he's done wrong, what you've both done wrong, that will make you want to kill yourself.
SCORPIO	He's charismatic and holds back enough to keep you interested.	Hello, psycho! Scorpio's temper is *from hell.*	Encourage him to express his anger via e-mail, then cancel your Hotmail account, change your phone number, and move far, far away.
SAGITTARIUS	All the other girls want him, but he chooses you.	That's what you think—*he cheats.*	Don't expect him to go through a mourning period—he'll have someone else lined up way before the door hits you in the rear.
CAPRICORN	He's a suit-and-tie guy—self-possessed, intelligent, goal-oriented.	He thinks doggie-style is risqué and is looking for a trophy wife.	Unless you live up to his expectations, you'll get the old heave-ho in a public place or via fax.

PISCES ASKS EVERY GIRL HE GOES OUT WITH, "ARE *YOU* MY MOMMY?"

	THE GOOD	THE BAD	THE END
AQUARIUS	Supercool hippie vibe where you love the one you're with.	He's a hypocrite who has big ideas about how people should behave that he doesn't apply to himself.	If you don't have *a lot* in common, run for your life.
PISCES	Sweet, dreamy, full of compliments.	Basically asks every girl he goes out with, "Are *you* my mommy?"	You'll never have your heart eaten out by anyone nicer. Expect the best of table manners. ʊ

CHAPTER
9

It's funny. You can go away, come back two days later, and have everything be totally different. I walked in the door, in a haze of depression after my abysmal weekend, and all I wanted was for Kiki to come over, preferably with beer, cigarettes, and pizza, so we could deconstruct every thing that happened until the inexplicable became explicable.

Except when I dialed her number I got the machine.

"Wait," I said, "where are you? Call me. Ummm . . . I'm home. Do I sound fucked up? Sorry. Are you out? Okay, then, call me back. 'Bye."

Then I considered how *Sunday Night Movie of the Week* my message sounded and called back.

"Me again. I'm not stalking you. I just wanted to say I'm okay so don't worry. I'm not lying on the side of the road or anything. I'm fine. Well, not really fine, but I'm in good actual *physical* health. Okay. Good-bye."

Now she knew without the slightest doubt that I was having a nervous breakdown. There was nothing left to do but wallow. So I wallowed, crying until my pillow was wet and soggy.

All I could think about was how much I didn't want the relationship to end. If it was, in fact, ending. Which I didn't know. I'd tried to broach the whole boyfriend/girlfriend mess in the car, but everything Max said only made me feel more confused. Even when we pulled up outside my house, I couldn't tell what he was thinking. He just dropped me off, kissed me on the cheek, and said he'd call me "soonish."

I finally fell asleep wondering how soon soonish was going to be.

I woke up the next morning with the phone ringing on the pillow next to me.

"Where have you *been?*" I said immediately. "I've been trying to—"

"I'm around the corner!" Kiki was shouting into the phone. I had to hold it away from my ear while frantically scrambling for the volume button. "Meet me at Back Door Bakery!" she yelled. "We have to talk!"

Now that's what I call a good friend.

I dressed quickly, putting on whatever I found on the floor, and dashed to the café. Kiki was already there, sitting outside the garishly painted purple restaurant, devouring a honey bun the size of her head and looking fabulous in black pants and a Marc Jacobs blazer. *Wait,* I thought, *those look like evening clothes.* "Honey," I said, "are you eating? What the hell is going on?"

"I met him!" she said, grabbing my arm and shoving me into the wrong seat (next to the busboy station, your basic auditory nightmare).

"Who?" I asked, shifting uncomfortably as a waiter dumped a pile of dishes into a plastic bin that was only inches from my head.

"*Who?* Ben, I met *The One!*"

It was the last story I ever thought I'd hear.

Last Friday, as I'd been getting ready to leave for my Palm Springs shit parade, Kiki had gotten so depressed she'd resolved to actually take my mother's advice and go on that walk. She figured she could at least get fresh air in her lungs, maybe put some color back in her cheeks. So she showered for the first time in days, combed her hair, put on her favorite pair of jeans and her beloved black sweater, and set off for a trek around the block.

Once she got outside, she found it so pleasant, she decided she'd actually walk to Aron's Records. The store isn't really that close to her house, but the new plan was to buy as much up-tempo pop music as it would take to get her out of her funk. So Kiki was walking along Highland and suddenly there was this loud *crack!* She looked up and actually *saw a human being falling out of a tree.* He fell through many branches, banging himself up pretty good in the process, and landed at her feet.

"Holy shit!" Kiki said. The crash site looked like a yard sale—his glasses went one way, wallet, keys, and one shoe another. "Are you okay?"

He said, "Grab the cat!"

Kiki looked up and saw a shabby-looking red tabby running headlong into the traffic. Now, she was about to say she hated cats. But then she noticed the guy's perfect hipster-boy pants from Sears, his carefully broken-in white T-shirt, and his adorable tousled hair (with bits of grass in it), and she dashed into the speeding cars after the crazed little thing, tackling it just before it would have been smashed to bits by a gardener's truck.

Kiki brought the stunned animal back to the cute boy, who was now on his feet and trying to get a cracked lens back into the frames of his glasses. She handed the feral beast to him, and he said, "That was a close one, huh?"

Kiki stopped telling me her story for a moment to shovel in another drippy piece of honey bun.

"What was his cat doing in a tree?" I said, watching the pastry ooze a glob of syrup onto her black top.

"Just wait . . ." Kiki said with a huge grin, mopping up the syrup and licking it off her index finger. "It wasn't his cat!"

It turned out he lived just over there and could hear the cat crying from his apartment window. When he'd gone out to investigate, he could tell from the kitty's chewed-up ears and dirty belly that it must be a stray, had gotten stuck in the tree, and since he was a saint he'd decided to *save it.* He climbed up, and he turned out to be a pretty lousy climber, which was how he almost killed my best friend.

Holding the cat in his arms, the boy named it Weezer, even though it was a female. Then he asked Kiki if she would want to share the cat with him since she'd helped save her life. Kiki said yes, deciding then and there that she loved cats (particularly little Weezer). They brought the cat back to his place, and he actually offered Kiki a diet Coke, solidifying his status as the perfect man. After some careful prying, the guy, whose name was Curtis, told her he worked A&R at a small indie record company. He also volunteered for an animal rescue group in his spare time. Oh, and he'd gone to Columbia where he was prelaw and in some garage band we would have heard of if we'd gone to Columbia. It was a true love connection, and they'd been together ever since. Going to brunch at Roscoe's House of Chicken 'n' Waffles, watching *Citizen Kane* on his DVD player, having sex every five minutes, and walking back to Kiki's apartment now and then when she needed clean underwear. They were already using the same toothbrush. Which meant this was really happening.

"He's so . . ." Kiki was at a loss. "My whole life I've been waiting for this guy, and there he was, just like"—she snapped her fingers—"*that!*"

"Guys aren't supposed to grow on trees," I said.

"I know! But they do! They really do!"

We spent the next hour going over every detail. But finally, after we'd rehashed this sudden change of events a third time, Kiki stopped midrhapsody: "Oh my God—how was your weekend? Was it just amazing?"

I couldn't hold back any longer, so I told her the whole story—Max basically sleeping his way through the trip, how he'd told me on the ride home he wanted to be "seeing each other," but not "going out," how he thought he "probably loved me," but didn't know if he'd ever been "in love." How he didn't like the terms *girlfriend* and *boyfriend* because they were "meaningless."

"If they're so meaningless then what difference does it make whether you're 'seeing each other' or 'going out'?" Kiki said.

"Bingo."

"Oh, so what the fuck? He brings you on this weekend away for . . . what, exactly? To make you fucking *miserable?*"

"So you understand why I've been crying nonstop."

"Uh, *yeah*. And what's this shit about his being sick?" She was becoming bloodthirsty on my behalf. "Like, as if he was *actually* sick and not just going through some insane commitment-phobic anxiety attack?"

"Right," I said. "Except that I'm such a wimp, I spent the entire time catering to his every whim, driving through the seventh circle of hell to find fucking cream for his coffee, and trying not to cry too loud in the bathroom. I felt like such a loser."

"*Well of course* you wanted to cry. *Duh.* He tells you he's not seeing anybody else, but he doesn't give a shit if you do? That's not what you want to hear. That's not what *any* woman would want to hear from a guy on a weekend that you are supposed to be together. Ben, look, I'm sorry. But the guy is . . . He's a total—"

"Wait." I had to interrupt her. *"Please don't say it."*

I could tell from the look on Kiki's face I was going to have to explain.

"I believe . . ." I started. "No. Okay. I know this sounds crazy. But I believe that Max might really love me." I paused, trying to gauge how this was coming across. She was withholding judgment, determined to hear me out. Even though it was killing her.

"I think maybe he's just scared because this is real," I said. "And I think, to just bail because things are getting hard, to just walk away, for what?" I took a deep breath. I was trying not to just lose it, in public, in front of all the Silver Lake cool kids stopping in for coffee before heading up the street to the dog park. "If he loves me . . . I want to stick this out."

"Why?" she said.

Wasn't it obvious? I put my head down on the table and closed my eyes. There was the way Max's face lit up whenever I walked in the door (provided he wasn't on the phone, of course). The juice by the bed in the morning. The fact that he knew Tater Tots were my favorite food, and he made them for me sometimes and they were never too undercooked, which I think can be one of the most disappointing things in this world. And I could never seem to stop myself from staring at him. I always felt lucky that he wanted to be with me. *It all has to add up to something real,* I thought. *It just has to. I can't accept that it doesn't.*

"It's complicated," I finally said. "He's just confused, okay? He's never been an out-and-out asshole to me. Ever. He brings me the juice, right? That can't be something he'd do for a girl he doesn't want to, for a girl he can't see himself with, you know, for a girl . . ."

"For someone who isn't his future girlfriend?" Kiki asked.

I nodded. "I don't think he wants me to walk away. I don't. I don't, I don't, I don't."

"Well, I guess he did leave things kind of up in the air," she said.

"So you don't think he's going to break up with me?"

I was starting to scare myself.

"No," she said. "Not yet, anyway."

Kiki sighed, pushed away what was left of her honey bun, and lit a cigarette.

"Look, to be honest, I kind of wish at this point that he would break up with you if this isn't going anywhere," she said. "I know that's not how you see it, but what's this guy wasting your time for? I mean, yeah, maybe he does love you. But I say *for all the good it does you.* If he can never make a real commitment, if he's just too young—"

I shot her a look. One that said, *Don't finish that sentence.*

"Look, he does seem crazy about you most of the time," she said, "which at this point is the only good thing I can say about him. So if you don't want to ditch him, then don't. If you're not ready, then you're not ready. I mean, you make a good point. He's never been a *complete* prick up until now."

She took another puff of the cigarette. I took it from her for a hit, but when I went to give it back, she waved it away. I got to keep it. "So what do I do now?" I asked.

"You want me to help you think of a way to keep him?" She was horrified.

"Yes."

"Shit. Really?"

"Come on. Be brutal. Tell me what you really think, and tell me how to fix it."

She considered this for a moment. "Okay," she said. "Then I think he's feeling smothered."

Ouch.

"It's not anything you did," she said. "That's what's pissing me off. But it's what's happening. He's got the Fear. So, I would guess that it's time for the Full Life."

"I was doing the full life already."

"No," she said. "You weren't."

I thought it over. Max had met all of my friends; I'd never even met his roommates. Max and I saw each other twice a week, but I always initiated the actual planning. And for some reason, I always slept at his house; he never came to mine. *Oh my God.* Suddenly the truth hit me: I'd been playing this all wrong.

THE FULL LIFE

Filly's BENJAMINA FRANKLIN **channels Anthony Robbins and takes on the very scary role of self-help guru.**

If men always did what we wanted, birds would sing, cherubs would serenade, and you'd never end up sitting across the dinner table from some guy, wishing you'd worn waterproof mascara while he breaks up with you, in public, which he does so you can't cause a scene.

Such is life. We can't change it. So the more important issue is: How exactly *did* you end up at that dinner table with the raccoon eyes? And who the hell *are* you anyway? What happened to the girl who was too busy to return most of her phone calls, kicking ass at work, and walking into bars and having men fall at her feet?

Where's the J.Lo you? The Get-Your-Freak-On you? *That's* the girl he was interested in, but she disappeared and in her place grew this monster of self-doubt and loathing.

You forgot that you have a full life. That you have friends. Work responsibilities. Family. Pets. Hobbies. An interest in writing prose poetry and an unbridled passion for growing avocados. Whatever. The point is, there were things that you enjoyed before you met *him*. After is a different story. You threw your life out the window and put him up on the fireplace mantel in your mind as the most important thing in the world. And he, like the caveman that he is, lost interest.

The Full Life is a way around this phenomenon. But it's not another cheery, bullshit mantra, nor is it the twelve steps to relationship happiness. There's no creepy group who can help you do it, and I promise I'm not gonna write a self-help book about it. But the Full Life works. If you want to avoid the embarrassing trip to the public rest room, the one where you dash from the dinner table and end up crying so hard that you distractedly plunk yourself down on a toilet without remembering to cover it with a seat protector, you have to *full-life his ass*.

What is the Full Life? It's the idea—no, the *complete and utter belief*—that with or without him you have everything you need. He can come to your party, sure. But the party goes on *whether he shows up or not*.

To do the Full Life, one must follow certain rules of empowerment. And no, these are not like "The Rules." Those are all about pleasing—and intriguing—him. No, the Full Life isn't about him at all. It's about you.

RULE #1: **A full-lifer doesn't leave holes in her schedule "just in case."** So it's Thursday, you haven't heard from him. Do you make plans for Saturday night? *If you're a full-lifer, you do.* And, just like when you're training a dog, if you do this enough times, he'll eventually learn that if he wants to see you, he has to make an effort *in advance*.

RULE #2: **A full-lifer knows how to take care of her own crises.** Sometimes when you're getting to know a new guy, you tell him your problems. You share because you're trying to establish trust. But while this is the foundation of a good relationship, you might be doing it before you're actually in one.

RULE #3: **A full-lifer doesn't commit to anyone until they've committed to her.** You don't know where you stand, but you act like you do—turning down dates, avoiding eye contact. *Don't do it!* You'll end up with expectations that, if you're honest with yourself, nobody told you to have in the first place.

RULE #4: **A full-lifer isn't instantly available.** Do you call everyone back the second they call you? Say you're running out the door and the phone rings. Do you leap for it? Stop the insanity. And finally . . .

RULE #5: **A full-lifer is fabulous.** Whether you want to learn how to crochet a tablecloth or drive a fire truck for the

A FULL-LIFER DOESN'T LEAVE HOLES IN HER SCHEDULE . . .

A FULL-LIFER IS FABULOUS.

local Red Cross, do it. Have the girls over for manicures, take that physics class, flirt. Don't change your life for him until you know he's interested in being a part of it.

TIME FOR TESTIMONIALS . . .

Don't believe it? Here's what the guys have to say:

Aaron, 28, physical therapist who was a full-lifer: "Most of the time, I'm out with a girl and I'm saying all the nice things, but inside I'm thinking, *How long do I have to listen before I get to see her underpants?* Then I met Nina. She was interesting, and frankly, if she would ever call me back, I'd go out with her again in a second."

Miles, 26, entertainment lawyer who talked to the hand: "Yeah, when I met Jeanne in college I knew I was calling the shots. But then, it was weird. She moved to L.A., made new friends . . . I think one time she actually told me I couldn't take her to dinner because she had to scrub her calluses. I recently proposed."

Gabriel, 30, actor: "Are you still in touch with your friend Jen? Could you ask her to please, please, *please* give me a call sometime?"

Surely you get the point.

Your money-back guarantee:

Okay, there isn't one. Life—especially when love is involved—doesn't give guarantees. But the one thing the Full Life *can* promise is that if he ever takes you out to that terrible I'm-breaking-up-with-you dinner, at least you'll already have something to do the following Saturday night. ∪

A FULL-LIFER DOESN'T COMMIT TO ANYONE UNTIL THEY'VE COMMITTED TO HER.

10

I was determined to get a full life if it killed me.

With Kiki's help, I devised a kind of mental checklist—all the things I had to do before I ended up relationship roadkill.

First, I planned to make plans with all my friends in order to fill my schedule.

Second, I would line up a safety boy for an ego-boosting flirtation and—depending on how desperate my situation became—possible physical contact.

Third, I had to repeat the following mantra to myself over and over: "I am not the hunter, I am the hunted."

And fourth, I would project an image of careless self-sufficiency and a complete lack of neediness.

The first, second, and third seemed pretty easy.

The last was going to be a little harder.

I dialed the number. He said hello.

I said, "Well, hello there, you," trying to sound as self-sufficient and un-needy as I probably did pre-Max.

"Who is this?"

"Duh. Ashton, it's Ben."

"Ben? Oh wow. Where you at?"

I explained that I was pulling into the parking lot at Fred Segal. I figured ringing my ex up after two months of no communication could look desperate, so I called from my cell while in the midst of a motive-camouflaging activity.

"So Ash," I said, "I only have a sec, but I've got this *stack* of Christmas party invitations and I wanted to know if you wanted to accompany me to—oh, hold on—"

Here I interrupted myself (always a good tactic) so I could exchange bastardized sign language with the parking attendant, who was waving me toward a row filled with SUVs. I couldn't see an open spot. Oh, there. I squeezed my car between a Ford Explorer and a Lincoln Navigator.

"I'm back," I said, turning down the radio.

Ashton said, "Which party?"

"Like it matters." I laughed. "Hey, what about the New Line thing at White Lotus this Saturday?"

"This Saturday?"

"Yeah, *this* Saturday."

"Uh . . . okay."

"Don't sound so excited. Hold on—"

Where the hell was my wallet? Oh, there.

"I'm back."

"No, I'm excited," Ashton said. "We just haven't caught up in a while. I have a lot to tell you actually—"

"Right, but listen, I'm in a rush so just pick me up at nine. We can get some food first so we won't get there too early."

Ashton said something about how that should be fine.

"Great. I gotta split."

Excellent, I thought as I snapped my cell phone closed. I was now officially busy Friday night, when I had plans with Chandra, and Saturday night, which I would spend flirting with Ashton. This would make it impossible for Max and me to do our weekend thing. That evening I planned to casually mention my hectic schedule to Max while we were watching our movie like it was no big deal. Take that!

THE FILLY LEXICON
girlie crack /'ger-lē 'krāk / *n.* **1:** highly addictive activities—clothes shopping, expensive beauty treatments, www.Sephora.com—that lead to painful withdrawal symptoms and maxed-out credit cards. *Related term:* GIRLIE PORN (fashion magazines, *Martha Stewart Weddings,* et cetera).
—*B.F.*

Feeling fairly fabulous, I crossed the parking lot and paused briefly at the front-window display—a dummy in a white Chloe suit with a mirrored ball where the head should have been. It was fitting. Ron Herman is more like a disco than a boutique. A place where it's as much about image and networking as fashion. I wasn't surprised when I opened the door and got hit full in the face with funk music blaring from hidden speakers. (Jamiroquai, naturally.)

I squinted my eyes against the track lighting and made my way inside, past a stylist balancing an armful of Katayone Adeli cocktail dresses and her cell phone.

"Girl, where have you been?" Allegra said from her place of honor, just left of the cash register.

"In hell." I slapped my credit card down on the counter. "But I'm back. I must find fabulous outfits immediately."

"Seriously, you have to because we have the cutest stuff right now." Allegra pocketed the card and took my elbow so she could guide me through the store. A stylist in her spare time, Allegra had impeccable taste. I trusted her to pull things off the racks while I tagged behind, every now and then adding one of my own choices to the growing pile. "So how's the boy?" she asked.

"Ugh." I nodded my approval at a top she held up. "Looks like he's got the Fear."

"Nunh-unh."

She deposited me in a dressing room and said through the door, "You have to show me everything, okay? Even the things you think don't work because you don't know."

"I promise."

I undressed quickly and pulled a white mesh dress over my head—her choice—and struggled to pull it down without tearing it.

"Finish your story," she said.

"Oh, right." I was desperately wriggling—this thing was so tight. My head popped out the top. "So this is just *one* example, okay?" I said. "I purposely stopped answering my phone earlier this week to see what would happen—he hasn't even called."

Now if only I could figure out how to hook the dress up.

"For how long?"

"Four days."

"Hi? You should *dump him.*"

I looked like I was wearing a tampon wrapper. I opened the door so Allegra could see. She glanced briefly up and down.

"Horrible. Take it off."

I resisted the urge to apologize and went back in the room, explaining that I wasn't going to dump him quite yet—I had better ideas.

I kept trying things on—some Allegra deemed cute, some she wrinkled her nose at and waved away—as we discussed the finer points of my Max plan. As the "yes" pile grew and grew, so did my confidence. Indeed, Max didn't stand a chance against the Full Life, I said. He would end up a quivering mass of jelly by the time I was through with him, I said. I mean, really, he just didn't get it, I said. And all the while Allegra, my fashion pusher, kept saying "I feel you," and "Right on."

Her enthusiasm made me feel just a little bit better when she rang me up and said the damage was one thousand five hundred and seventy-four dollars and thirty-six cents. It would have been too mortifying to go back now, so I handed her a second credit card and asked if she could put half on each.

Allegra smiled and said, "Of course."

By the time I got home, the shopping high had worn off, but I couldn't afford another hit. No, I'd have to ride out the detox stone-cold sober, without even a Banana Republic catalog to get me by. I couldn't believe I'd spent so much money—more than my rent and my car payment combined. Why? I pondered my new blouse, which looked like it could have been from Mexico and, if it hadn't been designed by Stella McCartney, would have cost only about $10 instead of $250.

It kind of reminded me of a top I'd seen another girl wearing recently. A couple of weeks ago I'd taken Max to a dinner for Collin's birthday. Kaitlyn, who's dating one of Collin's friends, was there. She's the kind of girl—faux tan, pixie cut, perma sneer—that Kiki and I call "ugly on the inside" because she's really pretty but incredibly mean to every girl she meets. (Of course, Kaitlyn's as sweet as pie to all our boyfriends.) So I, stupidly, asked Max if he thought she was pretty. He replied that he thought she was "adorable." I was crushed. I couldn't remember the last time he'd said that about me, and the brand-new skirt I was wearing—the skirt that cost 150 bucks—had gone completely unnoticed.

I was hanging my new blouse up in the closet when it hit me: I was being fantastically insecure at 21.99 percent interest.

That night I arrived at Max's house at the appointed time, as always. He'd called in the late afternoon to see if I was still coming over, and I'd waited until the last possible minute to call back. This would be the first time I'd seen him since Palm Springs, and I was nervous.

"Hey, B," he said when I walked in the door. He actually got up for a change, and kissed me full on the lips. I tried to contain my surprise.

"So, what's over there?" He pointed across the room.

"What's over where?"

"The brown box on the floor."

"For me?"

"It's not for me. Open it."

I pulled the cardboard apart, and inside was a *stack* of clothing.

"What's all this?"

"The Super Very Good women's spring line," he said, lighting a cigarette.

It was like I'd landed on the mother ship, and my people had come to take me home. There were pants, T-shirts, blouses, skirts . . . *Aw, why did I go shopping?* I thought. There I was spending money so Max would like me, while he was packing a box full of new clothes for me because he already did. I thanked him, but even though I was bursting with love and gratefulness and relief, I said it casually. Not like I was bowled over or anything. I tossed the clothes aside like they were my due.

Max smiled and turned to fiddle with the stereo.

"So," he said over his shoulder. "Should we order in?"

"Sure," I said nonchalantly. "Whatever."

He ordered Thai, like always. Our movie selection was *Aliens,* which Max had bought on DVD because he'd never seen it. We didn't make it to the "Get away from her, you bitch" part, though. Thank God. The sex was perfect—like last weekend had never happened.

After, Max said, "So listen, about Saturday . . ." and my heart sank. *Maybe I should just forgive him,* I thought. Because now that he was being so nice I *really* wanted to see him over the weekend. But I remembered what Kiki said—I'd been making it too easy. I had to tell him I was busy for our own good. I was about to do so when he said, "The Japanese buyers are coming into town and I've got to show them around."

I looked at him like, *Say what?*

"It's going to be crazy, B. They, like, want to go all over and they don't really speak English. And they obviously can't drive over here." He laughed. "I'm going to have to take them to all these big dinners. Probably Disneyland. Shopping. It's going to be madness."

This wasn't happening.

But maybe I should offer to help. I smiled. "You know, I love shopping. Disneyland . . ."

"Nah. I'm cool."

Why? Why? Why?

"So," he said, changing the subject, "the Japanese buyers are, like, totally into those skirts I just gave—"

I interrupted, "I'm busy, too. I have plans. All weekend."

"Oh. Great." He ran a finger up and down my arm. "Then it works out."

GO AHEAD, JUMP

BY BENJAMINA FRANKLIN

You're at the edge of a metaphorical precipice, unsure of what to do. But when you ask a friend for directional input, is she really giving you good advice? Take this Filly Quiz to find out if she's a true friend—or bitter foe.

1. You're in a fight with your boyfriend. Lately you're always picking *him* up, and you think he should do the driving once in a while. Your friend says:

a. "Dump him. If you capitulate any more you're just a wimp who's asking for trouble."

b. "At least you *have* a boyfriend."

c. "I know how you feel. The other day, my boyfriend and I were on our way to yoga, and he was all, 'Can I borrow your mat?' And I was like, 'Why didn't you bring your own mat?' And he was like, 'I forgot.' So I said . . ."

d. "He *could* be taking you for granted—talk to him and suggest splitting the driving time."

2. Your boss is a maladjusted skank and if you have to take any more of her mood swings you're going to brain yourself with your Rolodex. Then again, you *think* you're up for a promotion and you have –$172 in the bank. Your friend says:

a. "You can't afford to quit. You spend money like it grows like killer mold. Plus the job market is terrible, and frankly it's amazing you've been able to hold a job this long."

b. "See if that promotion's going to pan out. If not, quietly start looking for a better gig and don't tell her until you have a lock on something."

c. "Walk into that fat cow's office and tell her she's a flatulent piece of dung and she can take that job and stuff it up her you know what."

d. "Remember the time *my* boss told me to redo all the filing systems like five minutes after I got that manicure? I was totally pissed and she couldn't have cared less . . ."

3. Your cousin can be such a flake. The last three times you had plans with her, she canceled, but that didn't stop her from calling you drunk on a school night asking if you could pick her up. Your friend says:

a. "Send an e-mail telling her how you feel, but make sure you let your cousin know you want to hear her side and you'd really like to make your relationship better."

b. "At least you don't have brothers. I have four, and it's like they're in their own little club. Take the time when . . ."

c. "I would have let her drive her ass home. If she got in an accident, it would have been her own damn fault."

d. "I can't believe you'd talk about your relatives like this! She *loves* you. And what would you rather she do? Drive home drunk?"

4. In a moment of fashion lunacy you bought a new dress that's tight, bedecked with sequins, and extremely expensive. She says:

a. "Oh my God, that looks just like mine!"

b. "Oh my God, that makes you look like a prostitute!"

c. "Oh my God, I had no idea you had such bad taste!"

d. "Oh my God, please tell me you saved the receipt!"

→ THE FILLY **ANSWER KEY**

Match your answers to the following:

1.	a=M	b=N	c=S	d=BFF
2.	a=M	b=BFF	c=N	d=S
3.	a=BFF	b=S	c=N	d=M
4.	a=S	b=M	c=N	d=BFF

Mostly M's: The Mother You love your mom, but do you really need to be best friends with someone exactly like her? The guilt trips are too much—this girl needs to *relax* and let you take some risks, even if it means you may make the occasional mistake. And you need to ask yourself why you need to be treated like a child. (As in, do you act like one?)

Mostly N's: The Nazi We recognize this girl. She's so bitter she could turn a guy into a prune by giving him a kiss. Ask yourself: How many friends has she alienated? How many boyfriends ran screaming? Even scarier, she could put a contract on your head if you break off the friendship—you'll be confirming her delusion that the world is against her. Gently tell this paranoid freak you love her, and get her into group therapy.

Mostly S's: The Self-Obsessed Girl One time, I had a friend like this, and she was *so* annoying. I was shopping with her one day at Aero & Co. and she totally bit on my fashion, buying the same belt I had. And I was all, "Wait, if you wear that belt, then when am *I* going to wear that belt?" Besides the fact that it looked so much better on *me* . . . Sound familiar? Don't let your narcissistic friend use your life as a springboard into endless talking about hers. So, as I was saying about me . . .

Mostly BFF's: The Best Friend 4Ever This Christmas get her one of those cheesy heart necklaces—you know, the ones that break in half and say both your names? This girl's a keeper. She knows how to listen; she tries to help. She reflects your own feelings, always taking into account what you're going through, but she also knows when it's time to say enough is enough and call you on your B.S. And the really cool thing is, you must be a good friend, too—why else would such a great chick hang out with you? ♘

Even though Max was busy, I still had to go through with my strategic engagements, pointless as they now were.

Friday night I brought Chandra to a barbecue at Collin's. It wasn't the laid-back affair I was expecting—when we arrived, there was a cluster fuck of Industry PIBs (Personas in Black) huddled up on the outdoor patio. I was seriously not in the mood to talk about box-office reports and which executive had done what to whom—not to mention the fact the PIBs, who always claim to have recently quit smoking, help themselves to all my cigarettes. But it would have looked too crazy to run screaming back down the front walk, so I found a place to sit in the corner, where I filled Chandra in on my Max hell while watching Collin whipping around mixing sangria and grilling salmon.

I told Chandra about my attempt to make Max think I was superpopular and thus didn't have any time for him on the weekend, and how my ruse backfired. I was hoping for some sympathy, and maybe some strategic advice. But I ended up listening to Chandra rant about how we should stuff my pseudo-boyfriend's body in a wood chipper.

"You have to fuckin' *leave his sorry white ass,* Franklin," she insisted over her third sangria, alternating between the wine and her new inhaler. (She now has allergies, she explained, they're "serious," and she's never smoking again since if she does she will definitely end up with almost-emphysema like Christy Turlington. Which, she added, was definitely going to happen to me.)

While Chandra ranted, I let my gaze drift over Beachwood Canyon, quilted with hills, valleys, and million-dollar mansions. The eucalyptus trees were giving off a woodsy perfume. *This,* I thought, breathing deeply, *is what money smells like.* Not Collin's money, of course. The house—and the view—belonged to his roommate, a famous nobody who got his start on a reality TV show where he got buried alive with forty women in an underground town house, and had to marry the one he wanted to kill the least at the end of the season. Since the hunk was away on his book tour—four weeks on the *New York Times* best-seller list—Collin decided to throw a party and pretend this was his place.

Still, the liquor was free and the view was pretty. It would have been fine if Chandra wasn't crowing in my ear.

"Homeboy has *adult acne*," she continued.

"Oh come on," I said, snapping back to reality. "Max had *one* pimple the night you met him."

"It looked like a *bacterial infection*."

"You said you thought he was cute."

"Who's cute?" All night, Collin tripped over himself trying to horn in on our conversation. This time he was bearing a platter of roasted tomatoes as his excuse.

"Not the punk-ass bitch Ben's hooked on," Chandra said.

Collin nodded, and I noticed that, now that she had an audience, Chandra's voice got a *you-can-hear-her-in-the-cheap-seats* boom to it. The PIBs were starting to stare. "That fuckin' *bitch* treats her like fuckin' *dirt*, and she's so *whipped* she's willing to put up with it!" Chandra hollered. "What are you so afraid of, Franklin? That he's going to go out with some other 'ho instead of you?"

"Well, we *technically* haven't broken up," I said, "so I don't think that's exactly something to be worried about quite yet."

"Yeah, well you're *technically* not even together yet, either, so maybe *that's* what you should be worried about."

I looked to Collin for some assistance, but he just said, "You should listen to your homegirl."

The rest of the evening Collin cock-blocked me. He kept Chandra—who technically was my friend date—locked into a conversation by doling out compliments and generally kissing her ass. In the car on the way home Chandra kept talking about how "amazing" Collin was.

"He's fun," I said, "but watch out for him."

"Why?"

"He's so networking-obsessed, he tries to get invited to the right funerals."

"Girl, you are hi-larious!" Chandra whooped. Then, "Give me his number. I want to program it into my cell."

Saturday morning I was awakened by Audrey, who saw no reason why she shouldn't call me on her "Nokie" to discuss wedding drama while stuck in traffic.

"Aud," I said in the middle of her napkin-ring monologue, "I'm actually really busy today."

She said, "Doing what?"

I said I was working on a story for *Filly* but in fact I had nothing to do. When I'd gotten home from Collin's barbecue the night before, there was a message from Ashton saying he wasn't feeling well and wouldn't be able to go to the party with me after all. I couldn't believe Ash was blowing me off. Anyway, he said we could maybe do something next weekend instead, which I figured would work because I was going to have to full-life Max for a little longer than I thought.

This was how I ended up staying home on date night watching a *Touched by an Angel* rerun while writing clever Christmas cards to my editors in hopes that this would make them want to renew my contract in the new year.

In other words, I persisted with my newer, fuller life.

The next morning, my insides felt like they were made of sharp rocks, so I decided to meet Nina at her Sunday rejuvenation yoga class. It was in a trendy studio in West Hollywood where they played Sarah McLachlan in the changing room and burned vanilla-scented incense.

"I keep forgetting to tell you I ran into Ashton last night," Nina whispered, stretching into downward dog.

"You did?" I mentally reran the apologetic message I got from him on Friday—not feeling well, terribly sorry, thinks it could be the flu . . . "Wait"—I breathed into my hips—"where?"

"Some stupid party in Hancock Park I went to with the Producer. It was boring as lint."

"And?" I tried to relax my shoulders.

"I told you, it was boring."

"No, what happened with Ashton?"

We switched to lotus.

"What do you mean?" Nina closed her eyes.

"Did he seem sick at all?" I put my legs in a pretzel. "Did he look tired, or pale, in any way?"

"I don't think so."

I wondered if maybe Ashton had lied about being sick because he wasn't over me—maybe seeing me was too painful to bear—so I asked Nina if he seemed sad, or depressed. If he'd asked about me perhaps . . .

"Not once," she said. "He was out with friends, having a good time."

"Thanks," I hissed.

Nina breathed in deeply, then exhaled. "What do you want me to say? Maybe the night before last he was sitting at a bar alone and crying into his beer with grief, and I just didn't run into him. All I know is that last night he seemed like he was having fun."

I tried to stretch my fingers to the sun, weighing whether or not I wanted to tell Nina that Ashton had told me he was sick. I decided not, and said instead, "You're not being very helpful."

"Because you're acting like a child." Nina opened one eye at me. It had the beady look of the thoroughly exasperated. "*You* broke up with *him,* remember?"

I rolled my head one way, then the other. "I don't want to talk about it," I said, closing my eyes and straightening my spine, which was as tight as a rubber band stretched from L.A. to Vancouver.

"What's bothering you?" she whispered.

I kept my eyes closed. "Shush, I'm balancing my chakras."

I could feel Dr. Nina inspecting me, looking for soft spots. So I curled my lips up slightly at the ends, relaxed my furrowed brow, and tried to look rejuvenated. It was the most exhausting thing I did all weekend.

CHAPTER

11

One time, when I was sixteen or so, I had to go to school when I suspected a boyfriend was going to break up with me. He was so cool—owned a laminate machine, which meant he could make senior IDs for us so we could get off campus for lunch, and he was a really good skateboarder. But suddenly he was pulling away. And he kept saying, "What are you doing for lunch *Thursday?* Let's have lunch *Thursday*"—as though we didn't have lunch at Dan's Super Subs around the corner from school practically every day of the week. I told my mom what I thought was going to happen on Black Thursday, and all she said was, "I wouldn't wear mascara if I were you."

This should explain why, instead of talking to the Mother, I drove over to Kiki's, hoping my best friend would be home for a change. Lately she'd been falling into the Curtis vortex—I'd call and get the voicemail pretty much every time. I wasn't mad or anything. But I have to say I couldn't believe how much time they spent together. Days and days. *In a row.* Yet they never seemed to go anywhere, which was why I didn't even know what Curtis looked like until he answered her door. Standing in the entryway, I was suddenly aware I had on a mismatched sweatshirt over my pajamas, my hair was in crooked pigtails, and I was clutching a pack of cigarettes in each hand. While Curtis gawked at me, I took a moment to give him the once-over. Kiki's descriptions were pretty much on the money: He had brown hair, blue eyes, horn-rimmed glasses, and a kind of prep-school-meets-indie-rock vibe.

"You must be Ben," Curtis said, stepping aside so I could enter. Inside, the lights were turned down low, and there were a few lit candles scattered around. From the looks of things, they'd been snuggling on the couch, watching *Shakespeare in Love*—what is it with couples and that movie?—and I suspect they were actually enjoying it. I felt bad interrupting, but in between my stammered apologies Curtis just smiled patiently while he put on his shoes and located his car keys. He didn't complain once before he cleared out so Kiki could administer some much-needed heartbreak first aid, so I figured he was a pretty decent guy. He was cute. Quiet, but cute.

I hadn't seen Max or spoken directly to Max in over two weeks. After that horrible weekend when I tried to full-life him in hopes that this would get his attention, he'd left me another message saying that the Japanese were staying an extra few days and he was "all booked up."

I didn't return the call.

This didn't make him call again, though.

Where was he? What was going on? What did it mean? Every day I felt like I was being slowly squeezed to death. I couldn't breathe. I couldn't eat. I didn't sleep.

I thought about calling him and just asking flat-out what the deal was, but somehow I knew it would be a mistake. It was like Max needed space, but the more I gave him, the more he needed. I kept going back to that night—the night *we* were watching *Shakespeare in Love* and he didn't want to talk—and that hideous weekend in Palm Springs, which Kiki and I were now referring to as "The Debacle." How do you talk to someone who never wants to talk?

"So what are you going to do?" Kiki asked, closing the door behind Curtis with a wistful little breath.

"I'm going to fucking kill him," I said, finding myself a place to sit in the middle of her cluttered floor, next to some old newspapers and half a bag of kitty litter. "I know that Max does a lot of business with the Japanese but I mean, Jesus, they have to have left by now, don't you think?"

"Probably," she agreed, blowing out the candles and turning on a light. She offered me a beer, which I accepted gratefully. "So now what?"

"Maybe I should just go over there and say if this is the way he wants to treat me, then I'm out. I don't have to take this."

"What about the Full Life?" she asked.

I looked at her like, *You can't be serious,* and said, "His is fuller."

Kiki gave a small nod. She cleared away the newspapers, the litter, some shoes, and a raincoat so she could join me on the carpet. Then she put an ashtray on the floor between us. We sat in silence for a minute, smoking and mulling over my options. It didn't seem like I had very many.

"Maybe I should gather up all those great gifts he gave me, cart them over to his house, and dump them on his bed," I said.

"That works for me."

"Or maybe I should just show up and start screaming at him at the top of my lungs until the neighbors call the cops."

"Totally reasonable. Maybe you could, like, I dunno, B"—Kiki started to imitate Max, lighting another cigarette and schlumping her shoulders forward in a slacker pose—"act like you're really cute and sweet and harmless and then, like, take out a bowie knife and rip his heart out of his chest and eat it."

"*Hey.* That was good. Or I could like, bring an Uzi submachine gun, K, and totally, like, ram it up his butt and fire it."

"Or know what, B? You could, like, replace all the fucking half-and-half in his refrigerator with like, skim milk and watch him choke to death."

"And you know what his last words will be?" I gasped.

We yelled together, "This isn't cream, B!"

I rolled over on my back and tried to catch my breath. I had obviously been smoking too many cigarettes and it hurt deep in my chest, but I couldn't stop laughing—the kind of hysterical, all-in-a-whoosh laughing that, I imagine, people do right before they jump off a bridge into an icy river.

"Hold on a sec." Kiki went to answer her phone. It was Curtis. I could tell from the blissed-out look on her face. I looked at the clock—they had been separated for exactly seven minutes. "You have?" she said, holding up her finger. "You *do?*" She started laughing. "Later. No, *later.* I will. I promise. 'Bye."

"I should go, I barged in on you guys."

"You're not going." Kiki sat back down in front of me. "Come on, he's just being cute."

"So things are good."

"Amazing. Seriously. The other day, he told me he wants to come home with me for Hanukkah to meet my parents."

"That's so great. Meanwhile I can't even get Max to try my dry cleaner."

Kiki snorted. "So seriously, what are you going to do?"

"I have no idea." I lay down on the floor again, stared at the cracks in the ceiling that had been there since the last earthquake. "I don't want to end it, but I can't stand staying in it. Then again, if I *do* end it, I'm not sure I'll be able to stand it being over."

"You know I'll be supportive of whatever you decide."

"Oh, I know. Look, don't worry about me." I got up to leave. "I'm just going to go home and die alone so you two can get your fuck on."

I raised my eyebrow at Kiki and made my way to the door. "Are you sure you're going to be okay?" she said, just as her phone started to ring again.

I assured her I'd just needed a quick chat and I was going to be fine. As a good-bye, Kiki punched me in the shoulder. Then she gave me a hug.

"I'm a 'ho," she said, giggling.

"Yeah." I sighed. "Me, too."

THE FILLY WHEEL OF (IN)DECISION

Confused to the brink of insanity? Bashing your head in with that mercurial Magic Eight Ball? Does he love you? Love you not? Stop playing with toys! Stop murdering daisies! Use the Filly Wheel of (In)decision! Psychic energy was steeped into the paper by paranormal experts, and it has all the answers.—B.F.

INSTRUCTIONS*
— cut around the dotted lines.
—attach arrow with brass brad (or bent paper clip, knotted string, etc.).
— concentrate.
— Spin
— do whatever it says.

* FOR THE REALLY, INCREDIBLY, AMAZINGLY CONFUSED.

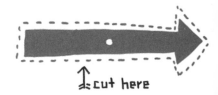

↑ cut here

THE FILLY WHEEL OF (in)decision

Wheel segments:
- Don't take it, call the tours.
- Pedicure, pronto!
- Cheeseburger Time!
- Face it, he's a total loser.
- Think of what you want to do, then do the opposite.
- Get in car. Drive for two hours while blasting rock music. Ask again.
- Never leave the house again.
- Would you just call and say sorry already.

I called Max at home every night for the rest of the week. We were going to have The Talk—the Are-We-or-Are-We-Not-Breaking-Up Talk—whether he wanted to or not. Putting it off at this point was just too painful. He never answered his phone, though, so I kept hanging up before his answering machine beeped. He was obviously avoiding me, and finally, with no other options, I called him during work hours on his cell. It felt like defeat.

"This is Max," he said.

"It's me," I said.

"Hey," he said. He sounded a million miles away.

"Look, I think we have to talk." I was trying to break it to him gently.

"I know." Oh, so he was ready for it . . .

"Today?" I asked, trying not to sound too desperate.

"I can't do it today."

"Tomorrow then."

"Can't do it tomorrow either."

"When then."

"Friday?"

"Max," I tried to keep the frustration out of my voice, "that's three days from now."

"I can't do it before then."

"All right. Fine."

"My house, six o'clock?"

"Okay." I tried to think if there was something more I wanted to say, but then he said, "See you," and hung up. I sat there, staring at the receiver. He didn't sound happy to hear from me. At all. *Did he actually expect me to just disappear?* I wondered. *Could that really be what he wants?*

But it didn't seem possible. I mean, he'd never said anything about us being over. Was I just supposed to assume that we were?

I spent the next few days trying not to lose it completely. But I couldn't pay attention to anything. I walked into walls. I stubbed my toe. I gave myself a bruise in the middle of my forehead when I distractedly opened my car door and slammed it into my own face. I cried—*a lot.* Curtis was away on a business trip, and so Kiki had time to discuss every conceivable outcome. We talked every day for so long my phone kept running out of batteries. She generously predicted that one of two things would happen. (A), Max and I would talk it out and everything would be fine. The less preferable, but more likely, (B), I'd break up with him and he'd be destroyed and would want me back by Christmas. The key, Kiki said, was not to be wishy-washy. I had to go over there and lay down the law. Tell him he couldn't treat me so cavalierly anymore if he really wanted me in his life. It was my only chance to get through this feeling remotely good about myself. But even with Kiki's cheerful reassurances that it would all work out in the end, the week dragged on forever, and I was overcome with the chill of impending doom. It was like that feeling you get just before you crash your car—you see it coming, you see it coming, you see it coming, and it's taking so long you should be able to do something to stop it. But you can't.

On Friday I didn't put on mascara before I left for Max's house. Melodramatic, sure, but I was in a melodramatic mood. I packed up the gifts, too. Into the trash bag went the Polaroid camera he'd given me to celebrate our one-month anniversary, along with the funny pictures I'd taken of us to document the occasion. In went the teddy bear hugging the red heart he'd tucked into bed with me one morning before he left for work—he'd probably bought it at Sav-On, but at the time I thought it was delightful. In went the Super Very Good sunglasses he'd presented to me for our trip to Palm Springs. In went the many CDs he'd burned for me, with covers from the albums carefully scanned, printed, and placed in the jewel boxes. And in went all the clothes. The bag was stuffed to bursting. After barely a five-minute conversation with Max in weeks, the presents hurt. They were like promises he didn't keep.

I pulled up in front of Max's house and wiped my sweaty palms on the legs of my jeans before grabbing the garbage bag full of presents. I took a deep breath and tried to remind myself that I was there to play hardball. *There will be no more of this,* I thought. No more waiting. No more guessing. No more wondering what he was going to do, or if I was ever going to hear from him again. It wasn't like I was putting all this pressure on him. It wasn't like I didn't have my own life. Whatever his problem was, he'd have to get over it because I simply wouldn't be able to take the silent treatment from him anymore. It had become physically intolerable.

For the first time since our first date, I rang the doorbell. Max usually left the door open for me and I'd wander in and find him upstairs listening to music. But this time, that seemed too informal, so I rang the bell and some shaggy-haired guy answered. At first I thought I was at the wrong house. Then I realized he was one of the roommates. *Of course,* I thought. *Now he's home.*

"Hey," I said, trying to act casual even though my eyes were puffy and I was carrying a giant green Glad garbage bag.

"Can I help you?"

"Oh. I'm Ben. Um. Is Max here?"

"Uhhhh . . . I dunno."

There was a three-foot bong and an open bag of Pirate's Booty on the table behind him.

"Could I check?"

"Uhhhh . . . I guess so. It's . . ."

"I know which way it is."

I suddenly realized the roommate had no idea who "Ben" was. He had never even heard of me.

I walked past him and up the stairs to Max's room. Inside, the curtains were drawn, even though it was still early. It took a moment for my eyes to adjust. Then I realized Max was lying on his bed, facing the wall.

"Hey," I said, putting my bitter bag of stuff on the floor by the drum set. Suddenly I wished I hadn't brought it. Seemed like I didn't want to work things out. But I did. Desperately.

"Hey." He didn't turn over.

I took my old reliable stool in front of the drum set.

"Max?" He ignored me. "Are you going to look at me or what?"

He rolled onto his back. His eyes flicked over in my direction. Then he looked at the bag. Then he looked away.

"So . . ." I said. "I haven't seen you around much lately."

Long pause.

Then he said, "I've been busy."

"Okay, but I think when you really want to be with somebody you kind of make the time, right?"

No response.

"What's going on, Max?"

The question hung in the air, until he said, "I don't know, Ben. You tell me."

"Well." I took a deep breath. "Look, I really want things to be okay. Okay? But that's kind of hard when I never see you, right?"

He didn't respond.

"I just feel like I'm in this totally alone. Like you're not even with me anymore."

Nothing.

"Is it something I did?"

Still nothing.

"Max? Isn't there *anything* you want to say?"

"What do you want me to say?"

I wanted to scream, *I want you to say that you can't live without me! That you're sorry! That you're making a mistake!* But all I could say was, "I just want you to say something."

He said, "Something."

And this was when I lost it.

"Okay, fine," I snapped. "You know what? I can't take it anymore. Seriously. If this is how you're going to act, then I'm out of here."

I stood up. My hands were on my hips and I knew how it looked and I didn't care.

But then I gave him one more chance.

"Max, please. Say something besides 'something.' Talk to me."

"Jesus Christ, Ben—" He sat up, and looked at me. His eyes were red, but not from crying. He was mad. I was surprised. I had no idea I was making him angry. He said, "What do you want from me?"

"What do I *want* from you?" I asked.

"Yeah. I mean, I already told you, *I don't want a girlfriend.*"

It was like being punched in the stomach. "You do," I said.

"I don't."

"But . . ."

His eyes said, *But what?*

"What about us, about all the presents—" I stammered. "What about *everything.* I mean, I thought we both felt the same thing. I thought this was . . . you know . . . going somewhere."

He shook his head. "I like hanging out with you," he said. "But it's not *going* anywhere. And I was happy with that. You're not."

"But I *am* happy," I heard myself say. "I am. And if you've been happy, too, then maybe we're not as far apart on this as you think—"

He interrupted. "The fact that we're having this conversation at all means we're far apart," he said. I stood there dumbly. Then he said, "I don't want to do this." And he lay back down on the bed.

"Max," I said. "We can work this out. Talk to me."

" "

"Don't act like this, come on."

" "

"*This* is how you want it to end?"

" "

"Fine. Have it your way."

I threw the bag down on the floor and was out the door so fast I didn't even have time to cry.

The first tear hit the pavement outside. Like rain, but smaller. Then a flood. *He never even saw how destroyed I am,* I thought. I couldn't decide if this was good or bad.

12

For the next several weeks I lurked around the neighborhood looking for him. In coffee shops. At parties. The grocery store, even though he rarely cooked. The bookstore, even though he didn't like to read. I got dressed up to go to the gas station. I felt self-conscious leaving the house if I had a pimple, or if my hair didn't seem right. On a good hair, blemish-free day, I'd manufacture reasons to go out. Maybe we'd bump into each other. He'd say he was sorry. He'd have answers.

I never ran into him.

I thought I saw him everywhere, though. I'd see his expression on an actor's face on TV. His haircut walking away from me on the street. His back at the prescription counter at the drugstore. I'd do a double take—usually it was someone who didn't even remotely resemble him. Those were the absolute worst. The ones that made me feel like the biggest fool.

My friends were getting sick of me.

"Do you think I broke up with him, or did he break up with me?" I asked Kiki at least once a day.

"You broke up with him," she'd say. "He was just torturing you, so you walked out. It was the right thing to do—you had to get out of that house."

"But I didn't *want* to break up with him. So then didn't he, in fact, break up with me?"

"No," she'd say. "Because even though you didn't say it exactly, his terms were not acceptable to you, and you made that clear. And you *did* want to break up with him, you just don't know it yet."

Then I'd ask her, "Do you think he's cooler than me?"

"That's ridiculous," she'd say.

"But he knows all those cool musicians . . . He owns a clothing company . . . Entertains Japanese hipsters . . ."

She'd tell me that in the end it wasn't about who was cooler. That deep down nobody ever felt like they were cooler than anybody else anyway, and I was just feeling insecure. Then she'd reassure me, again, that I wouldn't regret leaving the way I did. I tried to make myself believe her.

But as the holidays loomed, I started to miss Max more and more. I tried calling Ashton a couple of times, but he didn't call back. There was nothing much to do but sit around my apartment and brood, envisioning other scenarios, with different outcomes. In one alternate universe, just after I walked out Max came to his senses, grabbed the bitter bag of presents, raced out of the house, and shouted, "Ben! Wait!" He put the bag down on the pavement, stood before me, and said, "I can't lose you, B," and kissed me. It was a kiss that said everything he couldn't, and I forgave him instantly. In another, I walked into his room without the bag, acted like everything was fine, and, after a brief moment where everyone knew everything and all was understood, Max stood up, put a record on the turntable, lit a cigarette, and asked me what kind of food I wanted to order in. I smiled, and the tension between us evaporated like morning fog.

There were bad scenarios, too. The worst was when I imagined running into Max with another girl. Someone adorable. Someone his age. Maybe that girl Kaitlyn from Collin's birthday party. What if they ran into each other, and he asked her out, and she was able to date him the right way, and ended up being his girlfriend for real? This thought was so excruciating, I'd have to push it out of my mind with violent force.

"I want Max back," I finally declared to Kiki at the *Filly* Christmas party. We were at the Chateau Marmont, standing off to the side of the hotel's wide patio, which was peppered with heat lamps. People clustered around them like mosquitoes around those zapper things, because despite the fantasy that it never gets cold in California, tonight's temperature was hovering just above forty. The olive trees were decorated with little white lights, and you could sneak peaks through their branches and into guest rooms above. For a moment I saw a figure standing at a window, looking down on us, and I wondered who she was, where she was from. Another figure appeared, circling her waist with his arms. She turned toward him, said something, and drew the shades.

"You don't want him back," Kiki said, smacking my hand away from what would have been my tenth caviar beggar's purse.

"I do."

"You don't."

"I really fucking do." I grabbed a chicken satay skewer off the platter of a passing waiter and crammed it into my mouth. *"Maxth back now."*

Kiki took an anxious look around the room—it seemed Curtis, who was standing at the other side of the courtyard, was getting his ear talked off. Even from that distance, I could hear Steph telling him something about how "EVERYBODY KNOWS THAT ANGIE GETS HER TATTOOS DONE AT THE SAME PLACE AS PAMELA BUT THE THING THAT NOBODY KNOWS IS THAT THEY BOTH HAD THE SAME PLASTIC—" Kiki rolled her eyes. "Look, I have to go check and make sure Curtis is okay, okay?" she said. "I'll be right back and we can talk about Max some more. I promise."

You really can't blame her.

Meanwhile, on Christmas Eve, just after I asked the Mother if she thought the fact that Max had never called to say happy holidays meant he was devastated to have lost me or, conversely, over me completely, she snapped, "Oh my God Ben, *you have to stop.*" The Mother was serving mugs of very strong eggnog, and the table was decorated with a bouquet of "glitter-dipped" pinecones Audrey made with instructions courtesy of Martha. The house reeked of pine needles. My allergies were going nuts.

"She's right," Audrey said, handing me a napkin with a somewhat revolted look so I could blow my nose. "It doesn't matter how he feels; it matters how you feel."

I muttered something about feeling like I wanted to know how he felt, and the Mother shot Audrey a look like, *See what I have to deal with?*

And lucky me, Jamie was spending Christmas Eve with us. "I have two brothers," he said, leaning over so Aud could brush some cookie crumbs from the side of his mouth. "Maybe you can marry one of them."

At least I was keeping busy. Nina and I hit the day-after-Christmas sales, and I got a lecture that lasted from the Barneys Stila counter all the way to the rooftop deli, where we stopped for brunch.

"I could have told you that full-life thing wouldn't work," Nina said, carefully dissecting her tofu scramble. "If a guy is tracking toward you, you can goad him by playing off his insecurities. But if he's tracking away, well, it's best to accept his mental place and just let him go."

I took a big bite of my bagel, smiled with my mouth closed, and made a gesture like, *Hold that thought; mouth full.* Nina took this as permission to continue, saying, "Your neediness probably stems from childhood, when you competed for affection with Audrey and lost."

My eyes widened.

"Oh, don't be so defensive—I'm not saying it's your fault. Focus on next steps. You need to get back out there. Saddle . . ." Nina held up a bagel in one hand; then she held up a knife smeared with cream cheese in the other. "Horse. And remember"—she rested her elbows back on the table—"there's a fine line between mourning and self-indulgence."

And finally, the ultimate humiliation: I spent New Year's Eve alone. Kiki offered to do something, but I let her (and Curtis) off the hook, insisting that all I really wanted to do was watch movies with predictable story lines—Boy Meets Girl and They Get Together by the Holidays— and cuddle with my cat, if he'd have me.

I probably would have made it through the Cruelest Evening on Earth with nothing but Meg Ryan to keep me company, too, if only I'd stayed away from the cheap bottle of champagne I'd bought at the liquor store. The first glass went down okay, the second I drank without really thinking about it, but by the third or fourth the pathos started to wash over me in waves. The twinkle lights I'd put around my front door took on a depressing air, while the Christmas presents I still hadn't put away gave me incriminating glares from the kitchen table. Empty pizza boxes stacked by the door screamed at me, *Can't you see how pathetic you are?*

For reprieve, I turned on the news. They were showing a report about a huge snowstorm in Cleveland. B-roll showed people shoveling snow outside cute little brick houses, trucks sliding down the street. *So that's where Max is from,* I thought. I pictured him in a heavy parka, drinking cocoa and making snowballs, throwing them at some girl he met at a Christmas party who would probably kiss him when the ball dropped in Times Square. Suddenly I realized I was never going to meet Max's mother. Or his father. I used to fantasize about the day he'd bring me home to meet them. It was never going to happen.

I don't want to say I ended up lying facedown in my bathrobe, bawling into the floorboards and moaning, *"Why, Max, why?"* But I don't want to say that *didn't* happen either.

They manipulated me. Kiki. Nina. My mom. My sister. They manipulated me by acting like I had to get on with my life. But if they had asked me, I didn't think I had to get on with my life. I had to get my life back. I had to get *Max* back.

Of course, it wasn't Finlay's fault. I mean, he didn't even know me. But it was so irritating. All evening he'd been opening doors. Summoning waiters. Filling glasses. Asking thoughtful questions. And I drank, smoked, scowled, and generally ignored him. Talk about not getting the hint.

Finlay was best friends with Curtis. Kiki called me one day in the middle of my Max depression, ecstatic about how Curtis's friend, who produced MTV's *Rock the Vote, Spring Break,* and other painfully enthusiastic special-event programming, was moving here from New York. I could tell from her cloying tone that a setup was imminent. At the time I was playing Grand Theft Auto on my PlayStation 2, so the words came through as though she were on a staticky cell phone: "Great job . . . Black hair . . . Glasses! . . . You have to . . . The thing is . . ."

"Just give him my number," I said, and made excuses about needing to go to bed.

So now there I was. On a date with a total stranger. And I was supremely annoyed.

"Do you come to this restaurant often then?" Finlay asked.

It sounded like, *D'yew come to this rest-ront off-ten then?* His accent seemed vaguely hostile to my ears. Maybe it's because he'd gone to Cambridge, a late-breaking factoid that gave Kiki vicarious orgasms.

"Never," I said.

I took a look around. It was a grown-up place. Tablecloths. Wineglasses. A wood-fired oven that made gourmet pizzas, just like in Rome. Crusty bread, just like in Tuscany. Apparently Robert De Niro was a silent partner. Max and I didn't go to places like this. We liked to order in.

"I think it's quite nice, really." Finlay swirled his olive ciabatta around in a light green dish of oil. Suddenly, it dawned on me that with his glasses, floppy hair, and red scarf, he looked like Harry Potter.

But I figured I should at least make *some* small talk. That way I could tell Kiki I tried, he sucked, and that would be that.

"So, Finn," I asked, taking a big gulp of wine. "Where you from?"

"Oh." He stopped fidgeting with the bread and leaned forward like he was surprised I'd actually spoken to him without being asked a direct question. "I'm from Liverpool. Dad owns a small business. Mum keeps the house nice. Two sisters, which I guess makes me the sensitive sort. Never freak out about the tampons, heh, heh—"

I looked at him blankly.

He cleared his throat. "Have you been?"

"Where?"

"To Liverpool."

Just then Max walked into the restaurant. *Oh my God.* My heart flew up into my mouth, and for a second I panicked—what should I say, what should I do? But when he stopped to say something to the hostess, I realized it wasn't actually him. It was some other guy. Finlay was still waiting for me to elaborate. So I said, "Oh, yeah. I saw that clock. You know, whatsitcalled."

"Big Ben?"

Wait—was it definitely not him? I snuck another peek. No, not. But it looked like him—a lot like him. "Yeah, Big Ben."

"In Liverpool?"

"Right."

Max had better style, I observed. This guy was cute, too, though.

"You are aware that you weren't in Liverpool, then, you were in London?"

Hello, I thought. *I think I'm making an ass of myself.*

"What?"

"Big Ben. It's in London. I'm from *Liverpool,* which, as anyone who was listening to our conversation could tell you, is where the Beatles are from. Of course, that's all any American knows about the place where I grew up. But it's more than I can say for you."

I was shocked. Was this any way to talk to someone you hardly knew? I wasn't sure what I should do. Leave the table? Throw a glass of water in his face? Say something cutting? If so, then what?

"Ah," he said, "seems I've finally got your attention."

"I'm sorry," I said. "I haven't really been on a date in . . ."

"Quite a while. Yes, I can see that. And you're so charming, too. Not to worry." Finlay reached over and refilled my glass to the brim, then his own. "I love nothing more than a woman who drinks heavily on a first date, as you've been doing all evening, so let's both have a bit more of this lovely Pinot Grigio and you can keep me entertained with your interesting take on European geography."

My face was burning. I think I was actually blushing. I said, "Are you serious?"

"No," he said with a little smile. "But I think you're very beautiful. So I'm willing to put up with this inexcusable behavior for at least a few hours longer, if not for, let's say six, no, eight, weeks. After that I can't make any guarantees."

What an asshole.

Kiki called the next day to grill me for details and pronounced Finlay—despite my protestations that he was dull and not even remotely my type—"Marriage Material."

"Are you going out with him again?" she asked.

"No," I said. "I don't know."

"You will."

"Why do you say that?"

"Because you have nothing better to do."

She had a point.

Next, Kiki wanted to know what I would contribute to *Filly*'s "Sex vs. Love" issue. I didn't have the faintest idea. Last night's date had ended better than it began (I'd felt guilty so I'd let Finn kiss me when he walked me to my door), but it wasn't sex and it definitely wasn't love. Kiki said that was okay, because whatever I wrote, it didn't have to be "up." It could be "true." But "funny true." Not "down true" or "icky true."

"If you're suggesting I write about He Who Cannot Be Named, I'm afraid I can't help you," I said. "I've lost my sense of humor when it comes to him."

"Write about the breakup, then," she said. "An honest, heart-wrenching account. Ohhh, brainstorm: Write about the age difference!"

"I'm sure he'd really appreciate that."

"Who the fuck cares what He Who appreciates and doesn't appre-

FILLY

FACTS & FIGURES DEPT.

FIRST-DATE FACTS

We surveyed women from New York, London, Chicago, Los Angeles—even Hong Kong—to bring you fresh info on first dates. —*B.F.*

The Stats
- 25% of first dates lead to a second.
- 25% of first dates lead to everything but.
- The most common cuisine choices for a first date are (in descending order): Italian, sushi, French, Indian.
- 40% of women surveyed get intoxicated before their date picks them up.
- The average number of first dates a year for women surveyed is 4.6.

The Rituals
- "I wear good undies—just in case." —CLAIRE, VANCOUVER
- "I never get a bikini wax until the third date because I don't want them to get too used to it." —ALISON, LONDON
- "If the guy comes to pick me up, I make sure I'm 'finishing a phone call' when I open the door. Not sure why, but I do." —CHERYL, NEW YORK
- "I drink." —DARCY, LOS ANGELES U

ciate? I'm sorry, but you don't owe him *anything*. You could write about what a coward he is—"

"He's not a coward. He's just confused."

She ignored me. "Wait—does he have a small dick? Can you write about that?"

"No."

"Really." She lowered her voice. "How big was his . . ."

"Kiki."

"Spoilsport." She laughed. "Look, I'm sorry. I know you're depressed. But the Whip specifically asked for something funny-slash-true from you for the 'Sex vs. Love' issue so you're going to have to come up with *something*, honey. Just think *catharsis*. Now. Tell me more about Finlay. Has he called?"

"Do I care?"

I sat at my computer for the next two days, trying to think if I had anything to say about sex or love that wasn't down true or icky true.

On the third day, I sat down again, determined to write something if it killed me.

And I sat.

And sat.

Mmmmmm, bagels.

I was still sitting.

It dawned on me that I could have been a drummer in an all-girl punk band. I was pretty good at banging out beats on my desk.

Tap ta tap tap ta tappy tap tap. Tap ta tap tap ta tappy tap tap.

I hate him, I thought.

Tap ta tap tap ta tappy tap tap.

I miss him.

I hate him I miss him I hate him I miss him I hate him I miss him I hate him I miss him.

I ate him.

Har har.

I miss him.

HE'S TOO YOUNG FOR YOU
AND HE'LL RUIN YOUR LIFE

A cautionary tale by BENJAMINA FRANKLIN, who knows

The night M. and I broke up, I cried in a way I hadn't since I was a little girl. I was hyperventilating, sobbing so hard it hurt to talk, big gulps of air that choked, tears streaming down my face. I called my best friend to tell her what happened, and it sounded something like, *"Ah cant be lieve he jus leh me walk a way ah cant be lieve its ov ver ah cant take it wha have ah done wah did he not wan to be with me wha did he say he loved me wha . . ."*

And all she could say was, "Oh, honey, breathe. Oh, honey. Let it out. Oh, honey, breathe. You're going to be okay. I promise. Just breathe."

Eventually I breathed. But inside, I felt pretty much the same.

Breaking up with M. was my worst friggin' nightmare. Think you have it bad? Try falling in love with a guy who's *seven years younger than you are.*

I know. Right?

You probably think I just lost perspective. You probably think a mere child couldn't possibly do *that* much damage. I know—I used to think that way, too. I met him at a party. He was cute (of course). I fantasized that he'd be the Justin to my Britney. (Before the hideous breakup.) That he wouldn't be like all the jerks I knew my age—the ones who already figured out that when a girl's pushing twenty-eight (or thirty, or fifty-nine) she'll drop her underpants before he can say, "A dozen roses costs *what?*" My new boy was sweet. Unspoiled by heartbreak or cynicism.

> "THINK YOU HAVE IT BAD? TRY FALLING IN LOVE WITH A GUY SEVEN YEARS YOUNGER"

And because I had more experience, I told myself that, like Janet Jackson, I had the control. That after I had fun with his twenty-one-year-old rock hard torso, when it was time to settle down, I'd breezily move on to an older, more sophisticated guy with whom I could steam Chilean sea bass and breed.

Except that's *not* what happened. Here are the major plot points . . .

- M. started off bringing flowers, chocolates . . .
- I was easily seduced by such trivial gestures. And I didn't just take off my panties—I gave him my heart.
- I was ambushed by my affections. My fling turned into love.
- I became *obsessed* with the younger guy. And I started to want to have a *real relationship* with the younger guy. But I couldn't *talk* to the younger guy.
- This is when the younger guy became what he really was: a boy. One who didn't want to be in a "serious relationship." Who was terrified of getting "trapped." Who, metaphorically speaking, started checking the Trojans for pinpricks.
- He left, without ever really explaining why—if he was so sure he didn't want to be in a "serious relationship," then why did he get so involved with me in the first place?
- My heart was broken.
- I'm still trying to figure out how the story ends.

I recently met a woman who's married to a guy ten years her junior. I would have placed her somewhere around twenty-six years of age. Over dinner, I marveled that her skin was wrinkle-free and her frame model-thin. When she told me she was thirty-eight—and her husband was still in his twenties—I rejoiced. "What's the secret?" I asked her. "How does your relationship defy the odds?"

Her answer chilled my soul. "Aging simply isn't an option for me right now," she said. "It took years to get him to commit. He broke up with me so many times, went out with these little girls, came back, left again. I

never made a stink. And now he's finally mine. So you know what I do?" Her eyes locked onto mine. "I spend thousands of dollars a year on facials, trainers, and sunscreens. I do Power Yoga, I'm on the Zone, I take three Spin classes a week. I can't start aging until his hair falls out. Maybe when that happens, I'll be able to finish getting my law degree."

Clearly this isn't the answer.

Where is Mr. Right? Does he exist? I honestly don't know. When I started my romance with M., I thought my experiences with other men would give me the upper hand, but I came out on the bottom. I thought at least, if it didn't work out, the breakup with Junior would be less painful than the others, but it hurt more. I'm still hurt, confused, broken.

However, I do know this: When I go to bed at night, and those feelings—the *why did he do this to me*s and the *what have I done*s—come, I repeat to myself this one thought. No, make that prayer: The easy affections of a boy will be nothing compared to the love of a true man. Say it with me, The easy affections of a boy will be nothing compared to the love of a true man. All together now, The easy affections of a boy—I have to believe this, please, God, let it be true—will be *nothing* compared to the love of a true man. ⋃

Kiki turned out to be right. I really didn't have anything better to do. So I went out with Finlay again. And again. And again. Each time I told myself he was perfect on paper, and chances were he'd leap off the page into perfect in real life. Besides, as Kiki constantly told me, everyone knows the best way to get over someone is to start seeing somebody else.

Each date was carefully orchestrated, I assume because Finlay thought this would impress me enough so I'd keep returning his calls. We did northern Italian, sushi, Indian, minimalist Californian . . . On balance, each evening was fine, but not great. I still missed He Who.

Our fifth date was Franco-Moroccan, which, I discovered, I actually liked. The lights were low, the wine was flowing, and Finlay ordered some kind of pastry stuffed with chicken and dusted with powdered sugar, which sounded gross but was actually pretty good. I was all dressed up—decided making an effort was pivotal to my recovery—and fairly contented. *Finlay's not so bad,* I thought, taking a bite of the chicken thing. *He's cute. He's successful. He reads . . .*

When he picked me up, Finlay told me he couldn't contain his excitement anymore—he had to tell me that he "thinks there could really be something to build on here." My stomach did a little flip when he said it. I hoped it was a good flip. *I have to remember it's okay to be happy,* I thought. That's what Nina was always saying, anyway.

After dinner, Finlay asked if I wanted to see his apartment. I surprised myself and agreed. When we got there, I drank another glass of wine. Then he let me change into his pajama bottoms because I was sick of wearing what I was wearing. I was in an affectionate mood. I snuggled up to him on the couch and we talked and talked. Not the stilted chitchat we'd been doing on our previous evenings together, but real talk. He asked about the Mother, why she'd divorced my dad, how I felt about his endless surfing trip around the world. Whether or not I ever missed him. While I told him about my family, I suddenly realized I felt comfortable. Able to be myself. Free of worry about whether or not Finlay liked me, thought I was funny, thought I was pretty. I told him stuff about me— particularly about Audrey—that I never admit out loud, and Finlay was being kind about it, too. "It's hard with sisters," he said, putting my feet up in his lap and playing with my toes. "I know, I saw the battle firsthand."

"Oh yes, the great sister war chez Finlay," I teased. "The one where they used tampons as missiles and safety pads as armor, all so you wouldn't be freaked out by femininity."

"Good Lord, don't bring that up." He laughed. "What a conversational blunder."

"It really wasn't so bad."

"What a relief." Finlay lifted my foot and kissed my big toe gently. "Bless your little heart."

I got up to go to the bathroom, and while taking a quick peek into the medicine cabinet (antibiotics, Kiehl's products, several bottles of expensive cologne, and an old-style shaving kit—a mortar-and-brush thing—not the store-bought kind) it occurred to me that Finlay's apartment was an adult apartment. Everything matched everything. The marble tub sparkled, the chrome fixtures glimmered, and there was a jar of rosemary-scented bath salts on a little shelf. I made my way back to the living room, where heavy mahogany furniture gleamed—solid, dependable. And then, I don't know what came over me. I guess I was seduced by Finlay's ability to give foot rubs and buy antiquated Mission-style furniture from Restoration Hardware and I proceeded to jump him. Literally. I ran across the room and hopped onto his lap like a cowgirl ready to ride her favorite palomino, grabbed him by the hair, and kissed him.

"Wait," he said. Pulling back and looking at me in surprise. "Wait . . ." He took my hands down and placed them around his neck, and gave me a light, but sincere, kiss.

Which led to light, but sincere, sex.

In the morning I got up, got dressed, and got the hell out of there. Finlay was being ridiculously sweet—made me tea and toast for breakfast in bed, wanted to cuddle the morning away—but I couldn't wait to get home, shower, regroup. Things were good, it wasn't that. I just needed a little breathing room. He called in the afternoon, right on schedule. Said he wanted to see me that same night. Two nights in a row. Somewhere deep down, an alarm went off. It went to the tune of *too much too soon, too much too soon*. But I slammed my palm down on my internal panic button and said I'd love to. The other day at lunch, Nina had said something about how I was—for all my moaning and groaning about wanting a real boyfriend—emotionally unavailable and terrified of real intimacy, and that's why I'd found Max so attractive in the first place. I was determined to prove her wrong.

That night I went over to Finlay's and we ordered in Pacific New Wave. While we ate, we watched *Austin Powers* on DVD. It was extremely amusing—I love that movie. But then Finlay started with the kisses on the back of the neck. And his hands started moving under my blouse, where they lingered over the clasp to my bra and undid it. It seemed a little stagy—like he'd planned the whole thing in advance—and I was kind of into the movie. I shifted my weight on his overstuffed couch and said, "I really wish you wouldn't . . ."

"Sorry about that," Finlay said, sitting up and reaching over to rub my shoulders.

"Maybe not that, either."

"That, too." He took his hands away, sat on them in an attempt to make me laugh. Then he tried to kiss my ear.

It made me all squirmy. "That tickles."

"Oh, damn it all to hell, Ben. What's the matter?"

Finlay stood up in frustration and then, not sure what to do next, crossed his living room to get his Nicorette. "You know," he said, struggling with the packet, "last night this didn't seem to be a problem."

"No, I know. That was nice."

"*Nice?*" Finlay put a piece in his mouth, started chewing frantically.

"No, I mean nice as in *nice*, not nice as in, shit," I said. "The genuine nice."

"*Be-e-en,*" he said.

"What?"

He did it again, "*Be-e-en.*" It was a cross between a noisome whine and a cajoling niggle, three syllables long, and delivered in a sotto moan.

"*What?*"

"Don't be like this." He sat back down on the couch, and put his head on my shoulder like a puppy dog.

"Like what? I'm fine."

His chin was digging into my neck. I tried to shift my shoulders into a more comfortable position.

"*Be-e-en.* Come on, now, talk to me." He took my hand.

"About what?" I took it away to scratch my ear.

"Whatever's on your mind. I'd like us to be friends. More than friends, but friends first and foremost."

"There's nothing on my mind." I tried to shift my weight so I could look at him (or, maybe, so he would stop *touching* me) and I decided I hated his couch. It was enormous and I felt like I was being eaten alive by cushions.

"Just tell me what I've done wrong."

"Finlay, you haven't done anything wrong." I got up and switched to an armchair. It was overstuffed, too, and my ass sank to the floor while my knees rose to my chest.

"Tell me what's bothering you."

I got up again and tried another chair. Nope, puffy as can be. Your grandmother's kind of chair. Reminded me of the crap Jack was always buying—he'd sit in them and say, *Now this is more like it!* I got up and made for the ottoman.

"Ben!" Finlay yelled.

"WHAT?" I jumped. "Jesus Christ, you just scared the shit out of me."

"Stop bouncing around like the three bloody bears and talk to me."

"About what?"

"Ben," he said. *"Be-e-en. Be-e-e-en.* Come over here and give me a kiss."

Finlay was looking up at me expectantly, waiting for his kiss. I didn't see an alternative—I didn't want to start fighting with him already. And just yesterday, everything had seemed so promising. I didn't want to lose that feeling. So I crossed the room and gave him a kiss.

"Another," he said.

I gave him another.

"One more . . ."

Suddenly—scaring myself, Finlay, and probably half the neighborhood—I opened my mouth and I *screamed*.

I left in a hurry—didn't even bother to put my bra back on, just left it dangling. I'm sure my hasty departure offended Finlay, but when I walked through my front door all I felt was relief.

My heart leapt when I heard I had three messages. It was irrational, but I couldn't help thinking, *Maybe . . .*

First was Ashton. "Yo Ben, where you at? Listen, I know I've been kind of an asshole, made you miss that Christmas party, then I went out of town. But things should settle down soon, and I have news. I'll call you."

Second message.

"Hi, it's Audrey."

Oh.

"I've been thinking . . ."

Good for you.

"That what you need . . ."

Is a lobotomy and an engagement ring from De Beers.

"Is a sister weekend!"

Come again?

"Jamie has to go to L.A. for business so I'm driving down with him on Saturday, and you and I are going to hang out *all day Saturday* and *all day Sunday* and just do 'you' stuff. No wedding planning, no bridal boutiques, no bridesmaids dresses, none of the endless stuff I have to do before my big day. A sister weekend devoted to my favorite sister!"

Oh *fuck*.

And finally . . . Finlay. Naturally. "Well *that's* never happened to me before," he said in a tone of mock offense. "Don't worry about it, gorgeous. Am I moving things too fast? Okay, well, message received. We'll take it nice and slow from here. Listen, I'm just calling to make sure you made it home okay . . . Okay? Call me when you get in. I hope we're still on for that couples dinner with Kiki and Curtis tomorrow night. I'm quite excited! So call me. Doesn't matter what time. Just call. Call me."

The Mother phoned as I was drinking my first diet Coke of the day to remind me that since Aud was coming down—uninvited, might I add—I should probably clean my apartment.

"Hey thanks," I said. *"Terrific."*

Depression and cleanliness don't go together—my place looked like a refugee camp. So I spent my morning gathering up empty diet Coke cans with cigarette butts stuffed inside, throwing away the pizza boxes, emptying ashtrays and wiping them out with a T-shirt Max had given me that I'd mistakenly kept. I had to stuff several pounds' worth of dirty clothes, including the T-shirt, which I realized I couldn't bear to part with, into the hamper. It was overflowing and the lid wouldn't stay on, but I cleverly stacked magazines on top and it held. I even had to crawl around on all fours collecting dust bunnies with a paper towel because the vacuum cleaner was broken. I put a fresh roll of TP on top of the toilet and sprayed Lysol around. Done.

In the afternoon Nina phoned to tell me her latest theory—that I was addicted to "phantom lovers." I played Solitaire on my computer while she talked, so I can't say exactly what her hypothesis was, but it was something about how Max was a phantom who was so absent in my life that I could create a compelling fantasy in the space where a real relationship would have been. All of which was more satisfying for me than a real relationship, which I would most likely find intolerable. In other words, it was actually all my fault. I figured it could be true, but the fact that Nina then confided that she'd started carrying a trial-size bottle of Listerine in her backpack because she kept giving impromptu blow jobs to the assistant professor in her Pavlovian Response class made it a little hard to swallow.

That night, when Finlay picked me up in his brand-new four-by-four gargantuan mobile, I'd already decided to make the most of the evening and stop acting like such a freak. I was not going to obsess about Max anymore, and I was not going to push away the first really nice guy I'd met in the last year. Finlay, thank God, didn't mention what happened. He was too delighted with his new car, and eager to regale me with statistics on how big the sunroof was, how much horsepower he had, and how many pounds the SUV could pull if I were ever stuck on some snowy road and needed a tow. I pointed out that we don't get snowstorms in southern California, but Finlay just laughed and said that the ridiculous impracticality of the car was the whole point. "If you're going to go L.A.," he said, "you should bloody well go L.A." On the ride over, I felt like I was in a monster-truck rally, as emceed by Prince Charles. Finlay kept crying out in joy: "Look at this thing! It's a bloody *elephant!* It's the bloody *Titanic!* It's the largest car in Los Angeles!" He pronounced it *Los Anjelleeees.*

Kiki was already at the restaurant when we walked in. I saw her beaming approvingly from a spot by the bar, clearly excited to see me on a date with such a suitable match. Curtis was holding her hand. Le Petit Bistro was living up to its name—it was so crowded it took us a few tries just to make it over to them. Then Kiki, Curtis, Finlay, and I were led by a huffy hostess to a teensy booth where we were overpowered by screaming Frenchmen one table over. They were eating steak au poivre. "I'm getting that," Kiki said, hooking her thumb in their direction. "Oooh, and French onion soup to start!"

Curtis smiled and said, "I keep telling her she's too skinny."

"How cute is that?" Kiki said, beaming and slathering some butter on a large piece of bread.

After we ordered, I watched Kiki direct her attention to everything Curtis said. He told a story about the last time he'd been in Paris, something about calling a Frenchman a duck when he thought he was calling him a son of a bitch. (The punch line: "So I screamed, *'Canard!'*") I laughed out of politeness, but Curtis's wittiness sent Kiki right over the moon.

It was nice to see Finlay relax, though. He didn't fidget, or get all buggy and start Be-e-en-ing me. He dished us all the dirt on Carson Daly, and he was being attentive but not clingy. He got me a new fork when I dropped mine on the floor, and cracked up when I dropped the second fork, too, and the French waiter looked at me like I'd just squirted lemon in his eye. (When the waiter went to get me another, I yelled *"Canard!"* at him, and Finlay laughed so hard he had to spit his wine into his water glass.)

Midway through dinner Kiki and I excused ourselves to go to the bathroom so we could talk about the boys. On the way she whispered in my ear, "You like Finlay, don't you?"

I said, "I really want to." And for a brief second I thought, *Maybe I do.* But then, *"Ashton?"*

Sitting, stage right, at an intimate table for two with another girl. "Heeyyyy, what are you two doin' here?" He stood up and gave me a kiss on the cheek.

"Oh," Kiki turned around, saw Ashton, plus the date sitting at his table, and immediately took note—as I did—that she was a walking Jane Austen novel with long curly blond hair, a classic jaw, and clear blue eyes. "Hello, there," Kiki said. "You."

I hadn't found my larynx yet.

"This is Mina," Ashton said. "Mina, this is Ben and Kiki."

"Hi," I said.

"Nice to meet you," she said.

Awkward pause here.

"So. How do you guys know one another?" Mina said, looking around and blinking. "I'm always telling Ash I'd like to know his friends better."

"How do we know one another?" I said to Ashton.

"Just from around," he said with a smile. "The scene, you know."

"Right," I said. *"'The scene.'"*

"Hey, maybe we should all go out one night," Mina said. The girl was clueless.

"Wouldn't that be *fun?*" said Kiki. "Ashton, you should really set that up. Come on, Ben, bathroom time."

I excused myself.

When we got in the bathroom I locked the door, bent my head over the sink, and tried to focus. Kiki sat down on the toilet and said, "Are you okay?"

"Yeah, totally fine." I started to make myself busy, touching up makeup that didn't need touching up. "At least now we know why he's been dodging my calls."

"He should have told you."

"No, I was the one who broke it off. It's fine. I mean, we always said it was a casual thing."

"Well"—she started to pee—"I think the important thing to remember here is that Ashton wasn't the right guy for you. Maybe he's the right guy for pointy face out there, but not you."

"Yeah," I mumbled. "Except it seems like nobody is the right guy for me."

"Oh, come on. That's not true. This doesn't mean anything! He's nothing to you, honey." She flushed and joined me at the sink.

"Do you have to go?" she asked.

I shook my head. "I missed my moment."

I put my lipstick down and turned to look at her. "Do you think Max goes out on dates?"

"Max?" She waved her hands away, like *pshaw*. "I mean, who cares? Even if he does, they'll never go anywhere. That guy can't be in a relationship—you know that better than anyone."

"Yeah. I guess . . . I can't believe Ashton just said he knew me from 'the scene.'"

"That was completely crazy. And just for the record, she's not that cute."

"Kiki, I'm upset but you don't have to lie. She was totally cute."

"I thought she was gross. Her looks were totally predictable and her face was like this"—Kiki bugged her eyes out and sucked her cheeks in. "She was Milquetoast. I'm sorry. But she looks like a diet shake commercial."

"I'm going to die alone, aren't I?"

"Oh, cheer up. We all die alone," Kiki said, holding the door open for me. "It's the living alone that's hard."

CHAPTER

13

The sign outside The Standard Hotel on Sunset hangs upside down. Audrey wanted to know why. I told her I *thought* it was supposed to cutely suggest that they were setting a new standard. She looked at me like, *huh?*

All night over dinner Audrey complained (bragged) about her wedding. How she'd gotten so skinny and couldn't imagine why—she'd only been working out like four times a week. How she was in a tizzy over whether the bridesmaids should carry tulips or Gerber daisies. How she and Jamie had gotten more yeses than nos so they had to totally rearrange the seating chart. Oh, and she still needed to know if I was bringing a date to the wedding—it would be tacky for the seating card next to my place at the bridal table to say GUEST.

In self-defense I turned my personality up a notch. I wore a deconstructed skirt by Imitation of Christ, hoping the raw seams and hanging loose threads would put Audrey off. On the way to the hotel I gushed about Finlay, telling her how he had invited me to go with him to a live concert in Scotland that he was producing for MTV. "I'll probably get to meet Thom Yorke," I said.

"Who?"

"The guy from Radiohead."

Her eyes were devoid of recognition.

Of course, I left out the fact that I didn't know yet if I really wanted to go.

As we entered the lobby, Audrey's eyes widened. "Oh my gosh, are they real?" She stopped to gape at two models reclining in an oversize fish tank above the check-in desk. A guy with lips the size of basketballs was sitting Indian-style and reading *Wallpaper*, while a girl with boobs the size of thimbles slept in his lap.

"You bet your patootie they're real," I said.

"You can't put people in a fish tank."

"They're not people. They're *models*."

We made for the pool deck, and my spike heels sunk satisfyingly into AstroTurf. For once Audrey was in my domain. There were no Martha touches to take the edge off the asylum white walls. No crepe de chine to soften the steel stools in the minimal bar. In my world we mainline our aesthetic. It looked like it was going to be a pretty good party, too.

"Collin!" I waved. He was perched on the edge of a white chaise longue, wearing a T-shirt that said STAR FUCKER.

"Darlings." He air-kissed both my cheeks. "Do you believe this party? I hear the gift bag contains a fucking *mountain* of product from Kiehl's."

"Urban gift bag myth," I said. "The same rumor was going around that record release party at the Argyle a couple of weeks ago."

"I heard it from Tara Reid," he huffed.

"Sure you did. Collin, this is my sister, Audrey. Audrey, this is Collin. Nobody knows how he earns a living."

"I'm a celebrity stylist. Designer. Writer. Your basic hyphenate," he said, giving Audrey's outfit the once-over. I saw her cringe a little under his gaze, and felt an unexpected urge to protect her.

"Hey look, Collin," I said. "There's Jason Biggs."

"Oh my God, is the *entire* cast of *American Pie* here?" he said, turning around. "Gotta go—Jason's a pal."

"Of course he is," I said. Collin gave me the finger and left.

"Drink?" I asked Audrey.

"Okay."

On the way to the bar, she tapped me on the shoulder. "Look," she whispered. "I think I see Chandra McInerney."

"Where?"

"Right over there." Audrey motioned toward a white bearskin rug in the lobby, where a very imposing-looking group was spread out on the floor, drinking cocktails.

"Okay, let's get the drinks first."

"Chardonnay, please," Audrey said to the bartender, a girl of indeterminate youth in a spiked collar, white T-shirt, skintight sarong, and black combat boots. She gave Aud a withering glare.

"They don't serve Chardonnay, at least not for free," I whispered. "Two."

The bartender pushed two Johnny Walker margaritas at us. I handed

THE ART OF WAR

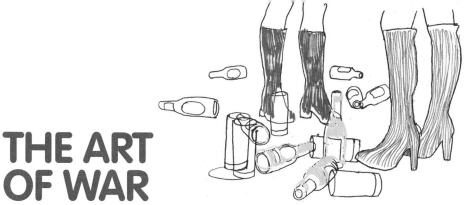

Plan a party like a Hollywood publicist, from vetting the list to cooking the crudités.
BY BENJAMINA FRANKLIN

In Hollywood a person's value isn't measured by her job title at the studio alone. To reach the apex of power, one must host the perfect party, planned by a publicist who will ensure that your next cocktail gathering or birthday celebration has the right people RSVPing and the wrong people sticking their heads in the oven and turning on the gas because their invitations "got lost in the mail." Not all of us can afford such an extravagance, but just because you can't hire a publicist doesn't mean you can't *think* like one.

Good parties, as any publicist will tell you, start with vetting the list. At studios, the pros list stars in a database where they're ranked according to A, B, and C. An actress on a low-rated sitcom, for example, is a C. Drew Barrymore is an A. You should do the same. Give prospective guests an alphabetic value. Admit it, you *are* being shallow. But just because you lack depth doesn't mean you shouldn't improve your social status! On your A-list should be: cool friends, hot guys, and "secret celebrities" whom it would be beneficial to get to know better. (Not actors, silly, but restaurateurs, yoga instructors, graffiti artists, and club promoters!) On the B-list will be those who'll do in a pinch, and on the C-list are people you'd

probably rather kill before they show up. Now, the publicist trick is to only start inviting B-listers *after* A-listers have declined. If you have to stack your party with too many C's, cancel. A troop of C-listers must never walk down your red carpet.

Next, consider your theme. Inventive ones—home theater (in which everyone puts on a prepared performance) or an evening of arts and crafts do the job. Avoid trends: A martini lounge is *way* too '00. If in doubt, go traditional—champagne, crystal, the works. You won't be creative, but you'll be a class act.

Once you've chosen a theme, make sure it informs everything at your party. Home theater is all about popcorn topped in real butter and chocolate-covered raisins from Dean & Deluca. Arts and crafts should come with gourmet peanut-butter-and-plantain sandwiches and freshly baked cookies served in designer lunch boxes.

When it all comes together, you'll reap the benefits of being a social diva. Invitations will flow your way, the promotion you deserve will be yours, and men will throw themselves at your feet. And consider this: If you have the stomach for using your birthday as a way to increase your social influence, you may have a future in Hollywood. ∪

> A TROOP OF C-LISTERS MUST NEVER WALK DOWN YOUR RED CARPET...

one to Audrey and she took a hesitant sip. "Ugh—this is disgusting," she said.

It seemed Her Highness didn't want a free drink. I tried to explain the concept of a party sponsor while she took these quick, wincing sips that were already getting on my nerves.

As we approached Chandra, I could feel Aud tensing up. "I don't really think we should ask for her autograph right now, do you?" she said. Then Chandra spotted us and jumped up, making Audrey almost leap out of her skin.

"Where the fuck've you been, dawg?" Chandra said, wrapping me in a bear hug.

"What up, McC?"

"Booyah, baby, booyah."

"Chandra, this is my sister, Audrey. Audrey, Chandra McInerney."

"You know each other," Audrey said. I thought she would be excited to meet a movie star, but instead she pointed to her glass and said, "I'll be right back."

"You've finished your drink already?" I said. "Okay, yeah, I'll see you in a sec."

Chandra gave Kate-o a nudge to move over so I could sit down next to her (I couldn't help thinking *ha-ha, bitch*) and proceeded to yell at me about how happy she was I finally got Max—or, as Chandra called him, "that fucking low-life punk-ass cocksucker"—out of my life. Then she moved on to a tale about how she was convinced her personal assistant was spiking her bottled water with LSD, possibly as part of an assassination plot.

"I don't know, Chandra," I said. I was trying not to look too incredulous. "I mean, I think it's pretty hard to kill someone with acid."

"Tell that to Charles fucking Manson," she said.

But before she really got going, Chandra turned her aggression toward the waitress, who'd forgotten she ordered her chicken egg rolls with tofu. Not that Chandra intended to eat them. "I ordered these for my friends," Chandra said, gesturing to the group, most of whom were already digging in, "and we can't have meat because *I'm a vegetarian.*"

"I'm sorry," the waitress said, "but they make all the egg rolls in advance. They can't take the chicken—"

"I don't give a *fuck* when they make the egg rolls," Chandra interrupted, looking around at us like *Can you believe this chick?* "I care about what *the people I love* put in their *fucking bodies,* mkay?"

The waitress was getting flustered, reaching for the egg rolls, then straightening up because half of them were already gone, unsure what to do. Krantz, who was in Chandra's armpit as usual, moved in to smooth things over. But, perhaps taking note of the crowd that was starting to gather, Chandra stood up and got in the waitress's face, stabbing her finger toward the poor girl's chest and yelling, "Do you wanna piece of this, you fucking bitch? Huh? *Do you wanna piece of this?*"

The waitress, scared out of her wits, dropped a tray full of drinks, and Johnny Walker margaritas splashed all over Chandra's Sigerson Morrison heels. That did it. Chandra grabbed the waitress by the hair, and, as she started to scream, started to wrestle her around—throwing her from side to side. The air got thick with busboys, a hotel manager, photographers, Krantz—who was wrestling with the photographers—and Collin, who rushed over, yelling "Get her, McC! Get her!" Chandra was screaming, "I'm going to fucking end you, 'ho! *I'm going to end you!*" Scared I might actually get hit, I leapt for the sidelines, where I'd be able to watch the spectacle from a safe distance. But as I tore my eyes away from the horror of Chandra trying to bite the waitress on the back of the neck so I could blot margarita mix off my skirt before it stained, I realized Audrey was nowhere to be seen. Where had she gone?

I scanned the lobby. No sign. Poolside? Nope, not there either. The bar? Huh. Chandra was stomping down on the waitress's foot in a very entertaining—and probably effective—manner as a busboy tried to pull her off, but now I was worried. I walked out to the front to see if maybe she was standing outside, but Audrey would rather gargle Drano than smoke, so I wasn't surprised when I didn't see her skulking around Sunset with all the banished nicotine addicts. I really wanted to sneak one myself, but I didn't want to leave Audrey inside alone, what with Chandra on the loose and Collin in a bitchy mood.

I finally found her talking on the far end of the pool deck with some guy who looked vaguely familiar—I thought maybe he'd been my waiter at Ammo the other day, but then again that didn't seem quite right. And, wait a minute, why would Audrey be *flirting* with my lunch waiter? She was perched on a lounge, and he started to lean toward her, his dark hair falling into his eyes. Then she laughed at whatever he said, throwing her head back as if to say *you are* so *funny!*

"Hi," I said, standing above them.

"Oh. Hi," she said, and they both started laughing again like I was the punch line for some in-joke.

I turned to the guy: "And who are you?"

"Jeff."

Jeff? I looked at Audrey.

"Jeff was in that Gap commercial," she said, looking supremely satisfied.

I said, "Ah."

"Something from the bar?" Jeff asked, standing up. She nodded, and he made his way past me—*without* asking if I wanted anything, by the way—and sauntered off with a smirk. From the looks of things, she'd had at least another margarita, if not two, since the last time I saw her.

"Audrey?" I said. "What the fuck do you think you're doing?"

She looked up at me, stuck her chin out. "What the fuck is with your tone?"

I was surprised she'd said the F-word. She never used the F-word.

Not to be outdone, I said, "What the fuck is with hanging all over some guy who screamed 'Mambo!' on TV?"

She stood up. "What the *fuck* is with you asking what I'm fucking up with when you're the one who's so fucking fabulous all the time and can't let anyone else have fun?" And then she flopped back into the lounge chair.

"Have another drink, Audrey."

She waved me off. "Ben, I'm having a good time. *Is that okay?*"

Oh, so *that's* how it was going to be. I told her that if she wanted to have "fun" with some complete stranger/cheeseball, it was fine with me. "Go ahead—flirt with the Mambo guy," I said. "And when you've come to your senses? Maybe I'll still be nice enough to drive you home."

I turned on my heel and stalked off, determined to find someone besides her to talk to. Before I passed through the sliding-glass doors, I saw Audrey downing yet another drink and putting her head on Jeff's chest because she was laughing so hard.

I grabbed another whiskey margarita and sat down in the bar to pout. I couldn't believe I'd thoughtfully cleaned my apartment just so Aud could come down and take over my party. *Besides,* I thought, *she's supposed to be my wingman while I flirt with new boys.* I looked back over my shoulder and—what the hell was this?—she was now *kissing* the Mambo guy. It was really unbelievable.

No, I decided. *This is too much.* I was going back over there, and I was going to knock some sense into her. *I* was the crazy sister who dated younger men and slept around with MTV employees. *She* would have to play the stable sister getting married—with the big fat ring that she waved in my face all the time to prove it. I grabbed the sticky glass and started to cross the lobby—*again*—when two things happened simultaneously.

One, I saw Jamie walking toward the pool in a powder blue Polo shirt, head swiveling from side to side like a lighthouse. It instantly dawned on me that Miss Party in Her Pants must have told him we were coming here to see if he'd want to meet up. Clearly she'd forgotten. We needed to spend some sister time together. *As if.*

Two, Max. Walking right toward me.

I stopped dead in my tracks, not sure what to do. Break right, and save Audrey's irritating marriage? Or stay put, and talk to Max for the first time in months? It was a toss-up. I looked back toward the pool—wait, Audrey was gone. Jamie was gone. Even the Mambo guy, gone.

Mmmm . . . Perhaps disaster had been averted without my help. Or they were all fighting in the bushes. Either way, I decided I could spare a minute. Just a superquick minute before I went to check on my sister. *Yes.* Max hadn't seen me yet, the party was crowded, but he was about to. He looked . . . really good. His hair was getting long—kind of John Lennon after the Beatles split up. I brushed my hair from my eyes and stood still while trying not to look like I was just cooling my heels waiting for him.

And he got closer.

And closer.

He was going to see me any minute now.

His eyes flicked in my direction.

I thought, *This is it,* and tried to think of my opening line—maybe something charming/casual/funny—and then

he walked

right

by.

"WHAT THE FUCK WAS THAT?"

"Sorry?" I was stunned into complete paralysis. Max was heading out the double doors onto the street.

"DUDE CHANDRA MCINERNEY JUST WENT APESHIT IN THERE THIS IS AMAZING EVERYONE WILL PICK UP THESE PICTURES DO YOU THINK THAT MAYBE I'LL GET INTERVIEWED FOR PEOPLE *OR* INSTYLE *OH MY GOD I'LL BE THE NEXT LIZZIE GRUBMAN BUT THIS TIME THE MOVIE STAR IS THE ONE WHO GOES POSTAL AND I'M THE HEROIC PUBLICIST WHO SAVES THE DAY!"*

It was Steph, beside herself with glee. Chandra's public detonation at her party was a true coup. But I was too busy gawking over her shoulder to revel. I watched Max give his ticket to the valet and then, when his car came, get in. He paused for a moment and I had the irrational thought that maybe he was having second thoughts and was about to run back inside to find me. But then he started the engine and peeled out. From what I could tell, he didn't look back. Not once. But I knew he'd seen me. *I saw him see me.*

"Steph, I'm sorry but I have to find a bathroom."

I walked/ran to the nearest facilities and locked myself in a stall, sitting down on the toilet seat and hugging my knees. It was as though I'd been physically hit. I squeezed my eyes shut in an effort to hold back any weird sobby noises I was about to make. There were two girls at the sinks talking loudly and fixing their makeup and I wanted to have my meltdown in peace.

"Did you see—I mean it was so . . ." one said.

"Amazing. Totally fucking amazing . . ." the other said.

"She took out the waitress and two busboys."

"She's *so* street . . ."

"Legit . . ."

"Love her movies . . ."

"Me too!"

Finally I heard them singing Chandra's praises as they walked down the marble hall back toward the lobby, hoping they'd get another glimpse of her. I was sure Krantz had whisked her off by now and at that moment was probably in the back of some limo actually telling Chandra the waitress deserved it.

I held my breath. I wanted to make sure there was nobody else in the bathroom. When ten more seconds passed without a sound, I sniffled. Then I blew my nose. And I sniffled again.

But then I thought I heard a sniffle.

I sniffled.

Sniffle.

Was that my sniffle echoing, I thought, *or someone else's sniffle?*

I sniffled.

Sniffle.

"Who's there?" I said.

No answer.

So I waited, completely silent, dying to sniffle but not letting myself, and then, *Sniffle.*

"*Who is that?*"

A little voice: "Nobody."

Unbelievable.

"Audrey, is that you?"

"No."

Great. I looked at the ceiling and sighed. *She had to be here for this, right?*

"Audrey, it's Ben."

Sniffle, sniffle. From the sound of it, she was about three or four stalls down.

"Oh," she said. "Great."

"Wait, are you okay?"

"I'm fine."

The booming echo of a blowing nose resonated through the empty room.

"He found you, didn't he?" I said.

There was silence. I read bathroom graffiti to pass the time. Right in front of my face someone had written the words, YOU ARE AWFUL. The room was amplifying everything, and I could hear Audrey breathing so I knew she was still there. The air was sharp with disinfectant and air-conditioning. My head hurt. After a minute, her voice bounced gently off the tiles.

"He's probably already driving back to San Francisco," she said.

"Oh, Audrey. What were you thinking?"

"I don't know. I just . . . I was having fun. For once."

"Come on. You have fun all the time."

"Yeah right." She blew her nose again. "Not like you. With your fabulous job. Your fabulous friends . . ." She laughed a little. "They obviously hate what I'm wearing. Even *I* hate what I'm wearing . . . Oh fuck it. Maybe marriage is just something to do."

"Are you joking?" I couldn't believe what I was hearing. "My friends are psychos."

"They are not."

"*Yes they are.* Nina's slept with half the staff at Whole Foods. Chandra is violent, she's a complete hypochondriac, and she thinks her assistant has put a contract on her head. That Collin guy is a professional ass kisser. And on top of it all I just saw Max outside and he totally snubbed me. Didn't even acknowledge my existence. Trust me, you don't want my life."

"Maybe," she said. I exhaled. But then she said, "Maybe I do."

Suddenly, inexplicably, I found myself rushing to defend her traditional choices, her commando fiancé . . . "Audrey, you're crazy!" I said. "Jamie *loves* you. He gave you a *ring*. He can *make a commitment. Do you have any idea how HARD IT IS TO FIND A HALF-DECENT GUY WHO WILL MAKE A COMMITMENT?*"

I begged her to tell him I'd gotten her drunk. To say that I'd left her alone to get harassed by some hideously drunken commercial actor.

"Blame it on me," I said. "Everyone will believe it if you blame it on me."

"Ben, calm down," she interrupted. "It's not like it's happening to you." Then she said, "Do you think you and I have nothing in common anymore?"

I thought about this for a second, fiddling with the toilet paper roll. "Well, we're both in the bathroom crying at the same time over our completely destroyed relationships," I said.

"Good point."

"And we probably both need a drink right about now."

"True. But can we go somewhere that has white wine? I like white wine."

"Sure."

"And Ben?"

"What?"

"Can I borrow your lip gloss?"

"The one I'm wearing?"

"I like it."

I said of course.

When Audrey was little, she used to break into my room and go through all my makeup, try on all my clothes, scratch my favorite records. I hated it. Begged my mom to have locks installed on my door. She refused, so I hung a sign outside my room that said, NO ENTRY PERMITTED WITHOUT EXPRESS PERMISSION OF THE MANAGEMENT! While I rummaged through my purse looking for the lip gloss, it dawned on me that maybe it wasn't the sign that made Audrey stop breaking in, but the fact that I'd hung it up at all.

I took a tissue and smeared it under each eye, checking to see if it came away black with mascara, and stood up, straightening my skirt. Aud came out of the stall doing the same. I handed her the tube of lip stuff. It was almost empty, but probably enough for one more coat.

"Know what, Audrey?" I said, putting my arm around her. "This'll probably look really good on you."

"Are you completely insane?"

It turned out Audrey didn't have to blame me. That had happened all on its own, and the Mother had been yelling since she'd called at 9 A.M., way before my scheduled wake-up time.

"But it's not my fault!" I said when she came up for air. "*She* wanted to talk to the Mambo guy. She wanted to drink drinks with the Mambo guy. And then *she* decided to *kiss* the Mambo guy. I tried to talk her out of it. I was like, 'Now, Audrey, you can't just go around . . .'"

She cut me off. "I guess your sister will just have to figure it out the hard way. She'll have to learn, just like I did, that you can party through your twenties, but you can never get back the years you wasted on men, and booze, and cheap sex."

"Yeah, well, those don't really sound like wasted years to me, Mom. *And you used to agree with me on that.*"

"I don't want to talk about it."

"Then why did you call me?"

"I can't remember."

She hung up.

Even my dad, Mr. Free to Be You and Me, was less than thrilled. He sent an e-mail from Costa Rica that was four words long: "Nice work. Aloha, Dad."

Audrey had been causing one to-do after another since the party. First she flew back to San Francisco and told Jamie she needed time to think. Then she packed her bags and took off to stay with a college friend who lived in New York and apparently had some great job doing product research for Urban Outfitters. Her wedding, which Audrey hadn't exactly said was on and hadn't exactly said was off, was exactly six weeks away. Not much time to reunite the happy couple. Not to mention the fact that if they didn't get back together within the next two weeks, the Mother was going to lose her deposit on the church. She was threatening to sue me for the expenses, plus emotional distress. I told myself she was just kidding.

The phone had been ringing off the hook all morning—so much so I didn't even have a chance to change out of my pajamas. The next call came from Audrey, and I braced myself for another tirade—she was probably regretting what she'd done by now and looking for a scapegoat. Except, surprisingly, she sounded like she was having a fantastic time.

"Can you believe I'm in Manhattan!" she gushed. "I've never gone anywhere alone before. Sharon lives in this great loft in Chelson—"

"Chelsea."

"Whatever! And she says she's going to introduce me to lots of cute guys who I can flirt with as much as I want!"

I made a last-ditch attempt. "And what will Jamie be doing while you're slutting it up in Chelson?"

"I'm not slutting it up. I'm doing what you would do and I like it." I heard a clink.

"Are you drinking?" I asked. It was only twelve-thirty in the afternoon in New York.

"Kiwi martinis, why?" she said. "Look, I want to hang out a little bit, do my own thing, not think about consequences. You should understand."

I lit a cigarette. Thanks to years of hanging out, the only constant in my life was my nicotine habit. And now I'd created this monster.

"So what happened with Max?" Audrey asked. It was probably the first question she'd asked me in years that didn't seem vaguely hostile.

"Nothing," I said, shaking my head. I almost started to gloss it over, but then I decided to just let the facts speak for themselves. "I'm positive he saw me at that party, but he hasn't called to explain why he acted like that."

"You're disappointed."

"Yes, I guess I am."

"You thought he'd change his mind."

"I thought he'd realize that deep down I wanted the same things he did." I sighed. "I mean, I was happy. I didn't need a *super*serious relationship, I just needed to know where I stood."

Audrey paused. Then she said, "You know, I never said anything before, because I didn't know how you would take it, but sometimes to get what you really want, you first have to admit to yourself what it is."

"So what are you saying?"

"I'm saying that I think you should have just skipped all the maneuvering and said out loud that you wanted a commitment from Max. That you wanted to be his girlfriend, that you wanted his love and devotion—the whole enchilada—and if he said he didn't want those things, too, at least you would have been able to just go on with your life."

"Well." I was taken aback by this sudden insight—especially from Audrey, of all people. I didn't know what to say. So I finally laughed and said, "Thank you very much, Mrs. Future Republicans of America."

She laughed too and said she had to go—she was meeting "friends" for drinks later at Bungalow 8 and wanted to go shopping in SoHo for something fabulous to wear.

On top of it all there was Finn, who'd been calling several times a day for the last week and leaving horrible messages that went something like, "*Be-e-en!* Come to Scotland with me! I leave in four days—still time to pack! The entire country awaits you! *Say you will Be-e-en . . .*"

In fact, that was probably him calling again. I still didn't know if I wanted to go—I changed my mind about every five minutes. If I did go, I had to get in some pitch ideas to Kiki first. Lately trying to think of a story was harder than a home bikini wax. Sure, I could have pitched "What to Do When You've Inadvertently Ruined Your Sister's Life." Or maybe "Go or Stay: You've Been Invited for a Thrilling Weekend Away with a Needy Maniac, Now What?" But those didn't seem quite right.

"Jesus Christ," I said to the ringing phone. "I'm coming."

I hopscotched over my latest shopping purchases—which were strewn around the room, still in their bags—and trod on Freak, who was sleeping on the floor in a patch of sun. He bit my ankle. Hard.

"Finn," I said, picking up, "if you keep calling me I'm never going to get any work done and then there's no way I'll be able to come with you."

"Who's Finn?"

"Hello?"

My breath. It was gone.

"Hey," he said.

"Hey," I said.

"Hey," he said. Then, "How are you?"

I couldn't talk.

"B, are you there?"

"I'm here." I tried to put some casualness in my voice. Max and I hadn't spoken in so long, I felt like I should at least sound okay. Even if I had no idea if I actually *was* okay.

"Well, how've you been?"

"I'm doing good," I said. "Doing really good, actually. Everything is just . . . good. How are you?"

"Good."

"That's good."

Enough with the goods already. I waited for him to say something else. He didn't. And just like every other time, I couldn't let the space be. I had to fill it. I opened my mouth to fill the void.

I said, "I thought I saw you at a party the other night."

"Really? Where?"

"The Standard."

"Oh. I didn't see you."

"You walked right by me."

"Huh." I heard his lighter click, and then he exhaled. "I didn't see you."

Okay, I wanted to say, *then what do you want?* Instead I waited for him to take the lead. But again, he didn't say anything.

"Max, is there something else you wanted to talk about?"

"Actually, there are a lot of things."

Intriguing, I thought. *Wait . . . shit.* "For example?"

"I read your article in *Filly.* The one about younger men."

"Oh."

"And I wanted to call"—he took a deep breath—"to say I'm sorry I hurt you."

There it was. The truth. I sat down on the couch and tried to figure out how hearing him say it made me feel. He did hurt me, of course, but what hurt the most was that I suddenly realized he must have known what he was doing the whole time and he didn't do anything to stop it. All my bravado and all my casualness and all the plans with all my friends—he probably saw through me the whole time, but he never wanted to talk about it. I'd never stood a chance. My throat started to swell shut. My nose started to run. My eyes filled and the sunlight coming through the windows started to look all watery. I let the tears go.

"I'm sorry you hurt me, too," I said. My voice sounded funny to me.

He said, "I think we need to talk, B."

"About . . ."

"About what happened. About us."

I felt my hopes start to rise. I didn't want them to   they just did.

"Nothing happened," I said. "You broke up with me." It felt good to say it.

He said, "That's not entirely true."

"Isn't it?"

"You brought the bag of presents I gave you, remember? I was really stressed at work. You were putting a lot of pressure on me—I know you didn't mean to . . . Look, this is the kind of stuff I want to talk to you about."

"But I'm a little confused. We haven't spoken in months."

"I thought about calling you every day."

Once, this would have been enough to get me right back in there. But all of a sudden, I was furious. *This is not enough,* I thought. *Not anymore.* I said, "If you thought about calling every day, then why didn't you?"

Max paused.

"Well," he said, "like, maybe I thought you wouldn't want to talk to me."

"I never gave you any reason to think that."

"You're right. You didn't."

"Then what?"

"Look." His voice was soft. Patient. Reasonable. I could close my eyes and see him, sitting on his bed, biting his lower lip, which he did whenever he was thinking hard. "I don't think we should try to fix our entire relationship over the phone, do you? I mean, come on B, I don't think we can."

I didn't say anything.

"Okay," he said. "You were right. I *was* happy. So I mean, maybe, if you could just give me the space I need, then it could all be okay. Maybe we can work this out."

Then he said, "When can I see you?"

It was like I was frozen, and I could see everything. Everything—and from all sides. I could see the dust sparkling in the light, dancing around the room. I could see every color known to mankind on the spines of books on the shelves in my living room. My CDs—scattered all over the table as usual—were refracting the sun and casting rainbows on the dining room walls. I could hear, too—Freak lick, lick, licking his paw. A car door slamming outside, then voices laughing. A baby crying. The slap of a basketball down the street. I could smell a neighbor cooking something spicy—something with curry powder in it. Under that, exhaust from a truck parked outside. And under that, the smell of flowers. Because underneath it all Los Angeles always smells like flowers. I could see and hear and smell everything, and for one perfect second I could keep everything in perfect balance in my mind.

14

So basically I got in my car and started driving. I didn't tell anyone I was taking off. Not even Kiki.

The crazed and colorful Vegas hotels looked psychedelic in the rain on my windshield. It had started pouring down the moment I'd pulled into a truck stop just outside of town. *Funny,* I thought. *Whenever I picture Vegas it's always sunny, dusty, hot.* Didn't matter though. I wasn't staying. Too many people trying to get the winning number, and I wasn't looking for the winning number. I wasn't even going to play the game.

I had this silly fantasy when Max and I had hung up the phone that I'd drive all the way to the Grand Canyon, where I'd never been, and take a look. Like the girl at the end of a movie. The girl whose heart got broken and yet, at the eleventh hour, gets out with her head on her shoulders and her dignity intact. As she drives away from the camera and the credits roll, we know for sure that even though it hurt, she'll soon find that a new, better road awaits. Maybe one with a cute hitchhiker thrown in for good measure.

Except then reality hit. I really didn't have time for this.

I had to get those story ideas in to Kiki.

I had to save my sister's marriage.

I forgot to leave food out for Freak.

I left my house with nothing but a sweater, a pack of cigarettes, and my entire CD collection, which I frantically pushed into a suitcase in a fit of misdirected cinematic romance.

And finally, if I just up and disappeared, Finn would probably have found me attractive enough for a marriage proposal and then he'd never stop calling.

I got out of the car for a minute to stretch my legs. I needed to get some gas, plan my next steps. I love truck stops, always have. The bathrooms are cleaner than at gas stations, you know. And they always sell funny cheap T-shirts and really good beef jerky. I wasn't in a mood to shop, though, so I told the guy behind the counter I just needed to fill my tank.

"Where you coming from?" he asked, scratching his arm.

"L.A."

"Where you heading?"

"L.A., actually."

"Not exactly good weather for a pleasure drive."

He pointed at the road, which was getting pelted with rain and, since the gutters were all clogged up, was starting to resemble a river. I shrugged and said, "It'll clear up."

He shook his head and laughed at me as I ran back outside with my sweater pulled halfway over my head in a vain attempt to stay dry. I could still feel his eyes as I pumped the gas, and then following my car as I made a U-turn back onto the highway.

Then I was just driving along, looking at landscape I'd already seen. I kind of liked it.

If Max had been surprised when I'd told him I couldn't make any plans because I was on my way out of town, he'd hidden it masterfully. "Just call me when you get back," he'd said.

I said, "Let me think about it for a little bit."

Then he seemed maybe a little surprised.

Rummaging around in my suitcase for something extra moody and good, I found the perfect CD and slid it into the player. There were no cars in sight, and the sun made a sudden appearance, lighting up clouds that were now so bold they looked like the print on a baby blanket. I was curious what fresh hell had occurred in the last three hours so I checked my voicemail. I had six messages. But before I listened to them, I decided I didn't care and hung up. I was sure it was just Audrey calling to complain about Jamie, the Mother calling to complain about Audrey, Nina calling to complain about my complaining, Kiki calling to see if I wanted to complain, Finn calling to complain that I hadn't called him back yet, and Chandra calling to complain to whoever would listen.

The smart money was that there would be no message from Max, though. Because according to the rules of the Full Life—and he was the master—Max had to bide his time. See if his silence grabbed me. Got me interested. Made me turn my metaphorical car around.

Perhaps it will. I wish I could say we'll never get back together, but maybe Aud's right. Maybe if I can get up the courage to tell Max what I really want, at least I'll find out for real if he's the right guy for me. It's possible that I'm just too scared to tell him the truth. Because I miss him. I really do.

At least Max will have to wait for me to call, for once.

I mean, six voicemail messages? If that isn't a full life, I don't know what is.